FORBIDDEN PLEASURE

"Alysha, you hiss and bristle like an alley cat when you're mad. And your eyes deepen to a beautiful cobalt blue. You really shouldn't do that, you know. It fires a man's blood. Better for you to be meek and submissive."

"Never."

"I'm going to kiss you," he said as if the warning made the act my responsibility. I was mesmerized by the soft curve of his lips hovering inches from mine. I felt the quickened heartbeat in his chest. Dark, sensuous eyes centered upon my face and mesmerized me with their intensity. . . .

FORBIDDEN TREASURE

LEONA KARR

LEISURE BOOKS ❧ NEW YORK CITY

To my aunt, Helen C. Campbell,
who encouraged my first efforts,
and placed them with a New York agent.

A LEISURE BOOK

Published by

Dorchester Publishing Co., Inc.
276 Fifth Avenue
New York, NY 10001

Copyright©1988 by Leona Karr

Printed in the United States of America

Chapter One

A French tapestry of variegated fields and
dark woods swept by the train windows as
we approached the small village of
Chambleau some twenty miles out of Paris.
Because low misty clouds shut the sun
from view, each passing scene was a
somber one in colors of dark forest green,
deep brown and burnt umber. It was a
cheerless, brooding June day to match my
melancholy mood. It would have been easy

to give in to fatigue, apprehension, and the overwhelming feeling of displacement that engulfed me. Instead, I took a deep breath and turned my gaze away from the window.

"We're almost there, Annette. Another ten minutes and I'll have you safely home," I said to the young girl sitting in the seat facing me. "And then, tomorrow early, it's on to Paris for me."

Annette de Lamareau's gloved hands tightened on her lap and I was not prepared for the surge of fright that suddenly widened her dark brown eyes. "I don't want you to leave me, Mademoiselle Grant. Please—"

"But you'll be home, Annette," I said brightly. "After months away at school, you'll be back with your own family . . . your mother, little brother, uncle . . . and your little kitten, Beau. They'll all be there waiting for you, *n'est pas?*" I smiled reassuringly. "You won't miss me at all, Annette. At school it was different. You were lonely. Ten years old is young to be away from home for the first time. I think the practice of putting older students as monitors helps ease some of the loneliness of the younger ones. I was twelve when I was sent away to school and I remember how lost I felt. When Sister Mary Josette asked me to see you home, I was glad to do it . . . since I'm going on to Paris, anyway. I'll meet your family, spend the night in your home . . . but tomorrow I must leave. Someone is expecting me." I hoped my voice didn't waver.

Annette continued to stare at me in her unblinking, disturbing way. She was a pretty girl—petite, with raven-dark hair, big somber eyes and a tiny, rosebud mouth. The kind of child you want to hug and spoil. Annette was richly dressed in a velvet traveling dress of deep rose, fashioned with yards of satin rouleau and tiny embroidery-trimmed flounces on her sleeves and skirt. A velvet bonnet framed her face and its pink color emphasized the translucent whiteness of her cheeks. The bonnet's deep brim put her face in shadow and made her features seem smaller than ever.

The girl's attire was a sharp contrast to my plain straw bonnet and the fawn-colored dress and short cape sent to me by my mother with the admonition that there was plenty of wear left in them. The garments were not my color, nor my style. It was my fate to have the same tall, slender build as my mother and my wardrobe was made up of cast-offs which she considered adequate for me but no longer becoming to her. As I caught sight of my blurred reflection in the train window, I thought that I looked twenty-eight years old rather than almost nineteen. My fair hair was pinned tightly under my straw bonnet so that only a small part of it showed on each side of my middle part. My mouth was held in a tired line and there was no glint of life in the dark blue eyes that were supposed to be my best feature.

"I don't want to go home," Annette declared in a stronger voice. Her lovely little chin jutted out. "Please, Mademoiselle Grant, don't leave me." Her small hand clutched mine. Her eyes were wide with fright and pleaded with me for understanding.

I didn't know what to say. Her fragile, vulnerable manner had appealed to me when she'd arrived only a few months earlier at the fashionable Swiss school where I had spent six years of my life. I had helped the younger girl with her studies and paired up with her on school outings but Annette de Lamareau had never talked much about her family. Looking back, I suppose I had been too busy trying to sort out my own life to really ask questions about hers. If the schoolmistress hadn't asked me to accompany Annette to her home, I probably would have put her completely from my mind and made my journey alone to Paris.

"I don't want to go home," Annette repeated, accenting each word as if I suddenly had lost my ability to converse fluently in French.

"*Pourquoi*, Annette? Why don't you want to go home?"

Her lip quivered. "I'm afraid."

"Afraid? What are you afraid of?"

"My Uncle Raoul . . . he's going to kill me."

The statement was so preposterous and melodramatic that for a second I could barely stifle an involuntary laugh. Only Annette's wide honest eyes stopped me. "You must be mistaken, surely."

She shook her head solemnly. "No, it's true."

I did not believe it. Her uncle had probably disciplined her too harshly at some time, I reasoned. Annette was a sensitive child. No doubt, she had taken some angry words too literally and now she feared him. "I'm certain that you have misinterpreted his behavior," I soothed. "I'm confident he means you no harm."

"Not just me," Annette said with a rush, tears brimming her eyes. "But my little brother, too."

Her earnestness dismayed me. "Why . . . why would you think such a thing?"

She leaned forward in a conspirator's

whisper. "My father's death was not an accident. Uncle Raoul planned it. My mother is certain of it."

"Your mother told you this?"

She nodded solemnly.

"Why . . . why doesn't she go to the authorities?" I stammered. I couldn't believe that a mother would share such sinister knowledge with a young girl and then do nothing about it.

"Mama did . . . she told them everything . . . but the *gendarmerie* didn't believe her. They believed Uncle Raoul. He said a poacher must have shot my father. But he lied. My mother saw my uncle go out with a gun that morning . . . the morning my father was shot in the back." Tears filled her eyes, easing down her cheeks. "Now Uncle Raoul wants to marry her . . . and get rid of my little brother and me—"

"Oh, Annette." I moved over in the seat beside her and pulled her close. The girl was trembling like someone caught in a chill and she clung to me as if I could make everything right and safe. "I think you've let your imagination get away from you."

"No, no, it's all true. You have to stay with me," she sobbed. "Please . . . please—"

"I can't Annette. It's impossible." How could I tell her that I didn't even have the ability to take charge of my own life . . . let alone interfere in hers? I had been at the convent-like Swiss school since I was twelve years old and it had become the only home I knew. Now, almost nineteen, I had reached the age where even those doors were closed to me. Because of my questionable background, Sister Josette had made it clear that there was no place for me there as a lay teacher. It was only through their Christian charity that they had accepted me as a live-in student in the first place. I drew my thoughts away from the quagmire of my own life and gave my attention to the frightened girl beside me. "I don't know what to think, Annette."

"It's true. My mother sent me away to school to keep me safe. I don't want to go back . . . I don't . . . I don't! Please take me with you to Paris."

The suggestion was so preposterous, my lips curved in an involuntary smile. "I'm afraid that isn't possible, Annette. I don't know where I'll be staying . . . or for how long. No, you have to go home. Surely some changes have been made in the months you've been away."

"No . . . Mama's letters are the same . . . full of fear. She does not want to marry Uncle Raoul and yet he pursues her."

"Isn't there anyone she can turn to? Some village priest . . . or relative?"

Annette shook her tiny head solemnly.
"Everyone is afraid of Uncle Raoul."

At that moment, the train began to slow
down with grinding wheels warning us that
we were approaching the station of
Chambleau. "You're not going to leave
me!" Annette pleaded, her voice rising in
panic. She clutched my arm.

"I'm going to accompany you home,
Annette," I said as firmly as I could. "Your
mother knows that I am spending the night
in your home . . . and taking the Paris train
in the morning. Come on now, Annette . . .
straighten your bonnet and smooth out
your skirts. That's it. And here's your book
. . . you have your umbrella?"

My firm voice seemed to settle her rising
hysteria. Quiet and obedient, she did as I
ordered but I could see that her lower lip
still trembled. We collected our things as
the Chambleau station slowly came into
view, a small brown and yellow clapboard
building similar to others dotting the
French countryside. The train whistled,
shot out billows of white steam, and ground
its wheels to a stop with a high-pitched
screech.

"There he is!" cried Annette in a
breathless sob. "Uncle Raoul! He's here."
Her fingernails bit through her gloves into
my arm. "Oh, no, Mademoiselle, what shall
we do?"

I looked through the window. "Where? Which one is he?"

"Over there . . . by the carriage."

I followed her gaze, with my own heart quickening a bit. "That's him?" I had expected her uncle to be an older man, perhaps thin and wizened, or even grossly obese. Raoul de Lamareau was none of these. The uncle who terrorized Annette must have been in his early thirties, with a wavy mantle of thick dark hair. He was standing by a sorrel horse hitched to a lady's fashionable phaeton and was lightly stroking the animal's head as it nuzzled his hand. As the train shivered and groaned to a stop, he gave the horse one last pat, then strode purposefully along the platform, looking up at the windows of the train. He wore riding breeches, a flared jacket and black boots with the comfortable, casual arrogance of someone who pleases himself.

As Raoul de Lamareau's gaze passed our window, the feeble sun played upon his face like the swift strokes of an artist's brush and cast light and dark shadows upon his crisp Teutonic features. The intensity of his brown-black eyes matched a firm full mouth which at the moment held no hint of a smile. His face was composed of hard angles and somehow I knew his hand-someness was a tool he used dispassionately and perhaps callously. No wonder Annette's mother's accusations against him had fallen on deaf ears. Everything about him exuded an aristocratic authority that few would dare dispute.

I turned my gaze away from the window, realizing that my heartbeat had strangely quickened. Even though I discounted Annette's melodramatic accusations, I did *not* want to meet this man. I wanted nothing to do with the sinister atmosphere that Annette had drawn around her home-coming. Even now, the young girl was cowering in her seat and I wondered if I was going to have trouble getting her off the train. "It's all right, Annette. Come on now," I ordered as briskly as I could. "You'll be in your mother's arms in no time."

"Why isn't Mama here to meet me?"

"I don't know . . . but I'm certain there's a reasonable explanation. We can't tarry here." Briskly, I herded the young girl down the aisle. As we made our way to the end of the car, I realized that my own mouth was peculiarly dry.

The conductor smiled, tipped his hat, and handed us down. We had tarried so long that we were the last passengers off the train.

Before we had reached the last step,

Monsieur de Lamareau stepped forward to greet us. He bowed politely but there was a hint of annoyance in his voice. "I had begun to fear that you had missed your train."

Annette kept her eyes lowered, refusing to look her uncle in the face, or acknowledge his greeting.

His jet black eyebrows drew together. "I see that a year at school has not improved your manners, Annette." Then his dark gaze shifted and settled on me. "Mademoiselle Grant . . . Raoul de Lamareau. We are in your debt for graciously seeing our young lady home."

"It was my pleasure, Monsieur de Lamareau," I replied in an equally formal tone. "Thank you for extending your hospitality to me for the night." He would not find my manners wanting, I determined, with a stubborn thrust of my chin. Under different circumstances I might have offered a friendly smile and some social repartee to ease the situation but I had no desire to converse with this formidable Frenchman.

Annette summoned courage enough to raise her fearful eyes and stare at her uncle. "Where is Mama? Why didn't she come?"

"Your mother is not feeling well, Annette. I volunteered to come instead. The carriage is waiting."

Annette's face fell and I thought she might burst into tears at any moment. I touched her arm and smiled encouragingly. "It will be good to get home, Annette."

As her uncle deftly guided us along the platform, I glanced up at the crisp, lean profile of Raoul de Lamareau with its cleft, angular chin and high cheekbones. It would be difficult to remain neutral and passive about this man, I thought. He was the kind who could dominate your life . . . and perhaps destroy it. Even though I did not believe the things that Annette had said about him, I was uncomfortable in his company. Suddenly I felt a great reluctance to be his houseguest for even one night. I must have slowed my steps perceptibly for Monsieur de Lamareau looked at me questioningly. "Is something the matter, Mademoiselle? Did you forget something on the train, *peut-être*?"

"No, I . . . I was just thinking that perhaps it might be better for me to continue my journey this afternoon instead of delaying until tomorrow."

"Mademoiselle Grant!" wailed Annette. "You promised . . . you promised. You said you'd stay—"

"Annette, control yourself," admonished her uncle. "If Mademoiselle Grant does not want to interrupt her journey, that is her decision and we must respect it."

His eyes locked with mine. For a moment I was shocked by the intensity there. He wanted me gone. It was as clear as if he had voiced the words. He was relieved that I was about to change my mind about spending the night at his chateau. This lack of hospitality made me wonder if Annette was right about him. Was she really in danger? I couldn't ignore Annette's ashen and pleading face. I would never forgive myself if something happened because I did not fulfill my responsibility to see her home.

"Yes, Mademoiselle?" Raoul de Lamareau raised an eyebrow and waited.

"Perhaps it would be better if I stay over one night as I promised . . . if you are certain my presence will not be an inconvenience?" My steady gaze was searching as it fixed upon his face, but his expression was inscrutable.

"It will be our pleasure, Mademoiselle," he responded smoothly. Only a tightness in his firm jaw verified the impression that he was disappointed I had changed my mind.

I could not rid myself of the feeling that he would have been most relieved to put me back on the train. I knew I should have gone. I sensed a controlled fury within

Monsieur de Lamareau that might be as dangerous as Annette had claimed.

Several people nodded and murmured a polite, "*Bonjour, Monsieur de Lamareau.*" They moved aside and allowed us ample room for passage along the platform. The deference they showed him was obvious. Curious eyes looked me over. Their scrutiny made me very much aware of my simple straw bonnet and my mother's cast-off traveling outfit. From my attire, it must have certainly appeared that I was in service to the de Lamareaus. My independent pride made me hold my head even higher as we made our way to the waiting carriage which I had seen from the train window.

A small phaeton with shiny black wheels and a tufted plush seat was comfortable enough for two but would be crowded with three people. I wondered if Monsieur de Lamareau was going to ride with us.

As if reading my thoughts, he indicated a beautiful chestnut stallion tethered to a railing. "I'll escort the carriage to the chateau. It is some five miles distant. I think you will find our home quite pleasant, Mademoiselle. It was in our family before the revolution and even though some of it has not been restored completely, I'm sure you will find it most comfortable." Was there a sardonic twist to his smile as if he knew from my attire that I was not used to aristocratic luxury?

"Annette has explained that only one half of the house is in use at the present. I understand that her father, the late heir, had some financial reversals," I said sweetly and was rewarded by a flash of anger in his deep-set eyes. He was a proud man, and not one who wanted the family's private concerns to be discussed. It was childishness on my part to taunt him with the knowledge but his condescending manner had riled me.

"Annette exaggerates," he replied curtly. Then he nodded to an agile, middle-aged driver who had been busy collecting and loading our luggage and now readily sprang up into the high seat.

Monsieur de Lamareau helped Annette into the carriage and then turned to me, offering his arm as assistance. I found his polite touch upon me rather disconcerting as his dexterous, firm hands guided me upward into the seat. His gaze settled on me and I pulled at my skirts to settle them respectably around me, an involuntary blush mounting in my cheeks. A slight curve of his lips was mocking as he turned away and swung his well-toned body up into the saddle of the sleek chestnut steed.

He touched his high-spirited mount lightly and led the carriage away from the station.

We had only gone a few yards, however, when the sorrel horse drawing our carriage suddenly reared up, gave a piercing whinny, and crashed backwards in its traces.

I screamed and tried to grab on to the sides of the carriage. The animal lashed out with his feet, threw his head from side to side, his mouth open like a crazed beast fighting unseen demons.

Our driver shouted, pulled frantically on the reins, and fought to bring him under control. But he couldn't. The horse had gone mad.

Annette and I screamed as we tried to stay inside the carriage. It careened from side to side and then tipped up crazily on one wheel.

The frantic horse lunged backwards and one of the traces snapped.

"Watch out!"

"It's going over!"

The carriage tipped again—higher and higher, then over on its side. I lost my frantic hold on the seat and screamed as I was flung out over the side. A peripheral view of Raoul de Lamareau mounted on his chestnut horse came to me just as the ground came up to hit me.

Instantly fierce colors spread like fire behind my eyes and jagged pain shot through a wrist that lay twisted under me. Sweet warm blood trickled from my forehead into my mouth. Voices came from far away, distorted as through layers of water.

"This one's hurt—"

"Get Doctor Duboise . . . he's in the station."

"What happened?"

"Horse went crazy—"

Horse went crazy. The phrase clanged in my head, over and over again. It demanded recognition. Spirals of pain tried to blot out all thinking but in some clear-cut corner of my mind, I knew what I was trying to remember. In flashes of stark perception, the scene came back—Raoul de Lamareau standing by the carriage horse, stroking its head as the train pulled in. *Had he been feeding something to the animal as it nuzzled his hand?*

Chapter Two

"It's all right, Mademoiselle." A deep male voice was reassuring. "We've brought you to the chateau and put you to bed. I'm Dr. Duboise. Just lie still. You're going to be all right. Just a nasty bump on the head. Your wrist is sprained but everything else seems fine . . . just fine."

My eyelids fluttered upward and my vision cleared. A square-faced, gray-haired man with a pair of square spectacles on the tip of his bulbous nose was bending over me. His full lips curved pleasantly and there were smile lines around the softest blue eyes I had ever seen. He was obviously pleased that I had pushed aside the murky curtains that had enveloped me since the accident. I groaned and lifted a hand to my forehead.

"No, don't touch," Dr. Duboise said gently and drew my hand down. "We're putting cold cloths on that nasty bump to keep the swelling down. You've suffered a small head cut, some loss of blood, but nothing serious. I've wrapped your left wrist securely to keep it in position because of a sprain. Do you hurt anywhere else?"

It was an asinine question, I decided angrily, for my whole body felt as though it had been pounded like pieces of laundry upon a rock. When my only answer to his question was a groan, he spooned some rather bitter medicine into my mouth. "There . . . that will ease some of the discomfort. You will sleep now and when you awaken you will feel much better, I promise you."

I was about to protest that I did not want to sleep. "Annette?" I croaked in a half-whisper.

"She's fine . . . thrown clear . . . just a few scratches, that's all. Very lucky. Both of you. The horse had to be destroyed. I can't imagine what sent it into such a crazed fit."

The horse . . . the carriage . . . Monsieur de Lamareau standing beside it. The scene I had viewed through the train window tugged at my memory. Had Annette's uncle cupped his hand under the horse's mouth, feeding it something? I couldn't be sure but I needed to tell someone. Even as I willed my mouth to shape the words there was no breath to give them strength. The bitter medicine was already taking affect. I felt myself slipping away even as I struggled to say something.

"That's it. Be a good girl and rest." He patted my shoulder. "I'll drop by and see you in the morning."

I heard him giving someone instructions about cold compresses for my head and then I drifted beyond the sound of his voice. Pain eased away from my body and I gave myself up to the magic of the laudanum he had given me.

When I awoke it was with a cold flash of terror, like the clammy cold cloth that lay on my body. My muscles were tense and rigid; my eyes darted about in a frantic manner. I was like a trapped animal poised for escape. My heart raced and my forehead was beaded with sweat. For a moment, I couldn't orient myself. I was like someone coming out of a horrible nightmare, deeply afraid but not knowing why. For several seconds I just lay there stiff, afraid to move. Slowly my shallow breathing began to deepen, the loud thumping in my heart eased and whatever had awakened me with such a lurch of fear was lost in the deep regions of the subconscious.

Soft, muted sunlight spilled into the room. Graying lace curtains billowed silently at three recessed windows flanked by deep brown drapes drawn back by tarnished gold cords. Even with the slightly opened windows, a musty, unaired smell filled my nostrils as if the room had been hurriedly "laid out" for my occupancy.

As I gazed up at the high ceiling, I could see dust webs caught in decorative moldings that crisscrossed in the high ceiling. I turned my head and the walls papered in a fading bold design swirled in a defeating vertigo. I closed my eyes against pain that seemed to come from behind my throbbing temple.

"Are you feeling better, Mam'selle?"

The voice startled me because I had thought I was alone. My gaze flew up to a figure standing by the bed. I saw a woman with thick shoulders and muscular build, dressed in a servant's black uniform and small white cap on dull brown hair. Her features were broad and flat and without expression as she took a cloth from my forehead and dampened it again.

"Please help me sit up," I croaked. A sense of urgency was back again.

"No. Mam'selle must rest. *Je m'appelle* Nela and I am here to serve you," she said in the same flat tone. "Does mam'selle wish something to eat, *peut-être*?"

"No," I croaked. The last thing I wanted to put in my queasy stomach was food.

"You must eat to regain your strength, mam'selle," she countered as if my answer to her question was of little consequence. "I will bring a tray."

She was out of the room before I could protest further.

The bed on which I lay was massive with high carved posts and a headboard decorated in a baroque design. A mammoth highboy, dressing table with marble top, and wide armoire were made of the same dark wood as the bed. There was one well-worn, deep cushioned black leather chair near the windows and a lumpy, scarred footstool stood before it. The furnishings were heavy and masculine and motes of dust floated in the air as if recently disturbed. I thought a faint smell of tobacco lingered in the room. It was not the kind of guest room I had expected to enjoy during my one night at the Lamareau chateau.

At that moment, I discovered to my embarrassment that I was wearing one of my mother's cast-off nightgowns which she had sent me just before I left school. It was a pink, lacy confection with only a pretense of covering my shoulders and the nipples of my breasts. The garment was a sharp contrast to the plain cotton nightgowns I usually wore. No doubt Nela had found the flimsy garment among my things and put it on me while I was unconscious. My mother's perfume lingered in the silken folds of the seductive nightgown and the familiar scent brought sudden tears to my eyes. I wiped at my eyes with my one good hand.

Why was I crying? For my mother? No, I had come to terms with the truth long ago that my presence only complicated things for her and I had finally accepted her lack of caring about me. My feelings about my mother had always been a mélange of resentment, deep affection, and hate. I could not understand how I could love her and yet entertain such profound lack of respect for her.

My English father, Byron Grant, had met my mother when in Paris on an assignment for the government in his role as Administrator of Foreign Trade. *La Belle*

Nicole Bizet, as my mother was billed in small letters on the marquee, had been appearing in a French comedy when the young Englishman first saw her and fell promptly in love with her. Later my mother admitted that she had no intention of marrying him but my father pursued her through several of her acting failures. Unfortunately Nicole Bizet's vivacious beauty and joie de vivre could not compensate for her lack of talent and she finally gave up the stage, married Byron Grant, and moved to London.

I arrived barely nine and a half months later, much to my father's joy and my mother's consternation. I was christened Alysha Marie Grant. We lived in a modest Queen Anne house just off Regent Street in the City of London. My mother's volatile personality was in sharp contrast to my father's stubborn, independent, Johnny Bull steadiness but the first six years of my life were happy ones despite their inevitable clashes of temperament. Much of the conflict between them was over me.

I was not a docile child. My mother's efforts to make me a miniature of herself failed miserably. My earliest dancing classes are memories of stubborn, willful fiascos; I behaved abominably at every lesson at which a retired French ballerina sought to instruct me. I hated the starchy tutus and the hours spent learning ridiculous feet positions. Proper, ladylike activities bored me. Racing along with my father in the park, my bonnet streamers flying and my pinafores all muddy from splashing in some puddle was more to my liking. My mother scolded and my father tried to appease her while he elicited promises from me that I would do as my mother wished. But I never did. Once I disgraced my mother by wandering off when we were having tea with a socially prominent dowager and hid in the servants' quarters of the mansion for nearly an hour. Then I returned to the drawing room and repeated all the odious things I heard the cook and butler say about their socially elite mistress and her guests.

When I was almost seven years old, my father unexpectedly died of influenza complications, leaving my mother and me with only meager financial resources. The warm safe cocoon that had protected me since birth broke apart at his death and the security he had provided for my mother was jerked away.

My mother decided to return to France. Perhaps she had hopes of returning to the stage but she soon discovered that her thespian skills were still inadequate for a professional career. Although she was still a very attractive woman, she was eight years older than when she'd married my father, and no longer an ingenue. She solved our financial dilemma by becoming the mistress of a middle-aged French businessman, Maurice Travois. He was a burly man in his fifties, thick-shouldered, with a wide trunk which was well-balanced by muscular legs and arms. He had a loud, booming voice, a strident manner, but strangely enough, I was never frightened of him. When he spoke to my mother and me, his gruffness was usually accompanied by a hint of a smile on his craggy face. He was married, but had no children.

Maurice Travois traveled a great deal in his import-export business and my mother and I accompanied him on many of these trips. As a result, I became fluent in French and Italian. He often took me to disreputable places which my mother never learned about. Later I realized some of the people from whom he bought his art objects must have been dealing in stolen or blackmarket goods. At the time, I just enjoyed each adventure. He would laugh and ruffle my hair. "You should have been a boy, Alysha." He seemed to appreciate my renegade spirit and, like my father had been, became my conspirator.

Those were happy years. Monsieur Travois was very good to me. Despite my mother's scoldings, Maurice spoiled me as if I were his own child. Then it all ended when I was almost twelve years old. Monsieur Travois became seriously ill, suffering a stroke in the front bedroom of our pretty little house. An ambulance took him to St. Mary's Hospital and Maurice's wife, whom we had never seen, took charge. We were refused permission to visit him and our letters were returned unopened. We learned later that his wife had taken Monsieur Travois to southern France and Italy to live. All contact was cut off between us and his financial support was withdrawn. Once again the stabilizing male force in my life was gone. Mother and I were on our own again.

As before, my mother used her sensuous good looks and outgoing personality to snare another "protector." Only this one was younger and didn't want me around . . . so I was sent off to Switzerland and kept out of the way for six years. Since her new lover paid the bills, Mama said the least we could do was accept the situation with as much grace as possible. I rather suspected she was at the age where she didn't want a twelve-year-old daughter underfoot, anyway. I rarely joined her and spent most of the holidays at the homes of other girls. Her visits to the school were fleeting. On these occasions, she seemed pleased that I seemed to be finally acquiring some ladylike attributes. On the surface I looked quite presentable—and mother was never one to look beneath the surface. Except for those few happy years when she was Maurice Travois's mistress, she had little time and energy for me. When I had been sent away to school, I had missed Monsieur Travois more than I had my mother. No, it was *not* homesickness for my mother that made me tearful. Her last letter had firmly cut any maternal cords between us.

I don't know what happened to her great *affaire de coeur* but a month ago, I received an unexpected letter from my mother. "Alysha, *ma chérie*. Such devastation. No warning. One moment a tender, considerate lover and the next—an utter cad. I hate to impart such sad news. *Vraiment*, I'm on my own again. It's a blessing that your schooling is now complete. I have approached a gentleman friend in Paris on your behalf. Monsieur Anton Roget will hire you as one of his *grisettes*. He is in charge of a successful dressmaking establishment. I am certain that the Sisters have instructed you in sewing a fine seam and Monsieur Roget is willing to train you in more sophisticated needlework. You will find him friendly and accommodating. Make yourself pretty and charming and appreciative. Under his patronage, you could do well for yourself. Remember, my daughter, a woman must look after herself as best she can. *Amour, toujours*, Mama."

Friendly and accommodating. She had not said so but between the lines my mother was admonishing me to look to my own future in the only way she knew how—as a paramour. Had Monsieur Roget already set the terms of my employment and was my mother cautioning me to go along with them? I knew what the working conditions were in such dressmaking establishments. Poverty-stricken *grisettes* spent twelve hours a day in airless rooms, straining their eyes and rounding their backs as they sewed delicate garments ordered by the affluent customers who demanded fine seams, elaborate beading, and miniscule embroidery. There was no security, and no future. Only the wiliest and the most unscrupulous women found a niche in the highly competitive fashion world. I had no special talent in designing or stitching women's garments. The wages would be a pittance. My stomach tightened at the thought. My father's stubborn, independent traits ran strongly in me. I was more like

him than my mother even though I had
inherited some of her fair beauty. I had to
find a way to take care of myself. But how?
I knew what could happen to young,
unattached women with no means of
support.

Why had the sweet scent of my mother's
perfume suddenly made my eyes swim with
tears? Because I felt helpless. I blinked
back the fullness in my eyes. Yes, that must
be it. The morning train to Paris was
leaving without me. I should have followed
my intuition yesterday when that brief
flicker of apprehension had slowed my
steps. It would have been easy to avoid all
of this. Raoul de Lamareau had been ready
to put me back on the train, I was sure of
that. He had not wanted me to stay. Under
the guise of his politeness, I had felt his
silent urging to go on to Paris without inter-
rupting my journey.

Had he known what was going to happen?
Now I knew that my presentiment to leave
before something happened had been valid.
But I had stayed and now I couldn't go on to
Paris as planned. My left hand throbbed
with pain just lying motionless beside me. I
certainly was in no condition to apply for
work. I could not earn any money as a
seamstress until the swelling in my wrist
went down and my fingers were no longer

in pain. To throw myself on Monsieur Roget's bounty would place me in exactly the kind of paramour relationship my mother had suggested.

But I couldn't stay here. Were Annette's melodramatic accusations true? The accident that could have killed us both was something I could not just wave away as an unfortunate happenstance. It could have been deliberate. Had I unwillingly been trapped by Raoul de Lamareau's villainy? A rise of anger diluted the wash of self-pity and I felt some of my usual resiliency surge back. I had never been one to meekly accept any predicament. Even though I couldn't do anything at the moment to change the situation, I did not intend to become a helpless pawn in Raoul de Lamareau's evil schemes. I would keep alert to anything that would confirm my suspicions that Annette's uncle had fed something to the horse which caused it to behave in that crazed fashion. He might be able to put the fear of God in everyone else but my stubborn English backbone would not let me cower before him or anyone else.

Nela came back with a tray clutched in her broad hands. She plumped my pillows so that I could sip the fragrant, spicy tea and nibble at the freshly baked scones which she spread lavishly with butter. To my surprise, under her steady gaze I managed to eat and drink most of what she had brought. The food sat queasily in my stomach but I did feel stronger for having eaten.

"The doctor will be here in a few minutes," she informed me briskly.

My good hand went up to my bare neck and shoulders. "I want to change into my flannel gown and robe," I told the servant. Even though I had inherited my mother's fair hair and ivory complexion, I was afraid of anything that might make me look and behave like my mother. I kept my hair drawn back tightly so none of the natural curl could betray me. I remade all her cast-off clothes so that they were sensible and without adornment. It was my father's sensible, strong, independent heredity that I cultivated . . . not my mother's guileless, flirtatious femininity.

Nela turned her broad back on me and brought the frilly peignoir which matched the lacy nightgown. Once again heavy, feminine perfume emitted from the folds and when I closed my eyes, I could almost believe my mother had entered the room.

Despite my protest that I wanted my flannel, high-necked robe, Nela raised me up and with one broad arm behind my back slipped the lacy, ruffled garment on me.

The peignoir was fashioned of the same soft pink silk as the nightgown and its neckline was equally seductive. Tiny pink satin roses decorated the bodice and sleeves and lace inserts showed white skin on my arms and neck. If I had had the energy I would have changed into one of my cotton nightgowns myself but my left arm was confined in a sling and my wrist was heavily bandaged. For the moment, I could do nothing but accept the administrations of this stubborn servant who turned a deaf ear to my wishes.

She washed my face and hands with warm water and to my surprise, her large hands were surprisingly gentle. She brought a silver brush that belonged to a set gracing the polished top of an elegant dressing table and began smoothing my hair which was in an utter state of disarray. Very gingerly she brushed the long strands. "Such a lovely pale color. And soft, natural curl," she murmured. "A wave over the ugly yellow bump on your temple? The rest without pins so that will be comfortable for you?" Her deferential manner suggested I had some say in the matter.

"No. I always part it in the middle and pull it straight back into a twist on my neck."

"This will be much more comfortable, Mam'selle," she said flatly.

I sighed. She would do what she wanted to do. I knew then that there had really been no choice. This stubborn woman could not be cajoled into doing anything she set her mind against. For the moment, there was nothing I could do but accept her decisions.

I don't care, I thought wearily. Let the woman do what she wanted with my hair. Evidently the medicine I had been taking had sapped my energy. Tomorrow I would be strong enough to pin it back properly, I thought, albeit with one hand.

When Nela was finished, she put her large head to one side and viewed her efforts. She nodded as if satisfied. Then her thick fingers retied the satin ribbon dipping low on the soft skin of my neck and she fluffed the ruffled sleeves falling halfway down my arms. "Mam'selle, rest now. Doctor will be here soon."

"I do feel tired," I admitted.

She nodded, deftly balanced the tray on one broad hip and left the bedroom, quietly closing the door after her.

I was glad that Dr. Duboise was coming. I was anxious to talk to him about the extent of my injuries and how soon I could expect to be recovered.

I must have dozed off because a firm knock on the bedroom door jerked me awake. I raised my head and said eagerly,

"Come in." Then the enthusiasm went out of my voice. "Oh—?"

It was not the smiling, blue-eyed doctor who entered but Raoul de Lamareau. "Good morning, Mademoiselle Grant."

The sight of him invading the privacy of my bedroom was so startling and disturbing that I couldn't think what I should do or say. I knew my expression was quite hostile.

He stopped a respectable distance from the bed. His expression was different from the one I had seen so briefly at the train station. It seemed softer, more relaxed. His broad forehead and long straight nose seemed less arrogant. It was a face of contrasts—a mobile, yet firm mouth, dark-lashed, brownish-black eyes which seemed to be calculating, sardonically amused, or genuinely sympathetic. I couldn't tell which. He was impeccably dressed in a burgundy morning coat, matching striped trousers, and a soft black tie which accented the whiteness of his starched linen. His high black boots were polished and the buckle on his leather belt shone like gold. "How are you feeling this morning?"

"*Très bien, merci,*" I said stiffly, resisting the urge to use my one good hand to pull the covers up around my neck.

I flushed as his bold gaze lazily examined

the loose waves of my fair hair which Nela
had draped softly around my face to hide
the ugly bump on my forehead and his eyes
lingered pointedly on the low décolleté of
the frilly peignoir. With that one measured
glance he was able to make me feel totally
undressed. I knew from his brazen manner
that a lady's boudoir was not an unfamiliar
place for him.

Anger diluted my embarrassment. How
dare he intrude upon my privacy like this!
"I was expecting Dr. Duboise," I said
pointedly.

His lips curved in a slight smile. "How
fortunate for Dr. Duboise. Your metamorphosis is startling, Mademoiselle
Grant. I must confess that I am surprised to
see you looking so . . . so enchanting." Once
more his deliberate gaze traveled down the
curve of my neck to the tiny satin roses
trailing over the swelling curves of my
breasts. "*Très ravissante.*"

I drew in my breath. "I find your manner
extremely rude and offensive, Monsieur."

"And I find the seductive scent of your
perfume quite provocative. Not at all what I
would expect of a young woman just
completing her studies at a proper
finishing school. You surprise me,
Mademoiselle Grant. I had thought myself a
good judge of feminine subterfuge but I

must confess that your charms lay quite
hidden from me yesterday."

Pride would not let me admit that the
feminine lingerie and perfume were not
mine but my mother's. Even though his
manner disturbed me, I did not want Raoul
de Lamareau to find me gauche. I was
caught between wanting to retreat behind
my usual defenses while at the same time
challenging his interest. At this point, I was
not about to admit to the high-necked,
cotton gowns of a schoolgirl. "I don't know
what you're talking about."

"You must admit that yesterday you
arrived with all your feminine allure
hidden like a drab bird under somber
plumage." His smile was infuriating.

"I admit nothing of the kind." I found his
description thoroughly insulting. A drab
bird, indeed! Just because I didn't flaunt
feminine fripperies, he dismissed me as not
worthy of his interest.

He stepped closer to the bed and I was
more aware of his virile presence than I
wanted to be. My chest rose and fell rapidly
as my heartbeat quickened.

An expression impossible to decipher
flitted across his face. He seemed to be
struggling to find the right words. "I want
to express my deep regrets for what
happened yesterday. I am completely at a

loss as to why the carriage horse suddenly became deranged like that."

"Yes, what could have made him behave in such a fashion?" I baited, waiting for his answer and keeping my eyes pinned upon his bold features.

"I don't know. I am completely at a loss to explain it."

"Do you think someone could have fed him something?" I challenged.

For a moment silence hung in the air. His expression did not change but I knew that my words had not struck him as innocent.

"And for what reason, Mademoiselle, would they do such a thing?" he countered, his wintry dark eyes delving into mine.

"To deliberately cause the accident." It was reckless and exactly the kind of thing which I had schooled myself not to do. This was a dangerous man and I had no doubt that he would hold to any course he set out for himself, regardless of how ruthless it might be. Some inner voice warned me that I was as much at his mercy as Annette and her poor mother and little brother.

"And who would want to arrange such a diabolical accident?" he asked. His forehead furrowed as if welcoming any ideas I might have.

"Who, indeed?" I could not keep from flinging the challenge, never lowering my gaze from his face.

For a moment he did not respond and
then he smiled. A devastating softness
reached his mobile lips and deepened a
cleft in his cheek. "I do believe that you're
about to accuse me of the foul deed,
Mademoiselle."

I did not deny it.

He startled me by laughing. "You are not
lacking in directness, Mademoiselle. But
then you are English. That is their way,
n'est-ce pas?"

"My father was English; my mother
French. My father died when I was almost
seven but Mother is alive."

"In Paris?"

"No, she is living in the Riviera at the
moment with . . . with . . . with friends," I
finished lamely.

He was not fooled. His dark eyebrow
raised knowingly. My stammering had told
him much more than I had intended. His
sardonic smile was an insult. New heat rose
in my cheeks as his eyes slipped to the deep
décolleté of my peignoir.

"And she is . . . fair like you?"

I bristled, not knowing where the
conversation was going. A glib response
escaped me.

"I assure you that I would never be a
party to risking such a lovely neck." His

voice softened as his eyes traveled over my bare shoulders. "I am heartily sorry for your injuries, Mademoiselle Grant."

Feelings I did not understand made me lash out. "Dr. Duboise said Annette and I might have been killed."

He sobered. "Yes, it's very fortunate that both of you escaped without serious injuries. By the way, I have dismissed Dr. Duboise and asked our own family doctor to tend you."

"No! I want Dr. Duboise."

"I know nothing about him. He is not a local physician. He just happened to be at the station when the accident happened. I understand he's only a visitor in the area."

"I don't care." I was suddenly fearful that Dr. Duboise might be the only lifeline I had to the outside world. The doctor had seen what had happened at the station. He knew I was here recuperating under this roof. Sister Josette and my mother would think that I'd gone on today and there would be no reason for Sister to check on me. We had said our "goodbyes" and her responsibility toward me had been dissolved. Monsieur Roget would think I had changed my mind if I didn't show up in Paris to assume the seamstress job that my mother had arranged for me. As for my mother, she probably would not be concerned about my whereabouts for months. I liked Dr. Duboise. It was important that someone outside the de Lamareau sphere of influence knew that I had been hurt and was recuperating here at the chateau. I feared that the family doctor might somehow be in league with Raoul de Lamareau. How could I trust his choice of a physician? I set my chin.

"I want Dr. Duboise!" I put all my strength into that declaration, not knowing what I would do if he dismissed my wishes as unimportant.

He shrugged. "There is no need to upset yourself, Mademoiselle. It makes no difference to me. If you prefer some stranger to our very competent Dr. Vanderley, I will not try to dissuade you."

I relaxed visibly. "Thank you."

"If there is anything else you wish—?"

"My only desire is to continue my journey as quickly as possible. I shall not intrude upon your hospitality any longer than necessary."

"You have someone waiting for you in Paris?"

It was an innocent question but I stiffened. For some reason I knew that I must not let him know that I was adrift without protection. "Yes. I shall have to write him today and tell him that I have been delayed." I knew I was giving him the impression that a romantic attachment awaited me in Paris. Somehow I felt safer if he thought I had someone who was personally watching out for me.

"Yes, of course. You will want to be on your way as soon as possible. I'm certain that Annette will enjoy your company while you are here. You mustn't let her monopolize you . . . or fill your ears with her fanciful imaginings." His eyes narrowed. "But, of course, she probably has already made me out as a monster, *n'est-ce pas?*"

I saw no reason to lie. Annette's behavior at the train had plainly shown her fear. "Yes."

"She told you of my brother's death?"

I nodded. I knew he could read from my expression what else she had said. His next words confirmed it.

"I was cleared of any implication in my brother's death. It is Annette's mother's misguided conviction that I'm responsible but I suppose Annette told you all of that?"

"Among other things." I was not going to offer any specific information. If it was true that he was trying to force his brother's widow into marriage, I would not do myself any good by confronting him with it. "I do not intend to involve myself in the de

Lamareau family's private affairs."

"That is very wise. You will not be disturbed by the regular household. This wing of the chateau has been shut off since my brother's death."

My eyes widened. "This was his room?"

"One of them. My brother was quite eccentric. He liked to shut himself away like a hermit for long periods of time. This room was one of his retreats."

"But I would rather be close to the rest of the family," I protested.

"At the moment I don't think that wise. I wouldn't want you further distressed. You would do well to confine yourself to this side of the chateau."

He smiled but his eyes were quite wintry, as if his thoughts were anything but warm. I knew then that he expected me to heed the warning he had given me.

Chapter Three

I had no more visitors that day and by the
next afternoon, I had decided that Raoul de
Lamareau must have dismissed Dr.
Duboise after all. I was not surprised. He
would not like having a strange doctor in
the house who might see and report things
to the villagers. I was positive now he had
not really wanted me to stay at the chateau
overnight. When I hesitated at the station,
he would have been quite happy to put the

"drab bird" back on the train. Now that I was under his roof, he had taken charge of my stay. If he wanted to cut me off from any outside contact, he was in a position to do so. I could protest the isolation but at the moment I was unable to do anything about it.

Neither Annette nor her mother came to inquire about my health. I reasoned that Annette might have been told to stay away but surely the mistress of the house would make a polite visit to inquire about my health. Had Raoul de Lamareau forbidden it? Did he intend to keep me away from the rest of the family and confined to this isolated room? Were there things he did not wish me to see during my unexpected visit? Like blind bats, these questions whipped around in my confused mind.

The servant, Nela, was the only person who came and went and saw to my needs. The large woman was pleasant enough in a stiff, unemotional kind of way but I knew that her strong, muscular arms could easily subdue me if it came to any kind of physical struggle.

I had decided against taking any more medicine to dull the pain in my wrist. I preferred the dull ache and occasional sharp knifelike jabs to the drugged, fuzzy state of mind which the laudanum induced. By the next afternoon, my head had cleared.

Like a prisoner bridling at unseen restraints, I waited until Nela had taken the lunch tray back to the kitchen and then threw back the light coverlet she had placed over me. Very cautiously I eased up on my feet, trying out my rubbery legs. I clutched a bedpost with my free arm as the floor rose and fell beneath me. I swayed on my feet but slowly the vertigo ceased.

After a few moments, I felt steady enough to let go of the bedpost. I felt my way around the edge of the room, going from one piece of heavy furniture to the next. A small throw rug on the wide oak planking felt gritty under my bare feet as if it had not been taken out and beaten for a long time. My head felt light enough to float away as I wavered across the room and sat down gratefully on one of the window seats.

I pulled aside one of the graying lace curtains and peered outside. Rounded gray stone walls stretched away from my high window in both directions. I seemed to be at one end of an E-shaped French chateau which was set in a wide expanse of grassy meadow cupped by a dark fringe of trees. A cultivated garden lay close to the house. Afternoon sunshine made dappled patterns under huge oak, maple and poplar trees which spread a grid of branches over silken lawns and flagstone paths. Dark hedges, precisely manicured, made intricate patterns of various heights. It was the kind of formal garden the French people put around their royal residences. Distant voices floated up to me and I stretched my neck until I could see below. A servant woman and young boy came into view along a path bordered by low-growing, carefully trimmed shrubs.

The young boy, about seven, was playing with a ball. I thought he must be André, Annette's younger brother. The woman's plain dress indicated a *bonne d'enfant* or governess. The boy's dark hair caught the sunlight like shiny blue-black raven wings and as he lifted his face, laughing, I saw a resemblance to the bold profile of his uncle, Raoul de Lamareau. For a moment my chest tightened.

I could not sort out my emotions. Was I suddenly afraid for the child? Or had the resemblance reminded me that once Monsieur de Lamareau had been such a laughing youngster? I reasoned that he must have skipped along the same path and chased a ball across the lawn just as André was doing now. Once he had been soft and vulnerable like André, I thought. I had seen hints of it in his clouded dark eyes but if Annette was right, he wanted the family inheritance for himself and was willing to eliminate anyone who stood in the way of getting it—even the happy little boy chasing a ball in the garden.

At that moment I heard scurrying, thumping noises in the hall outside my room.

"Beau . . . Beau . . . come back here, you naughty cat," a young girl's voice scolded.

I strained my ears to hear. "Annette . . . Annette, is that you?"

Annette's muffled voice came through the keyhole. "Mademoiselle Grant?"

"*Oui, entrez,*" I called.

The doorknob turned slowly and for a moment I thought the door was locked. Then a pair of dark eyes and two bright round furry yellow ones peered through the widening crack.

"Mademoiselle?"

"Yes, over here. On the window seat."

Annette peered in, her furtive gaze sliding around the room.

"It's all right," I assured her, delighted that she and her cat had found me.

"What are you doing here?" she croaked in a low whisper. "My father never let anyone in this room." She looked about as if he were about to rise out of the leather chair and reprimand her.

"It's all right," I said again. "Come in."

Annette clutched the cat as she rushed over to the window seat. "I didn't know where they had put you. Uncle Raoul said I would just make a pest of myself and you needed rest." Tears welled up in her eyes. "I didn't know how badly you were hurt or if maybe you were dead."

"I'm fine. Didn't your uncle tell you that my injuries were minor . . . that I'd be perfectly recovered in a few days?"

"Yes. But I didn't believe him. He lies. Even the servants lie. No one would tell me where you were. If I hadn't been chasing Beau into this side of the house, I never would have found you. Papa never allowed us to come into this wing." She cocked her head. "I wonder why Uncle Raoul didn't put you with the rest of the family. Why did he want you so far away from us?"

I wondered the same thing myself but I didn't say so, not wanting to add fuel to her simmering anxiety. "I don't know but I'm sure he had a good reason."

"What made the horse act so crazy?"

Again I had to admit I didn't know. I certainly wasn't going to voice any of my suspicions to Annette. She had enough emotional stress without my adding to it.

"They had to shoot it." Annette's voice quivered.

"I know. I'm glad you escaped injury. It

was a frightening experience."

"I'm sorry you were hurt." She blinked back tears.

I patted her hand. "It's only a sprained wrist and a bump on my head. I'll have to stay here for a few days until I can use my hand again."

"Good." The girl smiled and I saw how pretty she was when her eyes weren't clouded with fear and apprehension. "I'm glad you aren't going away."

"But I am . . . in a few days," I insisted. She had to accept the fact that this wasn't going to be an extended visit.

"Maybe you'll decide to stay longer," she insisted stubbornly.

I decided not to pursue the point. There was time enough for goodbyes later. "I just saw your brother in the garden. I bet André is glad to have you home again."

She nodded. "And Beau is too. He slept with me last night." Annette's face was luminous as she petted the cat. "He was lonesome for me."

The kitten she had talked so much about at school was now fully grown. The cat's long legs hung out of her arms in a haphazard fashion as she petted him. "So this is the famous Beau," I smiled. "He looks like a pirate with that dark patch of fur over one eye."

Annette nodded and smiled back, her
facial muscles relaxing. Beau contemplated
the pigeons fluttering outside the window
and his tongue shot out eagerly. Both
Annette and I laughed when he pushed his
nose against the glass and then looked dis-
gusted when they all flew away. He settled
himself in Annette's lap and began to work
his paws in purring contentment, peering
up at us with slanted, sleepy eyes.

"I'll bet your mother was happy to see
you, too."

Her eyes clouded. "I haven't seen Mama."

"You haven't seen your mother?" I
echoed, unable to keep the surprise out of
my voice.

Annette shook her head solemnly. "I went
to her room yesterday and again this
morning . . . but she's not there."

"Where is she? Didn't you ask someone
about her . . . the servants?"

"They won't say anything." Her lower lip
trembled.

"What about your brother?"

"André says he heard Mama fighting with
Uncle Raoul. She must have gone away."
Tears filled her eyes. "I told you my uncle
was bad, didn't I? I bet he hurt my mother
and she ran away."

I pulled Annette against me and
comforted her, not knowing what to say.

"There must be a reasonable explanation," I offered with as much reassurance as my doubts would allow.

"You're going to stay here with me, aren't you, Mademoiselle Grant?" She looked up at me with those pleading eyes.

"Until my wrist gets better," I repeated firmly.

"I told my brother that you would take care of us."

"But, Annette, I can't. I have to go to Paris as soon as possible." I tried to keep a rise of anxiety out of my voice. "You see, I must secure a position with a couturier before he hires someone else in my place."

"What if my mother doesn't come back?"

"Of course, she'll come back. She knew you were arriving yesterday. I wrote to her myself."

"Then why wasn't she here to meet me?"

"I don't know but . . . but I'm sure there's a reasonable explanation. Something must have happened to make her forget or—"

"Maybe she didn't get the letter. Maybe Uncle Raoul took it." Annette's eyes brimmed with tears. " I think he's done something with my mother."

"Stop it, Annette. You're letting your imagination run away with you." My mouth was strangely dry. "I'm sure your uncle will tell you what happened if you ask him."

In spite of my resolution not to get involved, I could not ignore Annette's need for support. I would have to try and find out why Madame de Lamareau was not here for her daughter's return. I deliberately turned the conversation back to Beau and all his feline charms. The cat took all the petting as his due and rewarded us with a purring monotone that grew louder and louder.

Nela came back a short time later and was obviously displeased to see my visitors. "You are not to be on this side of the house," she told Annette sharply.

"It's all right. I'm glad for the company," I insisted but in spite of my protest, she shooed Annette and Beau out of the room.

"Come back and see me again," I called after them before Nela shut the door. I wondered if the servant would keep it locked hereafter. I gave Nela a belligerent glare and asked her why Annette's mother had not come to see me.

"I don't know, ma'am."

"Isn't she at home?"

"I don't know, ma'am."

She was lying. Servants like Nela knew everything that went on upstairs and downstairs. I continued to ask questions about the mistress of the house but I got little information for my efforts. She answered the same "I don't know, ma'am" to all my questions as she helped me back into bed. I was suddenly too tired to pursue the matter any more.

"I'll be back in an hour with your dinner tray." She pursed her thick lips and left.

I slept fitfully that night and could not shake off a deep sense of depression when I awoke the next morning. The dark, somber room had become a prison and Nela my jailer. I didn't want to be in this isolated wing of the house. After the crowded dormitories at school with laughter and chatter bouncing off the rafters the deadly silence was like a rasp on my nerves.

When Nela suggested a bath, I readily agreed. The deep, claw-foot tub brought the water up to my neck. It was soothing to lie there and for a few minutes I was able to put aside my pesonal anxieties and those that Annette had heaped upon me.

I insisted upon wearing my cotton night-dress and high-necked flannel robe. I ignored Nela's blunt disapproval as she watched me secure my hair at the back of my head instead of letting it fall free on my shoulders. My mother's perfume no longer teased my nostrils and I felt in command of myself.

I dozed after my breakfast while

reclining in a deep leather chair near the windows. A faint odor of tobacco wafted up from the chair and I could tell from its well-worn contours that it had been occupied many times. I could not help but think about the dead man who had sat there and wonder if he had truly been murdered by his brother. About mid-morning, I awoke to a pleasant surprise. Dr. Duboise had arrived.

My eyes filled with tears and I blinked rapidly to hold them back as the burly doctor greeted me with a smile. "And how are you feeling, Mademoiselle?"

"Oh, I'm so glad you came. I was afraid that you wouldn't. Monsieur de Lamareau wanted to call his family physician but I insisted that I wanted you. When you didn't come—" I knew I was blabbering but I couldn't help it. "Now, now. No need to be upset." He patted my hand and his soft blue eyes twinkled at me. "I was told that Dr. Vanderley, the family physician, would be called in to tend you. And I understood completely. You see, I am a stranger in this area . . . a visitor, really. My brother and I are spending a little time here. I just happened to be at the station when the accident occurred. Of course, I had to offer my services in the emergency."

"I'm so grateful you were there and I'm

glad Monsieur changed his mind."

"So am I." His double chin wiggled as he chuckled. "I guess I miss my patients even though I left my Paris practice to enjoy some peace and quiet in the country. I received a message this morning from Monsieur de Lamareau that you were to remain under my care. I'm delighted to be of service. Now, tell me how are you feeling?" He peered at me through the small square glasses perched on his nose. His soft voice soon soothed my frayed nerves. He looked at the bump on my head and asked me about the pain in my wrist.

"How soon do you think I'll be well enough to leave?"

"Not for a week or ten days, I should imagine. You must give that hand rest. And a bump on the head should never be taken lightly. I suggest you avail yourself of Monsieur de Lamareau's hospitality until you are completely recovered. After all, it is his responsibility to care for you. The accident was caused by a horse from his stable."

"What would make a horse go crazy like that?"

"Hard to say. Very unfortunate. It does happen. Animals, like people, sometimes go mad without warning. I've tended patients who were nearly killed by animals who

were quite passive until a sudden derange-
ment overtook them."

I was tempted to tell him about my
suspicion that Raoul de Lamareau had fed
something to the horse but I hesitated.
Such an accusation was a very serious
charge. One I had better be able to
substantiate with more than some vague
impression, I decided. Besides, the memory
was not as clear as it once had been. It
would be best not to say anything for the
present. "I want to leave as soon as
possible. I have commitments in Paris."

"Is there someone there who could take
care of you until your wrist is healed?"

His simple question brought back the
reality of the situation. I was on my own
and my funds were very meager. The doctor
must have seen the shadow cross my eyes
for he nodded. "I see. You are on your own
then, mademoiselle?"

"Yes." I told him about the job of seamstress that was waiting for me in Monsieur
Roget's establishment.

"It is a hard life, Mademoiselle. I have
treated many *grisettes* who survive on the
edge of starvation. Long hours, demanding
work, low wages. Very little chance for
advancement. Surely, you must have other
options?"

"None at the moment. I . . . I didn't expect to be responsible for my own keep so soon. I didn't have time to pursue any other means of support."

"And what about your family?"

"My mother is in Italy. There is no place for me in her household."

He nodded knowingly. "I see. Well, then, I suggest, Mademoiselle Grant, that you relax and enjoy your convalescence in this magnificent gray stone chateau until you are fully recovered." He closed his doctor's bag. "I'm leaving some powdered medicine which will help you sleep and lessen the pain."

"I don't want to take any more medicine." Something in the way I said it caused him to raise one of his busy gray eyebrows.

"And why not . . . if it eases the pain and allows you to sleep? The dosage is very light. I don't think you should make yourself uncomfortable by refusing to take the edge off the pain. Your nerves are a little on edge, as is to be expected after such an accident. I sense that you are not at ease. Is there some way I can be of help?"

I hesitated and then shook my head. "Thank you for coming."

"Be sure to call me if something unexpected arises, and I will come immediately. Promise, Mademoiselle?"

I nodded and smiled. He did not know that this reassurance was worth more than all the medicine he could have given me.

Chapter Four

The next afternoon I told Nela I wanted to get dressed. At first I thought she might refuse to cooperate but she must have sensed that I was determined to do it with or without her help. "Dr. Duboise did not say I had to stay in bed . . . nor in my room." I argued with a pugnacious lift in my chin, watching her expression to ascertain whether or not I was really free to leave this bedroom if I wished.

Her flat features remained bland. "Yes, Mam'selle." Shifting her weight from side to side, she plodded to the wardrobe and brought back the best dress I owned—a willow-green moiré which my mother had briefly worn. When she sent it to me, I altered the low neckline by adding an ecru lace chemisette and modified the exaggerated trailing bustle. Sister Mary Josette, the head schoolmistress, had even complimented me on it when I wore it on a special occasion one evening.

"You're a talented seamstress, Alysha," she had told me. "A good sense of 'proper' style." She accented the "proper" for she had seen some of the discarded garments which my mother had sent to me.

I often wondered how the demure Sister would have reacted if I had decided to wear the seductive dresses without alteration, leaving the necklines scandalously low and sleeves cut to show bare skin on the shoulders. Of course, I never would have. Monsieur had been right in labeling me a "drab bird." I had felt enough embarrassment being around a mother who demanded the center limelight wherever she went and I had learned to avoid it whenever I could. I had inherited her coloring and features but I was not her child. I feared I was as boring and colorless as my mother was captivating and sophisticated.

As Nela fastened the tiny buttons at the back of the gown, I remembered the last time I had worn it. Early last spring, I had entertained a brief crush on our new male music teacher at the school and I had altered this dress especially for one of our afternoon teas when all the young ladies at the school practiced their social skills by conversing with members of the faculty. For days I dreamed that the rather gaunt, ascetic young teacher would notice me in my altered gown and pay more attention to me than all the other fashionably dressed girls. In my fantasy, we would retire to some quiet corner for an intimate discussion of Chopin and Mozart while we sipped our tea and ate the special shortbread cookies the Sisters always made for such an occasion. Of course, it didn't happen. That afternoon Fritz Swartz had nodded at me politely and then transferred his gaze to a cluster of smiling girls who ducked their heads coyly and peered at him with lowered lashes. I don't think he ever quite remembered my name even though I was in one of his music classes that quarter.

Remembering, I wished I had ordered Nela to bring one of my navy skirts and white blouses instead of this foolish dress. But I had seen the stubborn set of her jaw several times and I feared that if I argued with her too much she might refuse to help me at all and getting dressed with one arm in a sling was more than I could handle by myself.

We had removed the sling for bathing and dressing and my arm felt quite comfortable hanging at my side, my injured wrist held secure in the bandage Dr. Duboise had wrapped around it.

"I don't think I need the sling anymore," I said as I sat down at the rose-inlaid dressing table, determined to do my own hair. I gasped when I saw that the ugly swelling on my forehead had turned an ugly purple tinged with bilious yellow. A cut in the center of it still had raw edges. I looked like some fugitive from an alley fight.

Nela stood behind me, watching my expression in the mirror. I thought I caught a twinkle in those small hazel eyes. "Would Mam'selle prefer to cover up her forehead —until the wounds are healed?"

Even though I was not usually vain about my looks I felt the ugly goose egg had best be hidden and I tried to give in gracefully. "Please." I handed her the silver-handle brush and comb.

She brushed out the long flaxen strands letting them slip through her hands as if they were streams of pale yellow gold. Her large lips relaxed and an expression akin to pure contentment stole across her homely face as she worked with my hair. Her thick, broad hands should have been clumsy, but they weren't. The servant eased shiny, deep waves from a center part until both the cut and bump were hidden; then she lifted the rest of the hair to a fall on the top of my head which she rolled over her fingers, making a full, smooth twist. It was amazing to watch her and until she was finished I didn't realize what a transformation she had made in my appearance. I looked at my reflection and my stomach flipped over. The resemblance to my mother had never been so marked. Her beauty was mine and it frightened me. I did not want to be the lovely woman staring back at me.

"Mam'selle doesn't like?" Nela asked anxiously, standing behind me and meeting my wide eyes in the mirror.

"I . . . I just don't look like myself."

"Mam'selle does not need to hide, *n'est-ce pas*?" There was a wistful edge to Nela's voice and I suddenly felt sorry for this ugly, large woman who had no physical attributes to show nor hide.

"Thank you, Nela. I'm grateful for your efforts." I gave her a smile and was surprised to see a slight curving of her broad lips in return. "Now, I'll sit by the window and write a couple of letters."

"*Oui, Mam'selle.*" She settled me in the leather chair with a lap desk, pen and ink, and ivory stationery bearing the de Lamareau crest on it.

"Anything else, Mam'selle?"

"No, thank you, Nela. I'm fine."

She nodded, and left the room, her arms filled with a pile of soiled linen she had stripped from the bed.

I quickly penned a short note to Monsieur Roget explaining that an unfortunate carriage accident had detained me and asked for his kind consideration in keeping the seamstress position open for me. I expressed my gratitude for the opportunity of working in his establishment. After I signed my name, I wondered if I had set the right tone, apologetic but not fawning.

Although I knew my mother would not be expecting to hear from me, I feared that Monsieur Roget might alert her to my delayed appearance. I tried to be light and confident in my note to her for I knew my mother would resent any situation that was likely to put worry lines in her forehead.

The letters written, I set aside the lap desk. There was only uncertain sunshine brightening my room, for the day had dawned overcast and gray. More than ever the bedroom seemed to collect shadows.

Lowering clouds had cast a gray wash
across the landscape outside my high
windows. Floating mists had subdued the
bright hues of the garden and surrounded
the field stretching to the green-black copse
of evergreen trees. As if waiting for the
storm, the doves in the eaves were silent
and invisible. The air was heavy and still. A
deep sense of restlessness overtook me.

I walked to the closed bedroom door and
gingerly turned the knob. Was I free to
come and go as I wished? My melodramatic
imaginings made me feel foolish as the door
swung open. I peered out into the hall.

The corridor ran in both directions,
gathering darkness as it stretched away
from me and turned blind corners at the far
reaches of the wing. The same musty,
abandoned odor of the bedroom greeted my
nostrils in the hall. There was no sign of
life, no indication of the direction Nela took
when she came and went. I feared that the
deserted wing was a labyrinth of halls
which could completely lose me in a dark
maze.

Directly across the hall from my door,
framed by arched woodwork, was a pair of
elaborately carved doors with brass
doorknobs which caught dim light and
were the only points of brightness in the
gloomy corridor. Curiosity which had

motivated many of my childhood episodes
stirred as I stepped across the hall to stand
before the impressive doors. Gingerly I
turned a heavy brass doorknob. The door
surprised me by swinging open easily and
silently. I had expected a protesting creak.

I peered in cautiously, ready to retreat if
I saw that I was about to make an
embarrassing intrusion by entering an
occupied room uninvited and unan-
nounced. My caution was unnesessary.
There was no one in the long, high-ceil-
inged, gallery-like room. The dusty oak
flooring and the mass of furniture and
furnishings crammed into it told me that
the room had not been in use for a long
time.

Draped windows held back most of the
feeble afternoon light, allowing only long
shadows to touch everything in the room
with a ghostly patina. There was barely
room enough to move around the stored
furniture, mirrors, lamps, and tables
loaded with porcelain vases and sculptures
of rare quality. As my skirts swept along
the dusty floor, I passed magnificent
tapestries and clusters of huge paintings
which would have dwarfed most rooms but
which were displayed to perfection in this
huge gallery. In every alcove some
exquisite vase or sculpture caught my

admiring eye and I recognized several
bronze statues as the work of the Parisian,
Antoine-Louis Barye. A lovely set of Louis
XIV chairs were pushed together in one
corner and I wondered why they were here
instead of gracing some grand parlor.

I could not believe my eyes. The dusty
collection of beautiful furniture and
furnishings brought back memories of
buying trips I had enjoyed with Monsieur
Travois when my mother was his mistress.
He would have known the value of these
neglected furnishings, I thought. During
those years when we had accompanied him
on his buying trips, he had given me an
appreciation of fine furniture and objets
d'art and stimulated an interest which
continued long after my mother's lover had
gone back to his wife. As I grew older, I had
gone to museums and art shows and read
avidly about collectors' treasures. Now, to
be in a room like this, filled with such
treasures, was bewildering. My heart raced
excitedly.

It was unreal! Maybe I was not really
awake. Had the bump on my head caused
me to hallucinate? Was this room filled
with treasures only a figment of my
imagination, like a dream or a nightmare?
My skirts swished softly on the dusty floor
as I made my way through the fantastic

collection, touching and gazing and marveling at the rare and beautiful objects. Suddenly my pleasure fled and I stiffened as if intuitively aware of some evil that brushed my shoulders.

Hemmed in on all sides by massive pieces of furniture, tall screens, fluted pedestals, and large sculptures, I felt smothered and trapped. For a moment the room reminded me of a graveyard—a hushed, desolate burying place. It was unnatural, foreboding, and I was an intruder. I swung around, searching the room for a presence that seemed to be waiting and watching. I had never been one to give in to nervous flutterings or to believe in ghostly apparitions but the skin on the nape of my neck began to crawl. *Something or someone did not want me in this room*.

Clutching my skirts with my one good hand, I fled back to the hall door and shut it firmly behind me. Then I leaned up against it, trying to get my breath. Once more I asked myself why Monsieur de Lamareau had isolated me in this unused wing of the chateau. I was a usurper in a bedroom that had been a retreat for a dead man. I was positive of that. And I had viewed treasures lost in shadows and dust. What did it all mean? Maybe Annette could answer some of my questions.

Slowly I traversed the long hall, turning corners and going farther and farther away from my room. Windows along the passage had been partially shuttered and I soon lost all sense of direction. Since I had not seen the chateau before waking up in my room, I had no idea where my bedroom was located in the great structure. I could not orient myself in the labyrinth of halls and passages.

Closed doors on both sides of the passages gave little hint as to whether I was at the front or back of the chateau. I stopped and opened one of the doors. It revealed another large musty room filled with more stored furniture. I closed the door and continued forward down the endless hall until the walls on both sides seemed to close in on me. My mouth was dry, my nostrils choked with dust. The demands I was placing upon my body drained my strength. Panic began to rise and I held back a rising urge to scream for someone to come and find me.

I bolted down a narrow set of stairs and I lurched through a door at the bottom. Blessedly the smell of beeswax and turpentine, freshly starched linens, the faint smell of cooking filled my nostrils. This corridor was brightly carpeted and I knew I had reached the inhabited portion of the chateau. Relief was like the release of a taut spring.

I paused for a moment to get my breath and allow my heartbeat to regain its normal rhythm before I cautiously moved forward along the carpeted corridor to a wide landing. A central staircase curved gracefully downward and I knew I had reached the center of the house. Muted sounds of activity floated up from below. When a huge seventeenth century grand-father clock on the landing boomed the hour of two o'clock, I jumped like someone caught while engaging in illicit activity.

Slowly I went down the curved staircase. A white marble floor in a huge foyer stretched to a massive double door, heavily planked and gleaming with polished brass fittings. Above me, a fluted gaslight chandelier hung from the vaulted ceiling. It had been lit and its radius of light held gray afternoon shadows at bay.

As I reached the bottom step, I could see a stone front terrace and wide steps through front high arched windows hung with intricate lace curtains snowy white and crisply starched. Everything in the foyer was polished and shimmering. The fresh, clean smell was a sharp contrast to the musty, dank odors that permeated my room and the halls of the closed-off wing of the chateau.

My shoes clicked upon the intricate stone flooring as I crossed the massive hall. Uneasy, I expected someone to momentarily rush at me from one of the fluted archways and order me back to my bedroom. Now that I had reached the heart of the house, I didn't know where to go. Where would I find Annette? I would have to ask a servant to take me to her. Since the day was so dreary, she was probably entertaining herself indoors.

I turned away from the front door, took a few steps down the hall, and then passed through an arched doorway and found myself in a magnificent room which I determined must be the front parlor.

The furnishings in this room were as impressive as those stored in the deserted gallery upstairs, I decided. Huge mirrors reflected gilded chairs, exquisitely proportioned, embellished with scrolls and leaves, tables inlaid with satinwood, mother-of-pearl, ebony and ivory, and on the large wall a huge tapestry of Flemish origin. A pair of deep rose satin sofas flanked a white marble fireplace and on the mantel was a pair of seventeenth century Venetian vases whose beauty left me with my mouth open in astonishment. I had never seen anything so exquisite. They were deep amethyst, perfectly curved, trimmed in gold and ribbed with a translucent glaze.

I was staring at them entranced when I was suddenly brought back to the present by the demanding sound of someone knocking at the front door. The next instant the sound of the butler's quickening steps and a loud exchange of voices floated across the foyer. Through the vaulting archway, I had a clear view of the entrance hall. Not knowing what to do, I remained riveted where I was in front of the fireplace.

As a silver-haired butler quickly opened the door, the first person who brushed by him was an elegantly dressed young woman with dark auburn hair and a full figure. "We've brought Madame de Lamareau home," she said with a wave of her hand toward a sobbing woman coming in behind her, supported by a young man. The distraught Madame de Lamareau was petite, dark-haired, and even with her head bowed, I could see her resemblance to Annette.

A small reddish moustache gave the young man a jaunty look even though his expression at the moment was quite somber. "Now, now Yvonne," he soothed. "Everything's going to be all right." His hair was a deeper red than the young woman's and lay fashionably long on the shoulders of his riding jacket.

"Tell Monsieur that the Montaignes are here."

"Oui, mam'selle."

"Never mind, Frazer. I heard all the commotion from my study." Raoul de Lamareau's deep voice preceded him. With a nod of his head, he acknowledged the arrivals. "Louise . . . Maurey."

"We've brought Yvonne home," the lovely woman repeated, almost apologetically.

"So I see." Raoul's crisp gaze moved to his sister-in-law. "For heaven's sake, Yvonne, control yourself. Quit clinging to Maurey like some simpering child."

"I'm afraid she's a little distraught," Maurey said apologetically as if he were embarrassed to find himself in this situation. "Louise and I have done our best to reassure her but—"

"I didn't want to come back!" Annette's mother cried, swaying slightly on her feet. Then she covered her face with her hands and sobbed loudly.

"My brother and I thought it best, Raoul," said Louise Montaigne.

I watched them through the arched door-way and saw her eyes lock with Raoul's in

an intimate gaze. Louise's full mouth softened and a suggestive smile flickered at the
corners of it. I recognized the wordless exchange, the clinging eyes, and the knowing
look. I had seen the look too many times on
my mother's face to be mistaken about it.
They were lovers. I was certain of it. I dared
not ask myself why the knowledge made
something shrivel up inside me, like a
fragile thing suddenly brought out into
destructive light.

"I appreciate your concern, Louise." His
forehead furrowed and his dark eyebrows
drew together.

"We heard there was some kind of
accident at the station," said Maurey.

"My poor little girl," sobbed Yvonne, her
shrill voice rising. "I knew something like
this was going to happen. I sent her away to
be safe." She waved a trembling finger at
her brother-in-law and sobbed. "I was
afraid to let her come home. You can't get
away with it, Raoul. You'll have to kill me
first—"

Raoul's face became as hard as granite.
He took a deep breath as if to control himself. Then he turned to one of the women
servants who was hovering in the background. "Take Madame to her room. Keep
her there until she has composed herself."

Still sobbing but without protest,

Annette's mother allowed herself to be led away.

"I didn't know what to do when she showed up at our door," said Louis in a rush, touching Raoul's arm in supplicant fashion, half-adoring, half-pleading. "Father and Maurey insisted that Yvonne stay until . . . until she felt better. And you know how my brother is," she gave Maurey an indulgent smile. "Any woman in distress." Then she sobered. "She was really quite terrified, wasn't she, Maurey?"

"*Vraiment*. What are you going to do, Raoul . . . if she keeps on with these accusations? You'll have to do something."

Louise slipped her arm through Raoul's. "It's such a nuisance for you, darling. I wish I could help. There must be something we can do for poor Annette. We've come to spend the night," she said with a meaningful lift of a crescent eyebrow. "The inclement weather—" Then she smiled coquettishly. "Could you ring for some tea? I feel quite tired after being buffeted about by Yvonne's emotions."

"I could do with a spot of cognac, myself," her brother agreed sociably as he straightened his soft tie and smoothed the wrinkles from the sleeve of his coat which Yvonne had been clutching. He was as fashionably dressed as his sister and I judged him to be a couple of years her junior.

They started walking across the wide foyer toward the parlor. I realized to my horror that in another moment they would enter the room and find me standing in front of the fireplace, eavesdropping on the whole scene. My frantic gaze went around the room as I instinctively thought about hiding myself. Unfortunately, there was no time to turn coward and duck behind the closest concealment. I only had a few seconds to brace myself for the scene I knew would follow. As they came through the arched doorway, I boldly moved forward. My childhood escapades had taught me that there was always a chance that a strong bluff might rescue me from impending disaster.

Chapter Five

All three of them froze as if I were some
ghostly apparition suddenly appearing
before their eyes. The moment of weighted
silence was an eternity. Then Louise Montaigne broke it with a nervous laugh. Her
scrutinizing gaze traveled from the lace
ruching at my throat down the lines of my
secondhand gown and then back to the soft
waves of fair hair falling over my forehead.
My outfit was a sharp contrast to her *belle
mode* attire. "And who is this, Raoul?" Her

brown eyes hardened. "A new servant?"

I couldn't meet Raoul de Lamareau's eyes. He had thought me safely ensconced in a room far away from the center of the house, and here I was an intruder, embarrassing him and humiliating myself.

"A house guest," he stated in clipped tones which scarcely hid the anger simmering there. "Mademoiselle Alysha Grant."

"House guest?" echoed Louise in a dry tone. It was obvious from her brittle laugh that I was not the kind of house guest that usually graced these elegant premises. She obviously thought Raoul was playing some kind of joke on her.

"Yes, she arrived with Annette. Mademoiselle Grant graciously consented to travel with her and then—"

"*Mon Dieu!*" finished Maurey. "The overturned carriage! How fortunate you weren't seriously hurt, Mademoiselle. Please introduce us properly, Raoul. Perhaps there is some way I may be of help to this lovely young lady. Make her stay here a little less regrettable."

"Maurey Montaigne and his sister, Louise Montaigne." Raoul made the introductions evenly without looking at me but I saw muscles tighten in his lean cheeks.

In contrast, Maurey's grin was broad and

instantly flirtatious. *"Enchanté,* Alysha, if I may be so bold as to call you that." He took my unbandanged hand and lightly kissed it. His beaming smile was a contrast to Raoul's glare. I could not help but be grateful for his warm welcome and I responded with a warm smile.

"Maurey, really!" chided his sister, barely acknowledging the introduction. She gave her brother a withering look which he ignored.

He asked solicitously about my bandaged wrist. I heard myself answering but I couldn't have told anyone what I said. I was furious at myself for getting into such a situation. Even though I wished myself anywhere else at the moment, I managed to exchange polite amenities with Maurey Montaigne.

Louise flounced down on one of the French provincial sofas in front of the fireplace. Lifting a languid hand, she lightly smoothed a strand of dark red hair wisping out from under her velvet plumed hat. "I'm sure Mademoiselle Grant will excuse us, Raoul. We do have some private matters to speak about." The tone of dismissal was rude and unmistakable. I could have been a servant waiting for her command. In spite of myself I stiffened.

"Don't mind my sister," Maurey said, his

green eyes twinkling at me. "She loves to give orders but she's harmless. Come sit down."

For some perverse reason, I did not excuse myself as good manners dictated. I could be quite stubborn when someone wanted to embarrass me or try to control my behavior. I decided that the beautiful Louise Montaigne was not going to drive me away until I was ready to go—or until my glowering host escorted me back to my room. Maurey's hand was bold and familiar on my arm as he guided me to a parlor chair.

I knew that the young Frenchman was a practiced flirt, enjoying a woman's company wherever he found it, regardless of her social status. There had been plenty like him in my mother's train of admirers. He probably flirted with barmaids and countesses alike. I was under no illusion that my presence was anything more than a momentary interest. Under different circumstances I would have given Maurey Montaigne my "withering stare" and erased the hopeful gleam in his eyes. However, at the moment the flattering attention was like a drop of water in an arid land. His attention foolishly bolstered my courage.

Raoul de Lamareau kept an icy gaze on

me and I knew he was in agreement with Louise that I should leave. This aura of hostility coming from both him and Louise only increased my intent to stay and find out how much as I could about the relationship between them. I did not want to go back upstairs to my isolation. With the stubbornness learned in my childhood, I murmured halfheartedly, "I really should return to my room." But I did not move.

"Nonsense. Don't you agree, Raoul, that unpleasant matters can wait while Mademoiselle Grant joins us in some refreshment?"

Politely, Raoul responded with a nod which I sensed was slightly mocking. His controlled expression gave me little clue to the extent of his annoyance. Crossing the room, he pulled the bell cord and when a servant immediately appeared, he gave orders for a tea trolley and two glasses of cognac for himself and Maurey.

Maurey seemed bent on entertaining me. While Raoul watched from a casual stance near the fireplace, Maurey explained that the de Lamareau and Montaigne estates adjoined common woods and that the two families had common ancestors. I judged from the way Louise's possessive looks centered on Raoul de Lamareau that she was ready to unite the families once again. I wondered why he didn't marry her. She seemed most suitable to be chatelaine . . . but, of course, it was Annette's mother who had that position now as widow of the late Jacques de Lamareau, the oldest son.

As Maurey talked, my mind darted about collecting bits of information lodged in my memory. I tried to remember everything Annette had said about Raoul. Why would he want to marry Yvonne—unless she had inherited some part of the estate that wasn't entailed for it was the young boy, André, who had inherited the property as son of the deceased older brother, Jacques. As the second brother, Raoul de Lamareau could manage the estate until young André came of age—or those standing in his way were removed.

Was Louise also waiting for the latter to happen? It was easy for me to think of her as the villainess. She was beautiful, arrogant, and exuded the dominating presence that I lacked. It was obvious that Raoul de Lamareau deferred to her as we partook of our refreshments. He sat down beside her on the settee and she turned toward him as if there were no one else of interest in the room. I saw his easy smile for the first time as he responded to something Louise had said quietly to him. I wanted to eavesdrop on their conversation but Maurey kept up a merry banter that drowned out their softly spoken words.

"There's no need to play the gallant, Maurey," chided Louise finally as her brother once more expressed concern over my bandaged wrist. "I'm sure that Mademoiselle has been made quite comfortable under this roof." Her disapproving glance slid to the hem of my skirts which had been made dusty as they swept the floors upstairs. I realized then that the bandage on my hand was also dusty and I tried to slip it unobtrusively under the folds of my skirt. She gave me a brittle smile. "As I understand it, Mademoiselle Grant, you were hired as a companion to see Annette home."

"That's not quite true," I countered, my tone barely hiding my own rising indignation. Louise Montaigne seemed determined to impose the status of servant upon me. "I accompanied Annette home as a favor. Sister Mary Josette, the head schoolmistress, was uneasy about the young girl traveling alone and wanted to make certain she reached here safely."

"But she didn't reach home safely, did she? There was an accident," Louise said pointedly. Her full lips curved sardonically as if I had somehow been responsible for the near-disaster.

"Tell us, Raoul . . . exactly what did happen at the station?" Maurey asked.

"The horse went *fou* and overturned the carriage."

I searched his handsome face then for some flicker of guilt but his dark eyes were clear, inscrutable, like those of a consummate lair. "Fortunately Annette was thrown free and landed on some soft turf. She was not hurt . . . only shaken up and frightened. Mademoiselle Grant was less fortunate but Dr. Duboise assures me her injuries are not serious."

"Dr. Duboise? Who is he?" asked Louise. "I would have thought you would have called Dr. Vanderley."

"I wanted to but Dr. Duboise happened to be at the station at the time of the accident . . . he's visiting in the district. He offered his help and now Mademoiselle Grant insists that he continue to treat her. I know nothing about him."

Louise looked at me as if I had really crossed the bound of impropriety. "Really, I can't believe you would prefer a stranger to our reputable Dr. Vanderley."

"Dr. Vanderley is a stranger to me too," I said pointedly. "After all, little treatment is needed for a sprained wrist and a small cut and bump on my head. I appreciated Dr. Duboise's quick attention at the time of the accident . . . and I find him to be a very nice gentleman." I was tempted to tell her that he was the one person who did not exude cold animosity or indifference in my company. "Besides, he assures me I'll be able to leave in a few days."

"What a pity," sighed Maurey. "We must make certain you do not languish in this house for the remainder of your stay. Of course, you can't ride with that injured wrist but I think a nice walk through the chateau park would be most enjoyable for you. Don't you agree, Raoul?"

"I'm sure that Mademoiselle Grant and her doctor must decide on her activity. However, I think that she has overdone her first day out of bed. I will see her back upstairs now." He rose to his feet and waited for me to set down my cup and stand up. His smile was solicitous but there was a command in his unsmiling dark brown eyes.

"Really, Raoul, don't you think Mademoiselle Grant can find her way back to her own quarters?" Louise chided a little peevishly.

"I doubt it. She's in the west wing."

"The west wing?" Louise echoed with a raised eyebrow.

"Yes, I thought she would get more rest there. Annette and André can be a chore, at times," he said smoothly but I knew he lied. There was something deeper to his decision to isolate me from the family. "It is difficult to find one's way—"

"Then one of the servants, *peut-être?*" insisted Louise.

"No, I'll see Mademoiselle Grant to her room. Please excuse my absence for a few minutes. Maurey, why don't you take your sister into the solarium? The orchids are quite lovely. I'll join you there." Once more his tone was ribbed with authority.

Louise's eyes flashed with displeasure before she lowered them and said lightly, "Don't be long, Raoul."

Maurey clicked his heels and bent his auburn head over my one good hand and lightly kissed it again. "Perhaps you'll allow me to pay my respects tomorrow, Alysha, and see if you're feeling up to a tour of the gardens?"

"Perhaps. *Merci*. A pleasure to have met you." I gave them both a polite smile which Louise did not return.

Raoul did not speak to me as he escorted me with a firm guiding hand on my elbow. As we went up the curved flight of stairs, he looked very stern. "Thank you for showing me the way back," I said in a rather weak voice. "I'm afraid I found the main hall by trial and error."

He did not answer. His silence was the kind that always fired my anger. It infuriated me when people didn't come out and say what they were thinking. He was angry with me and I knew it. "I hope my presence in the drawing room was not an embarrassment for you," I said stiffly, my voice stronger and my tone more belligerent. "I had no intention of imposing myself upon your guests. I was simply curious to see my surroundings." Before I could launch a volley of indignant remarks born out of my guilty feelings, for snooping and eavesdropping, we reached the top of the stairs and came face to face with Annette.

The girl's dark questioning eyes went from my face to her uncle's and then fixed on the firm hand he had on my arm. Her eyes filled with instant panic. "Mademoiselle Grant," she gasped. "Where is he taking you?"

I smiled to reassure her. "Back to my room. I've been for a little walk."

"He's sending you away, isn't he?" Her voice rose. Her face crumpled. "Don't let him. I have to talk to you. Please, don't go away! Please stay."

"It's all right, Annette. I'm not going until the doctor says my wrist is well. I've had tea downstairs and your uncle is escorting me back to my bedroom. No need to be upset." I tried to soothe her. I could feel her uncle's patience drawn to a fine point.

"Mother's back . . . and she's frightened," she whimpered tearfully. "I have to talk to you—"

"Annette!" Her uncle's tone was sharp. "I will not have you behaving in this manner. Our family crisis has nothing to do with Mademoiselle Grant. Now go to your room and compose yourself!"

For a moment she acted as if she might defy him, then she pressed a fist to her mouth, turned and fled.

"Was that necessary?" I snapped, controlling an urge to run after her. I had looked after the little girl at school, helped her with her studies, walked with her to chapel, and let her weep on my shoulder when she was homesick. My hackles rose like a mother lion's. "Must you treat her like that?"

"Yes," he said flatly. "Do not concern yourself with things you do not understand."

"I'm perfectly capable of understanding any situation—if I'm told what it is!" I flared.

"I must ask that you not interfere. It is for your own good. Please respect my wishes. It is best that you remain separated from the upheavels that buffet our family at the moment."

"Is that why you have put me in a wing shut off from the rest of the family?"

"I thought it best. You are not likely to get much rest with all the dramatics provided by Annette and her mother. I wanted to spare you as much emotional disturbance as possible."

"Annette is my friend. I am willing to share her problems," I countered.

"I'm afraid a simple friendship will not quiet a deep-seated hysteria. There is no need for you to be drawn into the quagmire of our family problems."

We went down several long corridors and through several doorways before I found myself back in front of my bedroom door. He had taken a shorter route and I doubted that I could retrace my way back through the circuitous route. "Are you going to lock me in?" I demanded, my back rigid, ready to expend my fury upon him.

"You are my guest . . . not my prisoner." He surprised me by reaching out and lightly brushing back the soft wave covering the discolored skin on my forehead. "It's looking better." For the first time, I saw a slight twinkle in his deep eyes. "Now it looks more like a purple prune than a bird's egg." Then he lifted my bandaged hand gently and held it in his. "And your wrist? Does it hurt much, Alysha?"

I shook my head because I couldn't speak. The use of my first name was a shock. He had always been so formal with me. So distant. Now he held my hand and said my name in an intimate tone that made my heart lurch into my throat. "Alysha" had never sounded so beautiful as the way his deep voice said it. Then I stiffened. A few minutes earlier his soft smile had centered on Louise and I had seen the melting, adoring look on her face. He knew how to manipulate a woman's emotions, how to charge the moment with his smile and the softening of his dark eyes. I would not be such a fool as to react to his attention. "It is much improved, thank you," I answered formally and drew my hand away from his.

"Alysha," he said again. "A soft, melodious name. Sometimes it seems to fit you . . . and other times, *non.*" He smiled wryly.

"Perhaps your judgment is flawed, Monsieur," I dared to answer.

"Peut-être," he agreed, "but I think not. I suspect that there are many facets of your personality worth exploring." His glance traveled lazily over my flushed face. "I find

myself intrigued."

"And I find myself insulted." I knew that my mother would have replied in a light, coquettish manner which would have kept the soft smile on his lips. But I was not my mother. Nor did I want to be. I drew myself up as if he were about to assault my person. My thoughts floundered. I was not immune to a powerful physical attraction that threatened to overwhelm me.

"I think you lie to yourself. But then, maybe you are right. My judgment may be faulty. Well, if you will excuse me, I must return to my guests," he said abruptly.

"Yes, you must not keep Mademoiselle Montaigne waiting." There was an edge to my voice which I could not disguise. "She seems quite fond of you."

"Louise is a dear friend . . . as is her brother. And I feel it is my responsibility to warn someone like yourself, Alysha, that Maurey amuses himself whenever the opportunity arises."

"Like most gentlemen, I believe," I said tartly. "I assure you that I am not beguiled by his flattering attention. Thank you for your warning but it is not needed. I can take care of myself."

"Can you?" His wintry mask was back in place. "I hope that you will also abide by my wishes and not encourage Annette in her hysterics."

"She is my friend. I will do what I can to help her for the short time that I'm here."

"A matter of a few days, I believe? Is that what Dr. Duboise said?" asked Raoul hopefully.

"Yes."

He nodded and I knew then that he wanted me gone as soon as possible.

"This delay is not of *my* choosing," I flared. "I'm anxious to be on my way as quickly as possible." He needn't think I would delay my departure a moment longer than necessary.

"You are a bewildering contradiction. Perhaps we will meet at another more convenient time, Alysha." Once more he said my name with such softness that it was like a force pulling me to him. Our eyes met and held.

"Perhaps," I croaked, my breath suddenly short.

Once more his gaze bathed my face, then he bowed politely, turned away and left.

I stared at his retreating back until it was out of sight around a corner of the dim corridor. The deep gentleness of his voice lingered in my ears. *Perhaps we will meet at another more convenient time.* My heart raced crazily like a lopsided top and a fiery color swept up into my cheeks.

Bewildered by my reaction, I went in my room and closed the door, leaning up against it, wondering why my eyes were suddenly brimming with a foolish flow of tears.

Chapter Six

No use trying to sleep. Taunting thoughts
and emotions darted about in my mind like
swirls of devil dust. I could not deny a
rising, undefinable excitement that drew
me to Raoul de Lamareau. When he had
touched my face with the lightness of a
caress, for a bewildering moment, I had
wanted him to draw me close. Fool that I
was, I had wanted him to bend his arrogant
head and kiss me. Now such weakness
taunted me. I had always imagined that I

would be in complete control of my
emotions. Instead, anger, confusion, and a
newly awakened desire mocked me. I had
known from the first moment I saw Raoul
de Lamareau through the train window
that he was a man who would manipulate
people to his own designs. Everything
Annette had said about him had put me on
guard . . . and then I had let myself be taken
in by his seductive masculine charm. The
way he had said my name lowered all my
defenses. He was a master of manipulation
. . . especially when it came to women.

I remembered the sensual and fawning
eyes Louise Montaigne had fixed upon him.
There was no doubt in my mind that they
were lovers. Exposed to my mother's
numerous romantic dalliances, I was sensitive to veiled looks, casual touching, and
polite innuendos that had double meanings.
The romantic undercurrent was there. I
was sure of it. I angrily thumped at my
pillow with one good hand and winced as
pain spiraled through my other wrist. And
according to Annette, her uncle had designs
on her mother too . . . trying to force her to
marry him. The distraught Madame de
Lamareau feared for her own safety and
that of her children.

The atmosphere in the chateau was
seething with unrest and conflict. I wanted

to leave this house as quickly as possible. Then a stab of guilt weakened my resolve. How could I turn my back on Annette's distress? She needed me. It was a rare thing in my life for my presence to be of value to anyone. Not since my father died had I really felt important to anyone. My mother had kept me outside of her immediate relationships and, except for the few years she spent with Maurice Travois, I had never belonged in her life. Now Annette seemed to be in the same position as I had been, needing someone who would be concerned about her. She was probably as unable to sleep as I. "I need to talk with you." Her anguished voice came back to haunt me.

I eased out of bed and reached for my faded flannel robe lying at the foot of the bed. I pulled it on over my cotton gown and slipped my feet into some well-worn, soft-soled slippers. Very quietly, I opened my door and looked both ways down the deserted corridor lit by one feeble gaslight. Dark shadows crowded the long hall. At night the isolated wing seemed to belong to unseen spirits who challenged my presence there. Something cold crept down my spine as if the dead man whose room I was using was now walking the halls with me.

How would I ever find my way to the family wing where I had been earlier that

afternoon? I had not kept my wits about me
when Monsieur had escorted me back to my
room and I couldn't remember all the
twists and turns I had taken that afternoon.
Only the urgency to talk with Annette made
me put aside my uneasiness and start down
the echoing hall. The young girl needed me.
I could not put aside a compulsion to go to
her.

The storm had come. I could hear rain
beating against the gray stones of the
chateau. Like the high pitch of a wild
woman's shrieks, the wind rose and fell as
it caught under eaves and swirled around
gables and chimneys. I passed high, oval
windows. They were obliquely dark like
sightless eyes as they reflected the
darkness outside. I was alone and yet I
sensed there were specters around me. The
huge chateau slumbered uneasily and I
wondered how many restless ghosts
roamed these old halls. Did Annette's
father, Jacques de Lamareau, rest uneasily
in his grave, murdered by an unknown
hand? The longer I occupied his room, the
more I felt his lingering presence. He had
shut himself off in this wing of abandoned
treasures. His spirit seemed to be roving
the dusty halls, watching and waiting, an
insidious threat to those living within these
gray stone walls.

I drew the collar of my robe tighter around my neck, swallowing back my own breath as I traversed a labyrinth of halls through the deserted wing, stubbornly refusing to admit that I might be completely disoriented. An occasional gaslight on the wall broke the bank of wavering hall shadows. Several times, I paused within a lamp's radius, searching for some remembered clue that might assure me that I had been this way before. Finally I came upon a series of dark portraits hung along one wall which seemed familiar and I went in that direction, through a doorway.

Screams caught in my throat and I whirled about in terror, not knowing which way to run. The walls were alive with moving specters, all waving their arms and gesturing at me. Completely disoriented, I darted and the mocking wraiths darted and swirled with me. I froze and they froze. For a moment I stopped breathing and then I almost swooned in relief. The circular room was lined with mirrors—beautiful mirrors of all sizes and shapes, exquisitely framed. I had stumbled into a treasure house of silvered glass. It was my reflection that filled the ghostly chamber. My laugh was rather pitiful. It took a moment for my legs to regain their strength. I was too

shaken to appreciate the beauty of the
mirrored room. I circled the walls and gave
a cry of relief as I found the doorway once
more.

I was lost now, completely. Every turn
was like an endless twist in a bewildering
maze. I did not know if I had changed
directions and was now heading back to my
room. The sound of my night slippers
scuffing along the shadowy corridors
seemed loud enough to herald my passing . . .
but no one came to challenge my frantic
flight. Outside the wind and rain made
high-pitched noises that rose and fell eerily.

My heartbeat raced in my throat like a
frantic bird whipping its wings. I put my
good fist against my mouth to keep from
screaming. Perspiration gathered on my
brow. Every shadow seemed alive and
moving. I could not rid myself of the conviction that I was not alone in the dark
corridors. Was some human watching and
stalking my every step?

I bolted down another dusky corridor,
then I heard a noise—a lovely, wonderful
noise. A cat's meow!

I moved in the direction of the soft
meowing. With every step, I stopped and
listened. "Beau?" An answering meow
brought me to a remembered flight of
stairs, I bolted down them, threw open the

closed door at the bottom . . . and *voilà* . . . the second floor landing in the family wing. The familiar smells greeted me again and I sobbed with relief.

Beau was sitting there in the middle of the landing with his black and white head cocked and his dark tail swirled neatly around him in gentlemanly fashion. His whiskers twitched and his yellow eyes studied me with a look of surprise.

"Bless you, Beau. Bless you." I bent over and stroked his arched head. He gave me a deep meowing which I interpreted as "you're welcome."

I straightened up and listened. The only sound I heard was the rhythmic ticking of the huge grandfather clock on the stairway landing. It struck one o'clock in a loud vibrating note. Cautiously I moved forward and I peered over the railing.

Below me, crystal wall sconces sent a soft light over the deserted foyer. The cat twined around my legs, rubbing his back and purring. Then Beau headed down an upper hall, silent on his cushioned paws and almost an indistinct blur against the dark carpeting. He must be going toward the bedrooms, perhaps to find Annette, I thought hopefully and followed him, refusing to analyze my sudden willingness to depend upon the capricious activities of a cat for direction.

The black and white cat seemed to know
where he was going. I almost lost him twice
as we traversed several carpeted corridors
along the second floor. As I hurried along
past closed doors following the animal, I
wondered what feeble excuse I could offer
if one of the doors jerked open and Raoul de
Lamareau suddenly blocked my passage.
What if he drew me into his bedroom? The
thought of that possibility made my face
hot and I laughed at myself for the fool I
was. The Montaignes were spending the
night. There had been a meaningful,
unspoken message when Louise Montaigne
had said, "We've come to spend the night."
As I wondered behind which of these doors
they held their lover's tryst, I stilled a
rising emotion that I refused to identify.
What kind of a lover would he be? I knew
his touch could be gentle when he wanted
and that his eyes could seem soft when he
smiled. When I imagined the virile length of
his body pressed against mine, an unbidden
tingling swept through me. For one brief
moment, I almost wished I had my mother's
artful charms. Then a sensible, realistic
mocking chided my weakness.

We had reached the end of one hall when
Beau finally slipped through a half-opened
door. I took a deep breath and followed

him. He had not failed me. A small lamp upon a skirted dressing table revealed a girl's bedroom, furnished in white French provincial furniture, pretty silken curtains and pink bed drapings.

Beau jumped upon a pink velvet chair and began to preen himself as if his toiletries were utmost in his feline mind. It was almost as if he said, "Well, here she is. Now what are you going to do?"

I didn't know. Annette was sound asleep. Her dark hair spread like a fan upon the pillow and one arm curved gracefully above her head like a child in contented sleep. Her petite face seemed utterly relaxed and her quiet, peaceful slumber made my nocturnal rush to her side seem ludicrous and utterly melodramatic. To wake her up and tell her I was going to leave as soon as possible would be both cruel and purposeless. The last time I'd seen her, she'd had tears in her eyes, sobbing that her uncle was going to send me away. Now, looking at her deep in slumber, I wondered how much of Annette's hysterics might be a bid for attention. Had her mother really instilled such wild accusations and fears in the girl? If I really wanted to get to the truth of the matter, I should talk to Yvonne de Lamareau.

Now? Past midnight? Some prim,

chastising voice inside my head denounced
the idea and attempted to bring me to task
for even considering such an impropriety.
Unfortunately, it was a voice I had learned
to shut out years ago. Madame de
Lamareau might still be awake, I reasoned,
restless and lonely and needing to talk with
someone. Since I was in this part of the
house, it wouldn't hurt to see if she was
willing to talk to me about the situation
that seemed to have her and her daughter
terrorized. I did not want to think about
Raoul de Lamareau's reaction to my interference if he should find out. His warning
that I should keep myself separated from
the rest of the family only made my
determination to talk with Madame de
Lamareau greater.

Leaving Beau curled up in the pink velvet
chair in Annette's room, I slipped out into
the hall again, wondering where Madame
de Lamareau's bedroom might be. If I
listened carefully, I might hear her sobbing
or moving about in the agitated manner I
had seen that afternoon. Since she was the
mistress, she probably occupied a suite at
the front of the chateau, I reasoned.

My elongated shadow went before me as I
traversed a wide, carpeted, dimly lit hall
toward the front of the house. A waiting
silence mocked my erratic breathing. As I

remembered the distraught woman leaning heavily upon Maurey Montaigne, I began to waver in my decision to see her. Maybe Annette had not even told her I was in the house. What if she created a scene and brought Raoul de Lamareau running?

I stopped and finally considered the folly of my action. This was no childhood escapade . . . not like the times I'd run away to do some harmless exploring while my mother sat in a drawing room visiting. Raoul de Lamareau had warned me not to interfere and had put me on the far side of the huge chateau to keep me from interacting with the family. I shivered just thinking about that deep, cold voice demanding an explanation for my actions.

I turned around, intending to retreat— and then stopped. It was the sound of a child's soft whimpering that wiped out my wavering indecision. André? I stopped and listened. Yes, it must be Annette's little brother. The childish crying sounded as if it belonged to a young child. The low sobbing came from a room just beyond where I stood.

"André?" I walked a few steps down the hall, listened at the door, and then opened it, expecting to see a child's room, a nursery, perhaps. For a moment my eyes blinked as they adjusted to a dimly lit, utterly feminine boudoir.

Two lamps burned brightly on each side
of a large canopy bed which was mounted
on a dais and framed by amber-gold and
rose velvet hangings. The bed was smoothly
made up and empty. A cloak which I
recognized as the one Yvonne had been
wearing upon her arrival that afternoon
was thrown across the foot. Her bonnet and
gloves lay discarded in a heap on a chair
near the bed. Several bureau drawers were
open and the door of one wardrobe stood
ajar. I waited, straining to hear the muffled
whimpering that had led me here.

"André?" I said again.

No answer. The whimpering had stopped
with choked abruptness. I looked about and
listened. "André?" I said again and waited.
My ears picked up a whispered movement
on the far side of the raised bed. It was only
a furtive rustle, like a tiny creature trying
to find sanctuary.

Purposefully, I walked around the foot of
the bed. There he was—a little boy, huddled
on one of the steps of the bed platform.
André's dark eyes rounded and caught the
light like a frightened, trapped animal.

"It's all right," I said in a soothing tone.
"I'm Annette's friend. And I know you're
André, her little brother. I didn't mean to
frighten you."

André cowered away from my friendly outstretched hand.

"Please, don't be afraid of me." I smiled reassuringly, wondering what I would do if he suddenly started shrieking hysterically. "I came to talk with Annette but she's sound asleep. Is this your mother's room?"

No answer. Before I could manage some kind of response, he came at me with his little fists, clawing at me with the fury of a wildcat. I tried to ward him off with my one good hand, raising my bandaged hand to try to protect my face from his childish battering.

"Where is she? Where is she?" he croaked. "Why can't I see her?"

I finally managed to grab his little shoulder with my good hand. "Stop it!" I shook him gently. "I want to help you, André. I want to help." I repeated it a third time before his tense little frame crumpled and he stopped flailing at me with his fists.

I cradled him with my good arm and let him cry as we sat on the bottom step of the dais, side by side.

"Where is Mama?" he sobbed.

"I don't know. But I'm sure she's all right," I soothed, the assurance sounding false to my own ears. I had seen his mother arrive earlier in the afternoon. She had come to this room, her pelisse, hat and gloves were here. I couldn't see any sign of the portmanteau she'd had with her but it could have been emptied and put away. Or taken away—*along with Yvonne.*

"Where did she go?" André sobbed.

I stroked his dark head. "Maybe she just went out for the evening. See, her bureau drawers are open . . . she must have changed clothes and gone somewhere." I did not believe it. The disarray was not one of a woman dressing for the evening. There was little sign that Yvonne had spent any time here after Raoul had ordered the servants to conduct her to her room. "Perhaps she couldn't sleep . . . and went for a little walk."

His heaving chest quieted a little. As he contemplated my words, he peered up at me with those deep brown eyes so much like his uncle's, dark-lashed and expressive. At the moment they were filled with a childish pleading to make everything right. "Do . . . do you think so?"

"Yes," I lied. "And I think she would be terribly distressed to find you here and not tucked in bed. Where is your *bonne d'enfant*?"

"Don't call Mavis!" André'e eyes filled with panic. "Please, don't call Mavis." His sobs rose again.

"I won't. I won't. Come on now, let me get

you back in bed." I put my fingers up to my lips in a conspirator's whisper. "Nobody will know." I coaxed him up and held his hand as we left the room and walked a short distance down the hall to a room he indicated was his. It was only a few doors from Annette's.

His small bed was rumpled and I knew that his nanny had thought him tucked in for the night. He pointed to a closed adjoining door and put his finger up to his lips as I had done. I nodded, smiled, and indicated that I wouldn't do anything to wake up his nanny, Mavis.

He crawled back into bed, and I settled the covers around him with my one good hand. Before I could move away, he grabbed it tightly. "You stay," he ordered in a pleading whisper. Fear and loneliness filled his deep-set eyes.

"For a little while," I said. "Until you're asleep." Impulsively, I bent over and kissed his forehead. Thick shocks of wavy hair fell around his childish face and my heart contracted with tenderness. "Go to sleep. I'll stay right here."

Then I pulled a cushioned, upholstered chair close to the bed. I settled myself in it and watched the tense lines in his little face ease but André did not close his eyes. They watched me as if he dared not trust me to

stay with him. I didn't know what I should
do. His nanny was asleep in the next room.
Shouldn't she be the one to comfort and
reassure him? What if she knew where his
mother was and refused to tell him? No, I
couldn't do anything but stay close beside
him until he fell asleep.

The rest of the house seemed to slumber
peacefully. *Maybe Yvonne was with Raoul
de Lamareau.* It might not be Louise
Montaigne who shared his bed after all. The
thought was like a sharp knife stab. Maybe
André's mother had willingly gone to the
master's room . . . or had she been
summoned and obeyed out of fear? I didn't
want to believe that they might be sharing
the same bed and at this very moment
engaging in angry and passionate
lovemaking. On the other hand, if Madame
de Lamareau was not with the master . . .
where was she?

I closed my eyes and leaned back. My own
emotions were caught in a tangled
upheaval. I knew I should find my way back
to the deserted wing of the chateau but I
could not leave until André was asleep. The
storm brought claps of thunder vibrating
into the room. The wailing wind rose and
fell and sheets of rain beat against the
windows. André reached for my unbandaged hand and I engulfted his in a

reassuring squeeze.

I don't know when André closed his eyes but I fear that it was several moments after I closed my own. The last memory I had was of a warm, relaxing feeling settling upon me. I felt contented being there with André. I was needed and his tiny hand felt good in mine.

I did not awaken until a gray dawn was breaking and somewhere a rooster gave his coarse call in the wet morning. *I had slept the night in André's room!*

The boy was still asleep. I stood up and smoothed the folds of my robe and pushed back wisps of hair that lay wantonly around my face. Quietly I eased out of the room and hurried toward the main landing. I had to get back to my room. I did not want to be found in this part of the house in my nightclothes. As I darted across the main landing, I heard servants moving about in the lower regions of the house. Maybe Nela had already missed me. I would be mortified if she had mounted a search for me.

I reached the door leading into the unused wing of the chateau without encountering anyone. Now, to find my way back through the labyrinth of halls, I thought with some trepidation. My gaze fell to the dusty floor and I let out a sigh of relief. Dusty footprints on the oak flooring might lead me back to my room like Hansel and Gretel's crumbs in the fairy tale.

I had my head down, looking at the floor when I came around a corner of the dusky corridor and stopped short. A pair of black polished boots and muscular legs encased in tight riding pants stood in my way. I slowly raised my eyes with trepidation. I stood face to face with Raoul de Lamareau!

"I can explain," I said quickly, stiffening against his unspoken accusation. His expression was as cold as chipped ice and yet a fury burned in his dark eyes like red embers.

"I hope you can, Mademoiselle Grant." With one scathing look, he took in my tousled hair and nightclothes. "You didn't sleep in your own room last night?"

"No, but I can explain," I said again with as much composure as the situation would allow. I stiffened my neck and kept my gaze level with his.

"You were with Maurey Montaigne, perhaps?" he said caustically.

"I was not!" How dare he think I was returning to my room after keeping a romantic rendezvous? "How dare you insinuate such a thing!"

He held up a staying hand. "Spare me your virtuous indignation. Your romantic dalliance is of little importance. I am only interested in your whereabouts for one reason. The chateau was burglarized last night."

"Burglarized," I echoed. His words swept away the fury his accusation had aroused.

"Yes. At least a dozen expensive objets d'art are missing from the main floor and from the gallery across from your bedroom. You knew about the collection stored there, didn't you?" There was no mistaking the accusation in his crisp tone.

"Yes, I did, but—"

"I have just been there and the sweep of your skirts is all over that room. I noticed the dark edges of your gown yesterday but I thought it was from the hall."

"I . . . I was looking around before I came downstairs."

"So you knew the contents of the room? And their value?"

"Yes, but—"

"And you were aware of the valuable Venetian vases on the mantel—and other antiques in the drawing room which are now missing?"

My stomach muscles tightened. "I admired the amethyst vases—but you can't think I had anything to do with their disappearance."

His deep-set eyes were like honed steel.

"It would hardly seem likely anyone could have managed the burglary without inside help. The thieves were very selective . . . as if they knew exactly what objects they wished to take." His tone was as cold as his eyes. "It would seem that someone left a door unlatched. Someone let them in, Mademoiselle Grant."

Chapter Seven

It was a second or two before I realized that he was actually accusing me of being a thief. It was so preposterous that I managed to laugh and toss my head.

"I'm glad you find this so amusing, Alysha. When the *gendarmerie* arrives you can entertain them with your mirth."

"But . . . but you can't be serious," I gasped.

"A burglary is a very serious business."

"I agree. But I had nothing to do with it."

"You admit having knowledge of the contents of the gallery room?"

"Yes. I told you. I was in the room. I was curious and I did handle a few things . . . but I didn't steal anything nor did I make a reconnaissance for anyone else!"

"Would you mind telling me where you were last night, if not in your room?"

"I have nothing to hide," I snapped. "I decided I wanted to talk to Annette . . . explain why I couldn't stay here. You remember how agitated she was. I felt that the least I could do was to talk with her. I found her bedroom but she was asleep and I didn't want to disturb her. So—"

"So?" His lips curled nastily as if he thought I was making the lie up as I went.

My ready temper flared. "When I was in the hall I heard a child sobbing. It was André. He was in his mother's room and very distraught. He knew his mother had come back but he couldn't find her. At first, he lashed out at me, accusing me of taking his mother away. Yvonne's things were there . . . but the bed was still made up and the room empty. I thought it extremely bizarre myself." Now *my* tone was accusing "I saw her come into the house but she must not have remained in her room very long. I couldn't help wondering where she went—and why?"

"I thought I told you to stay away from the family side of the house."

He knew Yvonne was not in her room! He had trapped himself. He could not doubt my story because he knew I told the truth. I felt a sense of victory as if the scales had somehow tipped against him.

Taking advantage of this knowledge, I demanded, "Where is Madame de Lamareau? Apparently I wasn't the only one who was *not* in my own bed last night." I spoke sarcastically, tempted to add that perhaps that might include him and Louise as well.

My barbed innuendo failed to bring the tart reply I expected. He did not seem interested in my petty accusations. He was suddenly thoughtful as if his suspicions had sped away from me for the moment. Was he considering the possibility that someone else under the chateau's roof had broken the security of the house and let the burglars in? He could not fault my story of having been in Yvonne de Lamareau's room. For a moment his interest seemed to shift away from accusing me as the culprit and displayed more interest in ascertaining what I might have seen.

"Did you encounter anyone else moving about the house?"

"No." Then I shivered, remembering the

ghostly wraiths that had accompanied me through the labyrinth of halls.

"What's the matter?"

"Nothing." I managed a short laugh. "I'm afraid I let my imagination get away from me. It was dark, the storm was beating the house and . . . and I thought there might be ghosts—"

"Ghosts!" he echoed disdainfully.

"I told you I let my imagination run away from me. Especially when I got lost in that mirrored room."

His eyes narrowed. "You have managed to see quite a few things while you were supposed to be recuperating in your room, Alysha."

The implication that I was deliberately snooping about the chateau made me lash out defensively. "I don't understand why such a wealth of priceless furniture and objets d'art have been crammed in this wing of the chateau in the first place. Such beautiful things are ordinarily shown off to the best advantage . . . not crammed together in a dusty, attic-like abandonment. Why are all those things stored and not used? I'm sure they're worth a great deal of money."

At first I thought he was going to tell me curtly to mind my own business but he put a guiding hand on my arm and as we walked his shoulders suddenly seemed weighted as if he had carried a burden for a long time. "My brother, Jacques, was a collector of rare and beautiful things. If he liked a piece of furniture, a statue, painting or anything else of beauty, he had to have it . . . regardless of the cost. He had this sickness—I don't know how to explain it. He hoarded his possessions like a miser does his gold. And he always had to have more . . . more. Every bit of money he could scrape up or borrow went to feed his insatiable appetite. Like a gambler who can not rid himself of a weakness, he mortgaged everything to collect more and more things which he hid away. This wing of the house became his private territory. No one was allowed to trespass here . . . not even the servants were allowed to clean the rooms or dust his possessions. Jacques would disappear for days at a time in this side of the house and live like a hermit in the midst of his treasures. He let the estate and lands sink further into debt and ruin."

"But he's dead now." I pinned a sharp questioning gaze on Raoul. *Someone had killed his brother.* Had his addiction brought about Jacques de Lamareau's death? Was his widow telling the truth when she claimed Raoul had killed him? Had Raoul decided to put an end to the

neurotic collecting? If so, why did the
west wing remain crammed with such
treasures? "Surely, some of the collection could be sold now," I said aloud, voic-
ing my thoughts. From my experience with
Maurice Travois, I knew that the contents
of these crowded rooms would bring a
great deal of money.

Raoul sighed heavily. "My brother stipu-
lated in his will that nothing could be sold
or publicly displayed. He had made certain
that every item was carefully catalogued
and that a solicitor kept a careful
inventory. The collection must remain
intact and taxes paid upon every item.
There's no way to turn any of it into money
needed for upkeep of the chateau or its
lands."

I jerked my eyes away from his face,
fearful that he could read my thoughts. No
way, unless—? Was it possible that Raoul
de Lamareau had arranged for the burglary
to get needed capital for running the
estate? As administrator until André
reached adulthood, he had to worry about
the family finances. He might have chosen
this way to liquidate some of the assets.
Was he afraid that I might have seen
something during my wanderings that
would lead to their discovery? His next
words seemed to verify my suspicions.

"You spend the night looking for Yvonne?" he parried.

"No." I was trying to reorganize my thinking around my suspicion. He misunderstood my hesitation.

"Did you find company somewhere else, Alysha?"

"As a matter of fact I did," I answered sweetly. I knew he meant Maurey Montaigne.

I was rewarded by a flash of anger deeply reflected in his eyes. "I warned you," he growled.

"Yes, you did but as you can see I am not dressed for a romantic tête-à-tête." My steady gaze challenged him to admit I could have looked seductive if I had wanted to. He had seen me in my mother's peignoir.

He let his eyes travel over my plaited hair and the high-necked, drab robe covering up my cotton nightdress. I thought I saw his expression ease a little. "Are you going to tell me where you were, Alysha?"

"Why not? I have nothing to hide. I took André back to his bed, tucked him in and held his hand until he fell asleep. Unfortunately, I dozed off first. I only woke up a few moments ago and was returning to my room."

He did not challenge my story. I felt a sudden wash of relief as he asked, "Are you certain you didn't see anyone else on your nocturnal wanderings?"

"I'm sure. It was a little after midnight when I left my room and now it's—"

"Fifteen minutes past the hour of five. I arose early to take a morning ride before breakfast when I discovered that the chateau had been burglarized. The pair of Venetian vases were gone from the mantel."

I remembered having stroked the smooth glaze, running my fingers over the intricate design.

"You know the ones I mean?"

I nodded. There was no use denying it. "I . . . I admired them yesterday."

"Two small Louis XV chairs and a price-less wall tapestry are gone from the main entrance hall. A small ebony statue from the drawing room. I will not know what is missing from the gallery room until I check my brother's inventory but I could tell that several pieces have been removed. The thieves seemed to have been very selective. They seemed to know exactly what they wanted. As if someone had made out a list and they knew exactly where to go to fill it." Once more his penetrating gaze was like a diamond drill boring into my eyes.

"And you think I came here as a . . . what do they call it . . . front man? To arrange for the theft of certain items?"

"Which you might have easily identified ahead of time," he finished.

Once more I laughed, which I was pleased to see completely disconcerted him. "I suppose it's possible," I granted. Then I sobered. "But I can think of several other possibilities that are much more feasible, Monsieur. There are other people in the house who might benefit more from the theft. Someone who needed to liquidate some of the possessions into cash."

He flushed at the pointed barb. "Touché."

"It's just as reasonable to assume you had a part in their removal, Monsieur. However, I won't be rude enough to accuse you until some evidence is at hand to support the charge," I said rather primly.

A sheepish smile quirked at the corners of his lips. "I apologize. I'm afraid I did jump to conclusions."

"Yes, you did." I was not about to let him off easily.

"Perhaps you had best join us for breakfast this morning, Alysha."

As his deep voice softened upon my name in that devastating way of his, I felt a peculiar warmth sluicing through me. I wanted to be with him, hear his voice, and share the shadows that flickered behind his eyes. I wanted to share his troubles, if he

would let me. I felt that I had made a start.
He had shared the story of his brother's
eccentricity with me.

"I will have to send someone to the
village for the local *gendarmerie*. The police
will want to question everyone. If I were
you, I would not admit to leaving my bed,
Alysha. It sounds too . . . flimsy."

"But it's true! André will verify it."

"Perhaps but you could have left his bed
the moment he fell asleep. It is only your
word that you stayed there until morning.
There is no need to involve you in the
whereabouts of the rest of the family."

"I see. You want me to say that I never
left my room and never found Madame de
Lamareau missing from hers? Is that it?"
My tone was strident.

"It might be better all around." His lips
tightened in a warning.

A cold chill trickled down my back. All
warmth between us was gone. We were like
two gaming dogs ready to snarl at each
other. *He was trying to manipulate me for
his own evil purposes. He did not want me
to tell the constable that Yvonne de
Lamareau was not in her room last night.*

He left me at my room without any
further discussion. I rang for Nela and
despite her protests, I insisted on wearing a
simple, starched white blouse and dark

navy blue serge skirt which had been my
usual attire at school. As I stood in front of
the tall floor mirror, the familiar reflection
was reassuring. Even though I allowed a
soft wave to remain on my forehead, I told
Nela to draw the rest of my flaxen hair to
the back of my head in a familiar twist held
by long hairpins.

"You heard about the burglary?" I asked,
watching her bland face.

She nodded. "The servants have been
accused of leaving a door unlatched but it is
not true. The butler, Frazer, is very
responsible about such things."

"How did the burglars get in?"

"Through an unlocked window on the
first floor of this wing." Her small eyes
engaged mine. "The intruders must have
made noise removing contents from the
room across the hall. Did mam'selle hear
movement outside her door?" I shook my
head. "The medicine that the doctor left
puts me into a deep sleep." I readily lied as
if I had no choice but to willingly do as
Raoul de Lamareau had instructed. The
minute the lie was out, I wanted to draw it
back. Nela would know how much medicine
was missing from the bottle. She would
know that I had not taken the powdered
sedative that the doctor had left.

I could not meet her eyes. Perhaps she

already knew that I had not been in my bed
last night. One of the servants could have
been silently moving about last night and
could have seen me in the other wing of the
house. I suspected that a maze of servant
stairways accessed every floor. I could have
been observed without knowing it and the
gendarmerie would only have to question
someone who saw me to quickly discern my
lie. I felt as if I had just put one foot into a
treacherous quagmire and I didn't know
how to retreat from it. *Why had Raoul de
Lamareau instructed me not to tell the
truth? Why did he want me to lie?*

When I entered the breakfast room
nearly an hour later, I found it empty. At
first, I thought everyone might be in the
formal dining room, but tantalizing odors
wafting from a steaming row of silver
tureens lined on a magnificent buffet
reassured me that breakfast was being
served here. It was a lovely room, rounded
at one end with tall, stately windows overlooking a vine-covered terrace. Two French
doors stood ajar to the morning sunshine.

"Morning, Mam'selle." A small, gray-
haired woman appeared through solid
doors which led into the butler's pantry.
"Monsieur Montaigne is having breakfast
on the terrace. The morning is fresh and

clear after last night's rain. Would you care to join him?"

"Yes, thank you." The servant waited until I had made a choice of small crepes filled with fruit and clabbered cream, a side plate of country sausages, and a cup of deep, rich coffee and then followed me with a tray as I went out on the terrace.

"Mademoiselle Grant, *enchanté.*"

"*Bonjour,*" I greeted him.

Maurey immediately rose to his feet. He was handsomely dressed in fawn-colored trousers and a velvet morning coat, impeccable white linen and a soft dark tie. His auburn hair caught the morning light and waved handsomely around his face.

He held my chair. I was certain that my schoolish attire was a surprise to him but he was too practiced in the art of flattery to let it show. He immediately inquired after my health. His smiling eyes found mine and he gave me a delighted smile which I gratefully returned.

"I did not expect to see you until later this afternoon," he said. "You have not forgotten your promise to take a walk in the garden, *n'est-ce pas?* What is the matter, *ma chérie?* There are shadows around your lovely eyes. Did you not sleep well, Alysha?"

It was a natural, polite question but for a

moment I couldn't answer it. Was there something behind the polite inquiry? For a second I had the impression that he was after more than a simple yes or no. My suspicion seemed to be a many-legged monster. "The doctor gave me some medication to make me sleep," I answered evasively. "And you . . . did you sleep through all the excitement last night?"

"Didn't hear a thing. I can't believe someone made off with a half-dozen treasures while we all slept. Raoul said they were very selective . . . as if they really knew the house and where to go to get what they wanted. The pair of Venetian vases from the drawing room are gone."

"Yes, I know." Raoul had mentioned them to me earlier. I remembered how much I had enjoyed their lovely amethyst and gold color. Someone else had admired them too.

"You are quite pale, Alysha." He patted my good hand solicitously. "I'm certain you weren't in any danger, *chérie*. These scoundrels are not bent on harming anyone. This is not the first chateau to be burglarized in this fashion, you know. It's becoming quite popular, I fear. I must see that security at home is increased or we might be next, although we don't have the collection of rare art objects that is in the

de Lamareau family. Well, let us not
disturb ourselves with such an unfortunate
happening. It is much too pleasant having
breakfast here with you."

"Where are the others?" I really meant,
where was Raoul? An undefinable
emptiness made me inquire about him. In
spite of the circumstances, I had looked
forward to having breakfast with him.

"He and Louise decided to take an early
morning ride. A favorite pastime of theirs, I
fear. Our estate borders the de Lamareau
land not far into that band of trees. There
never have been any walls or fences to
divide our properties. At one time we
thought the two families might be united.
My oldest sister, Adeline, and Raoul's older
brother, Jacques, spent a good deal of time
together. Everyone thought they were going
to marry but Jacques surprised both
families by choosing Yvonne. Too bad. It
would be nice to see the families united."

"Maybe it will still happen . . . isn't there
a possibility that Louise might marry Raoul
de Lamareau?" I asked with feigned innocence.

He threw back his head and laughed.
"Touché. I'm certain my dear sister is
entertaining the same possibility. However,
at the moment Yvonne seems more in the
running. Not all of the estate went directly

to André at his father's death. In fact just the chateau and the immediate surrounding land is entailed to the first-born male of the family. A considerable inheritance, don't mistake me, but some of the chateau's vineyards and a few adjoining farms were deeded to Yvonne. She is land-poor, as they say, and it will take hard work and good management to realize much income from them. Although Raoul has offered to manage them, Yvonne is rather hysterical about the possibility that he may somehow wrench them from her. Raoul will only have control of the main estate until the boy becomes of age—or something happens to him. Then Raoul would inherit."

A cold draft hit my neck. Annette had said almost the same thing on the train.

"Of course, there's always the possibility that I might marry Yvonne myself," said Maurey. "Most women like younger men . . . especially a lonely widow as unhappy as Yvonne. Don't you think that would solve everybody's problem nicely?"

He was laughing and I wondered how much sober thinking lay behind his words. *Could Yvonne have spent the night with Maurey?* Maybe that was the reason Raoul wanted me to lie about not finding Yvonne in her room.

Maurey changed the subject and chatted quite pleasantly about the countryside and gave me some of the history of the area. When we had finished breakfast, he inquired, "Would you like to take our walk in the gardens this morning before the *Brigadier de police* arrives and burdens us all with his questioning?"

Suddenly my breakfast sat queasily on my stomach. "*Merci*, but I believe I'll return to my room and lie down."

Before I could rise to my feet, the sound of pounding horse hooves drew our eyes across a smooth expanse of grassy meadow. Two mounted riders galloped into view. The pair of horses moved together in beautiful rhythm. Streamers from Louise's riding hat trailed out behind her as she rose and fell in the saddle in a kind of liquid harmony. She kicked her white mount and it surged ahead of Raoul's, but only for a moment. In the next instant, his chestnut-colored steed quickly closed the distance and they raced side by side. My boarding school experience with horses had been limited to sedate walks around a bridle path. I was openly envious of the grace and skill which Louise Montaigne displayed. "They ride well," I said, thinking aloud.

"They probably rode out to the hunting

lodge. It lies in that direction."

"Oh?"

"Yes. Raoul's father had it built to accommodate his friends from the city when they came to hunt. Through the years, the game has been depleted and the lodge is not used much any more. It's a pleasant tryst for lovers, however." He winked at me knowingly. A sensual smile curved his full lips. "Perhaps we should ride out and see . . . as soon as you're feeling better."

I did not return his smile. I was not my mother. She would have lightly returned his sensual suggestion but I felt indignant hackles rising. "If you will excuse me," I said rather primly and rose to my feet. I did not want to be on the terrace when Louise and Raoul returned. "Thank you for a pleasant breakfast."

"May I look forward to a walk in the garden later in the day?"

"It will depend—" I said with my mouth suddenly dry as I pictured the interrogation ahead, "on what happens with the police."

Maurey waved his hand in a dismissive gesture. "Don't worry about it. The local officer will ask a few questions, sniff around like a bloodhound who has lost the scent, and then he will beg our pardons and be gone. Nothing will come of it."

"Are you sure?" I suddenly felt a wash of relief. Maybe it would be that simple. Undoubtedly the de Lamareau family would not be subject to any kind of interrogation that would be embarrassing. I had seen the deferential manner of those who greeted Raoul at the train station. But even as these hopeful thoughts skittered across my mind, I said, "Perhaps Monsier de Lamareau will not let them be so casual about it."

"My dear, Raoul has other things on his mind. And he will not want the authorities sniffing around. His brother, Jacques, was killed right over there at the edge of those trees. The verdict of an unknown assailant has rested uneasily with people like Yvonne. She thinks her husband was murdered—by Raoul."

"Yes, I know." He obviously had intended to shock me. I felt a vague satisfaction at his surprised expression. I quickly bid him good morning and found my way back to my room.

When Dr. Duboise came to see me after lunch, he mentioned the dark circles under my eyes. "Shame . . . shame. Haven't you been sleeping well? I left a sedative—?" He raised his bushy eyebrows questioningly.

I didn't admit that I hadn't taken it. "I
slept very well last night." Which was the
truth. I would have returned to my own bed
if I hadn't fallen sound asleep at André's
bedside. *Maybe I would have returned to
encounter the thieves as they burglarized
the room across the hall, too.*

I must have gone pale for Dr. Duboise
shook his head as he took my pulse. "You
are not resting as I advised," he said when
he had finished. "And look at that bandage
. . . so dirty. What have you been doing,
Mademoiselle, dusting the furniture?" His
blue eyes twinkled.

His friendliness was the tonic I needed. I
managed a weak smile in return. "When do
you think I can start using my hand?"

"The pain is still there, *n'est-ce pas*? The
swelling had not gone down. It will be
another week at least."

"Week!"

"Your deep blue eyes look pained,
Mademoiselle. Is it your head?" He peered
through his square glasses at the ugly
swelling on my forehead. "It seems to be
bleaching out. Nothing will remain to mar
your lovely complexion, I assure you." He
gave me his warm smile. "There is nothing
for you to worry about. I'm certain
Monsieur de Lamareau is most happy to

extend the hospitality of his home."

And I was just as certain that he wanted me gone.

"Have you met Madame de Lamareau?" I asked impulsively.

"Monsieur is married? I had the impression—"

"No, Raoul de Lamareau is not married. I meant his sister-in-law, Yvonne de Lamareau. She was married to the older brother, Jacques. I wondered if, by chance, you had made her acquaintance."

His answer was disappointing. "No, I have not had the pleasure . . . but you must remember, I am only a visitor to this area. My brother and I are on a holiday. You are my only patient at the moment and if you hadn't fallen into my lap, so to speak, I would not have broken my holiday to take a patient."

"I'm so glad you did. It's important to me that you do not turn me over to the de Lamareau's regular doctor."

He laughed and his heavy jowls shook. "I'm flattered, my dear. It has been a long time since a lovely young lady made me feel so special." He left with an admonition that I take my medicine and rest.

My nerves were stretched too tight to rest and I had no intention of getting myself into a groggy state with the medicine. I would

need my wits about me when the police
asked their questions.

When I heard movement and men's
voices in the hall, I knew the police had
arrived. I waited for a demanding knock on
my door but none came. The noises ceased
and an uneasy silence returned. Maybe I
was not going to be involved at all. Raoul
might have satisfied them that I knew
nothing. The knotted muscle in my stomach
had just begun to ease when Nela brought
me a message. My presence in the library
would be appreciated at my earliest
convenience, she said.

"Would you wish to change, Mam'selle,
to something more suitable?" she asked
with her broad nostrils twitching as she
viewed my prim blouse and plain walking
skirt.

"No." I smoothed back my hair. For some
reason I decided looking like a drab bird
might be to my advantage. Maybe the police
would believe the lies that were about to
fall from my lips.

As I followed Nela down the hall, I
rehearsed my story. I would declare that I
had slept soundly all night and knew
nothing about what had transpired in the
house. A small stab of conscience was
quickly dispelled. Looking back, I realize
that I did not even question my willingness

to do as Raoul de Lamareau had instructed.

I think I knew even then that I had fallen in love with him.

Chapter Eight

Nela knocked discreetly on the closed
library doors and then opened one of them
for me to enter. Like someone about to
make an appearance centerstage, my heart
raced crazily, and I swallowed hard to get
some moisture in my throat as I went in.

I had expected a room full of people,
including Raoul de Lamareau. But there
was only one person seated behind a wide
desk, a small, elderly, bald-headed man
with salt and pepper mutton-chop side-

burns along his narrow cheeks. Dressed
in a dark suit that did not fill out his
skinny shoulders and a black tie at a
white stiff collar encircling a scrawny neck,
he looked more like a judge than a
policeman. He immediately rose to his feet
at my entrance, put down the sheaf of
papers he was holding and gestured for me
to take a chair that had been placed in con-
versational distance at the side of the desk.
His steely eyes watched me like a bird
of prey, steady, watchful, and waiting.
"Mademoiselle Grant?" His raspy voice
was questioning.

Obviously my appearance was not what
he had expected of someone who was a
guest at this magnificent chateau. But after
that first questioning flicker, there was
nothing in his expression to betray his
thoughts.

I nodded, not trusting my voice to hide
the trembling I felt inside.

"I am inspector Davail. Please be seated. I
apologize for disturbing you. Very unfortunate, the accident."

His bald, age-spotted forehead furrowed sympathetically but his eyes remained the same, cold and steady. "I
hope you are recovering from your
injuries."

I nodded again and sat down, grateful

that my weak knees did not have to hold me up any longer.

"Do you have any idea how it happened?"

This was the time to voice my suspicions about the "accident." This officer of the law would listen to me. He would be interested in my speculation about Raoul de Lamareau having fed something to the horse as our train pulled into the station. I feared he saw the struggle going on in my mind.

"Yes?" he prodded.

Such was the state of my infatuation that I could not bring myself to point an accusing finger at Raoul de Lamareau.

"Yes, Mademoiselle? Did you wish to say something?" He had caught the scent, like a hound after his prey. He leaned forward. "You have some information, *peut-être*, that will shed some light on the matter?" His bird-like eyes were small and sharp, a peculiar color, like a kind of hard stone used for drilling. His voice had the same kind of abrasiveness.

"No," I shook my head, and summoned my wits. "Someone said the horse went *fou*. I guess it happens sometimes . . . to both people and animals. At least that's what Dr. Duboise told me."

"Ah, yes." He seemed disappointed at my innocuous answer. "Well, that is not the matter that brings me here." His speckled hand picked up a sheet of paper. "I have a list of things burglarized from the chateau. I understand that you are occupying a room directly across the hall from the one where several items were taken. Did you hear anything out of the ordinary last night, Mademoiselle?"

"Only the storm . . . before I went to sleep. My doctor has prescribed a sedative for me. I take it at night so I can have a good night's rest. My wrist sometimes pains me and I can't get to sleep. I didn't hear anything. Nothing at all." My answer was too pat, too well-rehearsed. Even as the lies spilled from my lips, I could see the disbelief in his stone eyes.

"You heard nothing? You *are* occupying the room across the hall from the de Lamareau collection, is that not so?"

I nodded.

"It does not seem reasonable that a burglary could take place across the hall and you would be completely unaware of it, Mademoiselle." It was not a question but a statement.

"I heard nothing. I did not know that a robbery had taken place until this morning." That much, at least, was true.

"And you did not leave your room last night?"

"No. I did not." I think I hated Raoul de Lamareau at that moment for making me lie. For some undefinable reason I could not do otherwise. I remembered his furrowed brow, the weighted slump to his shoulders, and I knew that I did not want to add to his distress, even if it meant lying to this vulture-like inspector.

"But you were aware of the treasures stored in the gallery room, Mademoiselle?"

"Yes, I was looking around yesterday and I discovered them."

"And you knew that they were valuable?"

I should have lied and said no, but his penetrating eyes seem to draw the truth from me. "Yes, I realized that some of the objects were very rare," I admitted. The minute the words were out, I wanted to call them back.

"I see. Then you became familiar with the contents of that room?"

"No, I just wandered through it yesterday, before I came downstairs and had tea in the drawing room."

"Ah, the drawing room. You noticed the pair of Venetian vases on the mantel, *peut-être*? The ones that are missing?"

A coil of panic began to unwind, making my voice shaky. "Yes, I admired them very much—but I did not steal them."

"No, of course not." His smile had no

warmth in it and did not change the hard penetrating glint of his eyes. "Monsieur de Lamareau tells me that you and his niece were together at a school in Switzerland. And you volunteered to see her home. Is that correct?"

"No, I did *not* volunteer. I was asked by Sister Mary Josette, *la directrice*, to see Mademoiselle Annette home. I was going on to Paris and Sister knew that I had become quite fond of the little girl, so I readily agreed when she asked me to stop over here for one night. If the carriage accident hadn't injured my wrist, I would have left on the train for Paris the next morning."

"I see." He tapped a lean finger on the desk as if he were thinking.

I could tell that the police officer did not believe me. All of a sudden, I saw where Inspector Davail was leading. I could read it in his flat eyes and the slow tapping of that finger. *He thought it was no accident that I had managed to get myself into this very private family chateau, in a position to be an accomplice for a burglary.* Raoul had inferred the thing earlier, only this time I wasn't laughing at the absurd accusation. Fright had replaced any righteous indignation. "I only planned to stay overnight," I repeated defensively.

Time enough to set up the burglary,

Inspector Davail's steady gaze seemed to say. "You knew nothing about the de Lamareau family? About the late Jacques de Lamareau's penchant for collecting valuable things?"

"No, I did not. I befriended Annette and tried to help her as much as I could at school but she didn't talk much about her family. It wasn't until I arrived that . . . that I became acquainted with Raoul de Lamareau . . . and Madame de Lamareau." He would think it odd that I had never met the mistress of the house. Raoul had put such a spell on me that I was lying to keep the inspector from knowing she had been absent from her room last night.

"I see that there were two other guests at the chateau last night. Louise and Maurey Montaigne. Are you acquainted with them, Mademoiselle?"

"I just met them yesterday."

"Not before that?" He raised a skeptical eyebrow.

"No." What was he getting at? Why didn't he believe me?

"You didn't come here at their request?"

"Of course not! I never met them before yesterday."

"You didn't know anyone before you arrived with Mademoiselle Annette?"

"No."

"You had no correspondence with anyone at the chateau?"

"I wrote to Annette's mother that I would be accompanying Annette home at Sister Mary Josette's request. Since I was going on to Paris—" my voice faltered. I didn't want to tell this austere inspector about my personal life. It was none of his business that I was without job or resources. Even as I choked off an explanation, I knew that he was not going to let anything escape his meticulous questioning.

"Your home is in Paris, Mademoiselle?"

Home? I don't have one! The truth flashed through my head and was like a key turning a lock against me. This calculating policeman would soon know that I was unprotected, a young woman who must depend upon her own resources, and defenseless against any charges he might level at me. I had only my pride and the knowledge that my personal reputation was beyond reproach. Mary Josette would testify to that. "I have a position as seamstress waiting for me in Paris," I said without lowering my eyes.

"And your family?"

"My mother is in the south of France . . . with friends." My voice landed on the last word too heavily. The plural did not hide the truth from him. Too late, I realized that

I had told him my mother was someone's paramour as plainly as if I had voiced the word. I thought there was suddenly a lewd glint in his eyes as they traveled over my face and I felt a flush mounting in my cheeks. Even though I wore my school attire of white bodice and dark skirt, he looked at me as if a deliberate effort at disguise had not fooled him.

"Would you mind telling me where you gained your knowledge of antiques, Mademoiselle Grant?"

All my life, I had taken great care to hide the fact that my mother was a kept woman. I wanted to lie now, make up some story that this scavenger-like man would accept. Under any other circumstances, I would not have revealed my mother's private relationshp as mistress to Maurice Travois but I knew that Inspector Davail had the means to check out any story I attempted to fabricate. I feared that he had already discerned that I had no family to support or defend me. I had no choice but to tell him the truth, however damaging it might be for me. "My mother and I lived with Monsieur Travois, a dealer in rare furniture and objets d'art until I was nearly twelve years old." I explained that the art dealer had taken me with him on many of his buying trips. "I continued to read and visit museums after I was sent away to school. But I am by no means an expert—"

"But knowledgeable enough to identify rare porcelain vases?"

"I recognized their value, yes, but I did not arrange that they should be stolen while I slept upstairs," I flared. My nervousness was laced with a growing indignation. I resented the implication that I had the background necessary to burglarize the de Lamareau chateau.

"And this Maurice Travois? Have you talked with him lately?"

I stiffened. The question was as barbed and direct as an arrow. "No. I have not seen Maurice Travois for nearly six years. He may even be dead by now. He had a heart attack and his wife took him south for his health. My mother and I have had no contact with him since."

"I see."

But I knew he didn't believe me. I wanted to shout at him that I knew nothing of the burglary or anything else that went on in this house. Why didn't he look elsewhere for the answers he sought? How convenient it was to have someone outside the de Lamareau family to place all the guilt upon. Their reputation would be protected. I had neither family, nor prestige, nor influence to worry about. I was made to order.

"You did not leave your room last night, Mademoiselle?" he asked again as if giving me one more chance to tell the truth.

"No." Had the inspector already questioned the servants? *And André?* I had completely forgotten the little boy. Had he told Mavis, his *bonne d'enfant*, that I had tucked him in bed last night and gone to sleep before he did. No, I didn't think so. André had not wanted me to tell his nanny that he had been out of bed. The little boy would not say anything, I was sure of it. I took a deep breath. Guilt was making me overreact. "I told you. The doctor gave me something to sleep."

"Ah, yes, you slept soundly. You have no knowledge of the culprits who made their way into the house and made off with several valuable pieces of Jacques Lamareau's hidden collection. Is that the statement you wish to sign, Mademoiselle Grant?" The warning was there in his voice, quiet and relentless, like the jaws of a steel trap.

Why was I doing this? My nocturnal wanderings had been innocent enough. I had gone to talk with a distressed young girl and had ended up comforting her little brother. I had *not* let thieves into the house. But who would believe it? Not this small, baldheaded man who terrorized with his penetrating eyes and granite voice. "I did not leave my room."

Even as he nodded, I knew that somehow he would prove that I had been wandering around the chateau last night. And when he did, he would know me for the liar that I was. I should not have listened to Raoul de Lamareau. He had wanted me to lie for some nefarious reason of his own. I had let him maneuver me into this position. *Had he deliberately set me up to become this law officer's quarry?*

Chapter Nine

As soon as Inspector Davail dismissed me,
I fled into the garden without even
returning upstairs for my bonnet and
gloves. I didn't want to see or talk to
anyone. My thoughts were like a swarm of
locusts. The inspector had abruptly warned
me against leaving the chateau until the
unfortunate matter was settled to his
satisfaction. I felt the tight cords of a mesh
tightening around me. I sensed that he
would be relieved to find a culprit outside

the de Lamareau and Montaigne families.
My being in the house was made to order
and I knew with sickening certainty that
the inspector wasn't the only one aware of
my vulnerability. Raoul de Lamareau had
played on my emotions so that I had
compromised my innocence by lying for
him.

Hot tears evaporated on my cheeks as I
hurried out a side door. A series of terraces
overlooked a wide expanse of cultivated
gardens. I stopped and looked about
bewildered. Except for the high, narrow
view from my window, I had not seen the
elaborate landscaping that surrounded the
chateau. Precisely trimmed green hedges
had been laid out in intricate patterns and
every flower bed planted with a single color
to heighten the design. Unlike English
gardens, there were no rambling roses,
untrimmed trees, rampant flowers, or
unshaped scrubs but every leaf and
blossom was precisely arranged in the
geometric pattern so popular in French
landscaping. I could understand now why
Maurey wanted to show the gardens to me.

I went down a series of wide terrace steps
and reached a pathway bordered by
carefully manicured hedges almost
shoulder high. Lavish plantings of greenery
provided a startling background for a

series of white marble statues. I tried to
give my attention to them but in my present
state of mind their graceful beauty was lost
on me.

A myriad of pathways branched out in
every direction from a wide corridor which
I could see led to a hexagonal pool where
streams of water from a fountain arched at
least ninety feet in the air. Instead of
continuing toward the fountain, I chose a
side path, hoping that I would lose myself
before Maurey could overtake me and
claim me for a walk in the gardens. I always
thought better out in the open air when I
could walk vigorously and take deep
breaths of air. My stride was bold and not
very ladylike in spite of Sister Josette's
constant reprimand. I enjoyed walking and
I could not stand taking mincing steps,
especially when I was agitated.

The beauty of the grounds was lost on me
as I followed a winding path away from the
chateau. I was only vaguely appreciative of
rose trees and flowers which greeted my
eyes and teased my nostrils with their
sweet scents. The path I had chosen led to a
small fountain where clear water descended in a gurgling rush over the backs
of frogs, stones, and capricious mermaids
to collect in a marble pool. Nearby,
numerous benches had been tucked in cool,

green corners shaded by a variety of
poplars, elms, maples and cypress trees but
I passed them all by. I was not certain my
exit from the house had gone unnoticed.
The need to be alone and sort out my
thoughts kept me from sinking down upon
a bench and giving way to my emotions.

My vigorous stride soon brought me out
of the formal garden, to an orchard
bounded by a clipped hornbean hedge. I
could see several gray stone outbuildings
only a short distance away which I
identified as carriage house and stables. I
gave them a wide berth as I circled around
them. I feared that Raoul might still be near
the stables with Louise. I couldn't bear to
see him now.

Anger and frustration made me clench
my fists. What a fool I'd been. He'd played
me like a fish on the line, telling me to lie
and setting me up as a conspirator in the
burglary. I could see now how the whole
thing had been engineered. Somehow he
had learned about me—maybe Annette had
mentioned me in her letters and Raoul saw
the opportunity to have a stranger in the
house when he arranged for the burglary.
He could have requested that Mary Josette
have me accompany his niece home. I had
assumed that the request came from
Annette's mother but having seen Yvonne, I

knew now that Raoul managed the family.

Glad that I wore my school walking skirt, I left the landscaped grounds and headed across an expanse of meadow tinted green and yellow with tender grass and blooming cornflowers. When I reached a copse of trees, I breathed a sigh of relief. Now I was hidden from any of the myriad windows facing this direction. I saw a bridle path on my left and I realized I must be in about the place where Raoul and Louise had emerged from the trees earlier that morning.

I turned and looked back at the de Lamareau chateau, seeing it from a distance for the first time. There was little grace to the mammoth structure. Gray stone walls darkened and ravaged by time were stark and unrelieved. From this distance, its turrets and belfries looked stiff and harsh as they rose jaggedly from the steep roof line. Even in the bright sunlight, it looked brooding and forbidding. Windows that rose from arches on the first floor to dormers in the attic were blank and dull and as I let my eyes scan the chateau, I could not locate my bedroom window in the unoccupied wing. Obviously, it was an old chateau which had weathered France's turbulent history of royal tyranny and peasant uprisings. I wondered how many members of the de Lamareau family had come to a violent death within it. The thought made me shiver and I turned away to lose myself in the soothing quiet of the woods.

I filled my lungs with invigorating, deep breaths of air. My head cleared as I walked. I was glad that there was no sign of anyone coming after me. I didn't want to suffer Maurey's flirtatious company. My thoughts centered on him for a moment. Since I had not let the burglars into the house, someone else had. Was Maurey Montaigne the guilty one? He undoubtedly knew of the cache of vaulable objects collected in the west wing of the house. Although I had just met him I could guess that he was the kind who would always need money for his social obligations. Maybe his father had tightened the Montaigne purse strings and he needed to pay off some debts. Maurey and Louise could be in on the theft together, arranging for a percentage of the stolen articles to be returned to them.

And then there was Yvonne. Maurey had said that she was "land-poor." With Raoul holding the purse strings for young André, she might have decided to hire someone to help her turn some of her husband's collection into cash. I knew that such a rationale was feeble but it was not impossible. I much preferred to think that the

Montaignes or Yvonne were responsible than to put the blame where it more likely belonged. The suspicion that Raoul had deliberately manipulated me so that I would lie to the inspector was so painful that I deliberately pushed the possibility away. In my emotional state, I would have gladly accepted anyone but Raoul as the culprit.

Leafy trees stretched overhead and a musty, cool odor touched my nostrils as heavy moss carpeted the ground around me. Walking in the woods around the school had always been a favorite pastime of mine. Since I never had visitors, I had made it a point to go off by myself when other students were having Sunday afternoon guests. Somehow, I felt less lonely with wild bushes and flowers offering me berries or blossoms and fluttering birds darting about scolding me with caws and chirps. I reached out for that solace now, but it escaped me as I continued further along the narrow bridle path.

There was a silence in these woods that was different from the woods around the school, I thought, with a sudden uneasiness. An infinity of trees stretched in every direction, blocking out any view of what lay beyond. I remembered then that Jacques had been murdered while hunting in these

woods. The memory of Annette's tearful
face came back. *My uncle killed my father.
My mother is sure of it.*

My expectation of enjoying a walk in this
thick forest faded. I felt more alone than
ever. More vulnerable. I was just about to
turn around and go back when I caught a
glimpse of a low stone building through a
narrow break in the trees. The hunting
lodge! Maurey had told me this morning
that it was only used as a "lover's retreat"
now. *This was where Louise and Raoul had
been when they appeared on horseback that
morning.* I walked closer until I could see
the long, vine-covered stone lodge and a
large stable that lay beyond it. It resembled
a style of architecture that was popular in
Germany: made of heavy stone blocks, the
lodge was one story with rounded heavy
doors, mullioned windows and a turret
rising above a deeply slanted, gray tile roof.

As I gazed at it, I could visualize a
shadowy bedroom within those walls, a
rumpled bed and Raoul claiming Louise's
clinging body in a heat of passion that shut
out the world. My fantasy was as real as if I
stood in the shadows of the room and
listened to their passion-laced whispers. I
hated myself for a sudden wish that I could
have been the one in his arms. I had thought
myself immune to appetites such as the one

that rose within me at the thought of Raoul's body claiming mine. Even though I hated this man for what he had done to me, making me lie and bending me to his will when I knew that he was exploiting my presence in the house, I could not control a deep ache within me as I visualized him making love to Louise in that lodge beyond the trees. I hated myself for the weakness that brought tears into my eyes and a sudden ache into my chest.

I swung around, intending to flee back to the chateau. Then I froze. My breath caught in a short gasp. I couldn't believe my eyes. Yvonne de Lamareau appeared like a dark specter, stepping out from behind the trees. She stood purposefully within firing distance, pointing a rifle at my stomach.

"Madame—" I stammered, not knowing what to do or say.

Her dark eyes fixed on my face as if I were some hunted quarry that had stumbled into her snare. There was none of the hysterical blubbering that I had seen upon her arrival with the Montaignes. This woman was in command of herself. Her dark eyes did not flicker and her gaze held me immobile like the hypnotic stare of a coiled snake.

I knew I must say something and I forced my dry mouth to croak. "I'm Alysha Grant

. . . Annette's school friend. I wrote to you . . . that I would accompany her home."

She still did not speak.

"I'm very fond of Annette," I said with a rush. "She's a lovely little girl."

"Silence!" The order was like the sting of a whip. "He told me you were coming," she said in a hateful tone that sent shivers up my back. "He thought he was clever. But I wasn't fooled."

"I . . . I don't know what you're talking about," I stammered. I struggled for some understanding of her vitriolic words. "He" must refer to Raoul. There was undisguised hatred in Yvonne's eyes and I knew then that Annette had not lied. Her mother despised her husband's brother with a diabolical intensity. The woman looked as if she would pull the trigger at any moment.

"You lie," she spat.

Terror rose like a wild surf within me. Surely Yvonne's hate did not encompass me. Even as I struggled to reassure myself, I knew from her malevolent glare that it already had. She had linked me with whatever treachery she assigned to her brother-in-law. How could I convince her of my innocence?

I forced a smile to my stiff lips. "There's some misunderstanding. Sister Mary Josette asked me to see Annette home.

There was an accident—" I held up my bandaged hand. "See, my wrist was hurt and I couldn't leave. I've been wanting to talk with you. I'm very fond of Annette . . . and I tried to look after her at school." I thought I could see a flicker of her eyelashes but the mention of her daughter had not brought a slackening of her finger upon the trigger. "Can't we talk about Annette?"

A long, long moment went by. My heart thumped loudly and all moisture left my mouth and throat. Would she pull the trigger as her answer? When she finally gave a wave of her rifle toward the lodge, I didn't know whether my weak legs would carry me there.

She made me walk in front of her and I could sense the gun barrel inches from my back. My mind raced to find some kind of strategy that would convince her that I was not deserving of the hatred she felt for Raoul.

We entered the lodge through a side door that opened into a shadowy, long sitting room. Heavy fireplaces at both ends were almost large enough to take a man standing up and their darkened hearths, massive mantels and broad rock chimneys dwarfed everything else in the room. Heads of stuffed animal trophies with glassy eyes stared down from dark panelled walls and a variety of bearskins dotted the wooden floors. Overhead the ceiling was ribbed with heavy walnut beams and unpolished copper chandeliers hung on long chains at both ends of the room. They were not lighted and draperies hanging at the long, narrow windows added to the oppressive, closed-in feeling of the lodge.

Yvonne kept her rifle leveled on me as she backed up and reached into the nearest fireplace and took out a bottle of whiskey that must have been hidden on a ledge inside. Still keeping her steady, unblinking stare on me, she took a healthy swig from the bottle, so deep that it would have set most sailors to gasping. Not knowing what to do, I sank down on a leather chair and moistened my lips with a dry tongue that threatened to stick to them. Before I could say anything, she set the bottle on a nearby table and demanded, "Where is Raoul? I'm going to put a bullet between his deceitful eyes. I was waiting for him. Where is he?"

"I . . . I don't know."

"You're one of his women, aren't you?"

"No. I told you, I brought Annette home."

Yvonne took another hearty swig of whiskey. Then she gave a bitter laugh. "Raoul's smart. Sneaking you in like this. That bitch, Louise Montaigne, isn't enough for him. They think they've got me fooled.

Even Maurey thinks he can play up to me
and get my lands away from me. They all
want what is mine. Raoul killed my
husband . . . and now I'm going to kill him."

"No," I protested. The thought of Raoul
dead in his own blood outweighed any fear
I had for my own safety. "No, you mustn't."

Yvonne smiled then, a knowing, cruel
smile. "That's what I thought. Gave
yourself away, didn't you? You don't want
me to kill the deceitful bastard."

"No, please—"

Yvonne had obviously drunk enough now
to make her tongue thick. Eyes that had
been stark and clear began to cloud over as
the liquor began to have its effect. I had
never seen anyone drink the way she did.
The bottle of whiskey was nearly a third
gone in a matter of a few minutes. My God,
she would be raving drunk with another
few swigs, I thought in panic. How could I
reason with her then? She leaned up
against the wall, bracing herself as she kept
the rifle aimed right at me. It wavered as
she took drinks from the bottle but her eyes
never left me. There was no chance of
wrestling the gun from her.

"You have to listen to me, Yvonne," I said
in a brisk tone that belied the trembling
that lay beneath. "I like Annette and André
very much and I want to help them . . . and

you in any way I can. They are worried about you."

"He's going to kill them." Yvonne shouted at me as if I had defied her in some way. "But I'm going to kill him first." Her voice rose in a shrieking rage and any hope I had of reasoning with her fled.

At that moment a door at the far end of the room jerked open. A servant woman who had a family resemblance to Nela came into the room. She stopped short when she saw Yvonne standing there with a rifle in her hands. Then she moved forward very slowly. "'Madame . . . Madame—'' she said soothingly. Her hazel eyes were the same as Nela's, the same homely features, with a hint of gray in the same lackluster brown hair. An older sister, I thought, as she tried to coax the gun from her mistress.

"Stay back," screamed Yvonne, swinging the gun in her direction. "You're one of them, Alveretta. Don't think I don't know he pays you to keep me here."

"It's best for you, Madame. Until you get well—"

"Until he kills me! That's what he's going to do. But I'll kill him first. When he comes, I'll—"

"Do what, Yvonne?" demanded a strident voice from the same side door where Yvonne and I had entered the room a few minutes earlier. Raoul stood there, his legs slightly apart, his arms at his side. There was a rigidity in his carriage that belied the calmness of his voice. Raoul must have quietly opened the door as Yvonne was screaming threats about him.

At the sound of his voice, Yvonne swung the gun in his direction. I wanted to rush at him and scream a warning of the danger he was in. He must have sensed my terror for his eyes flickered to me and a warning in them halted any movement I might have made. I forced myself to remain seated, not knowing how I could remain quiet when any moment, the crazed woman would carry out her threat to put a bullet between his eyes.

"She's been drinking, m'sieur," warned the servant.

"So I see. Put down that rifle, Yvonne," he ordered.

She gave a drunken laugh. "Your new mistress got here before you. But I saved the bullet for you."

"Don't be—" He took a step forward but he never finished the sentence.

Yvonne pulled the trigger. The window behind Raoul exploded at the same time a jagged streak of blood appeared on his left temple. I screamed and leaped up. Yvonne lowered the gun and covered her face with one hand.

Raoul looked surprised but not injured. He wiped at the blood trickling down his cheek, and I realized then that the bullet had grazed his forehead. Yvonne's aim had been off only a fraction of an inch.

I was so weak with relief, I sat back down in the chair. Raoul brushed by me and quickly took the gun from Yvonne. She was sobbing hysterically. Raoul handed the rifle to the servant and then put his arm around Yvonne's trembling shoulder.

"You little fool," he said gently.

To my astonishment, Yvonne pressed her tear-streaked cheek against his chest. "I love you . . . I love you," she sobbed.

Raoul met my eyes over her bowed head and for a moment I thought there was a plea for understanding in his anguished dark eyes.

Chapter Ten

Raoul ordered the servant, Alveretta, to take Yvonne to her room. He had reprimanded her for allowing Yvonne to gain the keys which gave her access to the gun cabinet and the outside door.

"I thought Madame was sleeping," she explained, obviously flustered and fearful. "I didn't think there were any more spirits about, Monsieur, really I didn't. She had the bottle hidden." The woman was obviously flustered and fearful. It was not a pretty sight; blood was caked on her master's forehead where the bullet had grazed him and Madame held her head in a drunken, sloppy wailing. The servant put her thick arms around Yvonne. "It'll not happen again."

"See that it doesn't." Raoul's tone was like granite. "I brought Madame to the lodge to regain herself and I expected you to be with her every minute of every day and night until she's ready to move back into the main house."

"Yes, sir. I understand, sir." Alveretta led the weeping Yvonne away.

Raoul turned to me and I braced myself against the anger that flared in the dark-lashed eyes. "And what, Mademoiselle, are you doing here?" His tone was the same one he had used with the servant.

"I was not prying into your affairs," I bristled. "If that's what your rude tone implies. I assure you I had no idea that a quiet walk would put me in danger of being shot."

He touched his bloodied face with his handkerchief, wiping away the red dribbles that coated the ugly bullet crease. "I thought you were sàfe enough in the west wing. Then André told me he had seen you walking in this direction. My God, there is no telling what Yvonne would have done to you if I hadn't come. I'll speak to Nela about her lack of duty. She is supposed to be attending you."

"Don't blame her. She thought I was with the inspector. I slipped out a side door without speaking to anyone."

He swore softly. "Well, I guess there's no help for it now. You and Yvonne have met—"

"Yes," I shivered. "She's in a terrible state, isn't she?"

His jaw muscles flickered. "Yes. I tried to keep you apart, sending Yvonne here when she arrived home angry and drunk. I didn't want her to see you . . . especially not while she's drinking. There's no telling what she'll say or do. Any young woman who comes to the house is in danger of Yvonne's jealousy."

"But I thought she hated you?"

"Hate . . . love—" He shrugged. "They intermingle in her disturbed, befuddled mind. When she drinks she accuses me of murder, seduction, of plotting to harm her and the children. Or goes into passionate rages about how much she loves me. I do my best to keep her condition as quiet as possible. Maurey and Louise are a great help. She usually runs to them in her drunken tirades. Yvonne is a very shrewd woman at times. This robbery makes me wonder if—"

"You think she had a part in it?"

"I don't know. Yvonne has brought some unsavory characters home from time to time. She drinks and gambles when she goes to Paris. And she's always talking about her late husband's fortune in antiques and art. She was here at the lodge last night but she could have arranged for one of the windows of the chateau to be left unlatched. I just don't know."

"I see. Now, I understand why you wanted to protect Yvonne—at my expense." My manner was not generous as I accused him. "You persuaded me to lie about not being out of my room to protect a woman who is in love with you. Are your feelings for her more than just those of a considerate brother-in-law?" It was a petty question, unworthy of me, but I couldn't help it. After all, he had used me to protect her, and I felt I had the right to know the depth of his feelings. He didn't give me an answer but instead assailed me with questions of his own.

"What happened with the inspector?" Raoul's forehead furrowed and his dark eyebrows drew together in a worried line. "Didn't he believe you?"

"No, I'm sure he didn't. No doubt he'll talk to André or some servant who saw me in the main part of the chateau last night.

Once he does that, he'll know I was lying."

Raoul sat down on the arm of my chair and took my hand. "I'm sorry, Alysha. I really thought it would be better not to get you involved. I didn't think anyone would believe your story about wandering around, following a cat in the middle of the night—"

"Since you don't!" I flashed.

He smiled ruefully. "A young desirable woman roaming about in night clothes has only one interpretation for most people."

"You, included," I snapped. I hadn't forgotten that he had assumed I'd been with Maurey. I pushed aside my own suspicions that he had spent the night with Louise. I would not humble myself to ask him for an accounting of his own whereabouts.

To my surprise, he raised my hand and lightly kissed it. "I apologize, Alysha. I suppose I shouldn't have asked you to lie. I didn't intend to get you in trouble with the inspector but I think your fears are groundless. There's no reason for him to be interested in your innocent comings and goings."

"I don't think he considers them all that innocent."

"What are you talking about?"

For years, I had struggled to keep my own identity separate from that of my

mother and her romantic entanglements.
Divorcing myself from her had not been
easy. I had paid the price by being alone,
reticent, and forced to be satisfied with
friendships that I could hold at an arm's
distance. As I grew up, I had clung to my
dead father's respectability, willing myself
to be like him. In every way I could I had
shunned the things in me that were my
mother and I had thought there would be no
way that her way of life could dominate
mine. Now, I realized that such a hope was
folly. The inspector was very much interested in my past and he would bring it
out for everyone to see. My mother was a
kept woman, a courtesan, and my own
livelihood had been provided by a series of
her lovers. He would look into our relationship with Maurice Travois and all of it
would come out. My own reputation would
be besmirched. Like mother, like daughter,
I could hear the whispered judgments.

"What is it, Alysha?" He looked
concerned. "Tell me what the inspector
said."

I took a deep breath and kept my eyes
centered on a place just below Raoul's chin.
I did not want to look into his eyes while I
told him about Monsieur Travois. "The
inspector thinks I may be part of a burglary
conspiracy. If I remember rightly, you said

something similar this morning when we met in the hall." I smiled wryly.

"Not finding you in your room, and thinking that you might be with Maurey, well, I just lashed out. I'm sorry. It was unfair and quite ridiculous."

"Inspector Davail does not think so. You see, he knows that I have some familiarity with antiques and objets d'art. I admitted that I had been wandering around the house the day before, touching and examining things in the gallery room and in the drawing room. He thinks I could have made up a shopping list for the burglars."

"But that's ridiculous. Where would you learn about such things?"

"I was taught by one of the best dealers in France, Maurice Travois. My mother was his mistress. For over six years he was an important figure in my life." I still could not look Raoul in the face. It was easier to avoid his discerning eyes. "Monsieur Travois took me with him on buying trips. I realized later that I had viewed transactions which must have been illegal and blackmarket but I was too young to be concerned about any ethics. I was very fond of Monsieur Travois and he said I had a good head for beauty, line, and proportion. Young as I was, I picked up a great deal of knowledge. Since then I've done considerable reading and increased my ability to recognize valuable antiques."

I heard him let out his breath. "My God!" he swore.

I raised my eyes then and looked into his shocked expression. He stared at me as if searching my face for the truth. Did he believe me? And if he did, what chance was there that he would ever speak gently to me again? I lowered my eyes and my chin. "My mother is a courtesan. She has lived with numerous men since my father died and is in the south of France with her latest lover. I was on my way to Paris to work for a Monsieur Roget as a seamstress but the inspector thinks that the carriage accident could have been arranged for me to gain entrance into the chateau." I kept my gaze on a brown bear rug under my feet and the animal's glassy eyes stared up at me in an unseeing trance.

Raoul's hand reached out and tipped my chin up. "Did you come here to commit a robbery, Alysha?"

"No, I did not." My chest filled with an indescribable emotion. I don't know what I would have done if he'd rejected me at that moment. I felt naked, vulnerable, and poised at some point of no return.

He searched my face. "I believe you."

I blinked back foolish tears that eased into my eyes.

He bent over and lightly kissed my fore-head. "Come on. We'll take a ride. I need time to think things out. I'll put a side-saddle on my horse and we'll ride double."

My own thoughts were in such a state that I went willingly, clinging to this moment of understanding between us. Outside, he ordered me to sit on a low stone wall while he went to the stable for a lady's saddle. I did not know where we were going or why. For the moment it was enough to feel his protection and his acceptance.

He knew about me! I had told him every-thing and he had not turned away. I felt as if I had faced some kind of emotional dragon and routed it. I had never felt so free, so unencumbered. I wanted to laugh as I held my face up to the sun and let its golden light touch my skin. There were no shadows within me. The sun's afternoon warmth matched the burst of spring that flowed through my veins.

When Raoul brought his large horse out of the barn, a small woman's sidesaddle had replaced his larger one. With his hand steadying me, I stood on a mounting block and I was glad for the training I had at school of swinging one leg over the horn and tucking the foot under my other leg. Even with my bandaged hand, I handled it quite nicely. My walking skirt was shorter than a riding habit and I feared that my slim ankles showed clearly under the serge cloth. I caught an appreciative glance in his eyes as he surveyed me in the saddle.

"Very nice," he said, making me flush more with pleasure than embarrassment. Then he swung himself up behind me. His arms reached around my waist to hold the reins and the sudden closeness of his body pressed against mine sent a peculiar tingling up my spine. I could smell a spicy shaving tonic on his face and his warm breath was teasing and intimate upon my neck.

Raoul reined the horse away from the lodge. I was glad I wore no bonnet or gloves. My indiscreet attire did not bother me. My penchant for flaunting convention mingled with my childhood enthusiasm for enjoying the unexpected. It had been a long time since I had felt the wonderful excitement of a spontaneous adventure. So complete was my infatuation that it never entered my head that I might be in danger.

Raoul set the horse in an easy gallop away from the lodge in the opposite direction of the chateau. Thick gray-green branches interlacing overhead made a green-gold canopy that filtered slivers of sunlight down upon the bridle path. On every side, heavy undergrowth of shrubs and ferns clogged passages between the trees. Only the sound of rhythmic horse hooves hitting the ground broke the muffled silence as we rode through a tunnel of trees, following a well-worn, circuitous path deeper into the forest. It was obvious from the light rein Raoul held on the horse that he had ridden this way many times before. He was an easy rider and I thrilled at the speed which whipped branches by us and kept the air bathing my face and teasing my hair.

As our bodies rose and fell in rhythm with the horse's gait, I entertained a delicious sensation of leaving the rest of the world behind. At another time, I might have found the deep copse oppressive, threatening, but as Raoul tightened his arms around me, I did not care that I was completely lost and alone with this man who had challenged my senses from the first time that I saw him. For once in my life my rational, self-disciplined mind was dominated by feelings. I did not understand what was happening to me. The thrill of being with a man was too alien for me to understand. Why should I delight in the encompassing hold of his arms and his

body pressed against mine? These were
questions for which I had no answer. Every
pore in my body was alive, drinking in the
sensation of his nearness.

I smiled with pleasure as we reached a
small, shallow stream, banked by soft
green grass and spanned by a graceful
arched bridge. The small stream of water
flowed like a silver bank through the trees,
rippling and changing like a liquid
sculpture as it foamed over rocks and
around sandbars.

Raoul reined the horse a short distance
above the bridge. A clump of overhanging
cypress trees shaded the grassy plot where
flat smooth rocks lay at the water's edge. I
delighted in the mystical beauty of the spot.
The air was perfumed by dank crevices and
spring-green shoots of grass and flowers.

Raoul helped me down from the horse.
His hands lingered for a moment on my
waist. "This is a special place for me. I want
to share it with you."

Then he drew me to the water's edge and
we sat down on stones warmed by the sun.
"This is my boyhood retreat. Used to come
here to be King of the Mountain or the
Scarlet Pimpernel."

I grinned back at him for I could visualize
him bounding over these rocks brandishing
a willow stick as his sword. "The two of us

would have made a great pair," I said. "I always found some hideaway of my own, a forked tree whose branches I could hide in or a sheltered cove under a lilac bush. None as special as this. Did you ever run away from home?"

"More than once," he laughingly admitted and there was a boyish gleam in his eyes that I had never seen before.

"Me, too." I had a foolish resentment that I never would be able to share those youthful experiences with him. Suddenly I wanted to know everything about him . . . as if I knew I must store up these moments like someone hoarding for the future when there would be no more. "Did you have boyhood friends?"

"Not really. Guess I've always been pretty much of a loner. I like to ride and be by myself. I found this spot years ago and still come here a lot when I have dragons to slay," he confessed.

"It's lovely."

"I've never brought a girl here, somehow they didn't seem to belong on wet ground and dusty stones—but you do."

"Because I'm a 'drab bird'?" I teased. I trailed my fingers in the cool water and delighted in the ripples that radiated from my touch. I smiled to soften the retort. At the moment I really didn't care what he had called me. I was here with him and that in itself seemed a miracle.

"Ouch, I guess I deserved that one." He leaned back on one arm as he surveyed me. "I must confess I made a mistake. I know now that clothes are not an extension of your personality. Not that ugly traveling dress, nor the fussy green floral, nor that prim blouse and girlish skirt you're wearing now. None of the things you wear blends with the real you."

"Oh, really?" I raised one eyebrow. "And what clothes would be the real me, may I ask?" I picked a green strand of sweet grass and set it between my teeth. It had a delicious, fresh taste.

"Nothing."

"Nothing becomes me? That's not very flattering." I laughed but I was piqued by his remark. It implied that I was wrong for all kinds of clothes. I knew I had inherited my mother's fair hair and ivory complexion, her high cheekbones, well-shaped mouth and attractive figure. If anything my bust was a little fuller and my waist an inch smaller. "How dare you smile at me and say that there aren't any clothes that would enhance my appearance?" I challenged.

"You misunderstood me. What I meant is that you don't need outward trappings to

enhance your beauty. Your natural loveliness comes through no matter what you
wear . . . or don't wear." His eyes and smile
were as warm as I'd ever seen them. "Even
though you do your best to camouflage her,
the real Alysha won't be hidden."

"And who is the real Alysha?"

"I've only had glimpses but I've caught
tantalizing hints that beyond that stubborn,
willful guardedness of yours, I might find a
very passionate woman. The rare kind that
a man is always looking for."

"I'm not my mother," I flared, stiffening.
I did not like the turn the conversation was
taking.

"I never said you were. Although I
suspect she's a very beautiful lady."

Suddenly I knew why he had brought me
here. I had told him I was the daughter of a
courtesan and he thought he could dally
with me as if I were some cheap wench
brought up in an immoral household. A
deep sickness swept through me. All this
talk about the real Alysha was just a
smooth manipulation to get me in the right
mood for his advances.

I jerked to my feet. All the pleasure of
being here tarnished. He had been very
clever. "You thought that my confession
about my mother gave you license to bring
me here and take your pleasure, didn't

you?" I flared. "As soon as you found out, you suggested this little ride." I put my hands on my hips and glared down at him. "I'll put scratches on your face deeper than that bullet did if you try to take me."

Lazily, he sat up and rested his arms on his pulled up legs. "Alysha, you hiss and bristle like an alley cat when you're mad. And your eyes deepen to a beautiful cobalt blue. You really shouldn't do that, you know. It fires a man's blood. Better for you to be meek and submissive."

"Never."

He grinned. "I know. Now sit back down."

"No." I started to flounce away.

In the next instant he was up and had swung me around to face him. Blood was still caked on his temple and for a moment I remembered the terror I had felt when I thought Yvonne had killed him. My foolish pride dissipated in a deep thankfulness that I had not lost him. If her aim had been an inch closer, he would be dead now. My eyes must have softened for his embrace became quite gentle. I probably could have moved away from him then but I didn't.

"I'm going to kiss you," he said as if the warning made the act my responsibility. I was mesmerized by the soft curve of his lips hovering inches from mine. I felt the

quickened heartbeat in his chest. Dark,
sensuous eyes centered upon my face and
mesmerized me with their intensity. He
waited for some sign that I would commit
myself to his embrace.

I had never been kissed by a man before.
In my girlish dreams I had thought about
such a momentous event but my Prince
Charming had always been vague and
ethereal. And there was nothing ethereal
about the man who held me in his arms and
bent his face near mine. His bold handsome
visage, masculine stature and commanding
virility filled my senses. He was a man, not
a fantasy, and I knew that no woman would
be passive in his arms. Palpitations of
fright, excitement and a deep longing
sluiced through me. Without understanding my own need, I closed my eyes and offered my lips to him.

A wondrous sensation spiraled through
me as he gently but possessively pressed a
kiss upon my waiting lips. As his mouth
met mine, my arms slid up around his neck.
At first I feared that my innocence might
betray itself but no experience was
necessary to return the devouring kisses.
With instinctive willingness, I allowed his
flickering tongue to taste my lips. When his
hands slipped down my back and pressed
me against him, my whole body caught fire.

The exquisite pressure of his firm length radiated upward and spilled out in the ardor of my kisses. Like floating bubbles bursting in my head, I could not control the effervescence of my rising desires as he kissed me.

If he had pulled me down to the softness of the grassy bank, I would have surrendered to the mounting hunger building between us—but it never happened. With a force of will, he lifted his mouth from mine and dropped his arms. "You must go away." His dark velvet gaze traveled over my flushed face. "You were right, my tantalizing Alysha. I want to pursue my pleasure with you. Come on, I'll take you back."

I was too bewildered and shaken to even stammer a reply.

It wasn't until I was back in my room at the chateau that I lashed out with tears and unspoken words for the fool I'd been.

Chapter Eleven

By the next day, anger and pride coated
my humiliation. I could view the wild,
passionate scene with Raoul as one more
evidence of his artful manipulation. The
fact that he had resisted taking me fully I
credited to some motive other than protecting my virtue. He had admitted that he had
wanted me for his own pleasure. Rage like I
had never felt before fueled my intent to
leave this house as soon as the inspector
allowed. And that would be soon, I

reasoned. Once Davail checked my background and it was confirmed that I had
spent the last eight years in a private school
in Switzerland, his suspicions about me
would be laid to rest.

My wrist was much better. I removed the
binding and no sharp pains accompanied
its movement. Yes, I was well enough to
leave. But first I must talk to Annette. I
couldn't tell her the truth about her mother
and of the protection her uncle was providing for her but I could reassure both her
and André that she was safe.

As Nela helped me dress in another one of
my white, high-necked bodices and a full
brown skirt with matching jacket, I asked
Nela where I might find the children. I
could tell from her expression that she had
been reprimanded for allowing me out of
her sight yesterday. "They are in the school-
room with their teacher. Mademoiselle
Lapotaire does not like interruptions." I
could tell from the set of her broad chin
that Nela wasn't going to let me get her into
more trouble.

"Is that your sister who is attending
Madame de Lamareau at the hunting
lodge?" I asked boldly.

Her tiny eyes were suddenly guarded.
"*Oui.*"

"I saw her yesterday. Alveretta is her

name? She really has her hands full, doesn't she?"

Nela nodded but she set her mouth in a way that I wasn't going to pry any information out of her. Gossip was not a part of her stoic nature. Raoul had chosen his servants well. "Are the Montaignes still here?" I asked, desperate enough to allow Maurey to pry me loose from my stalwart jailer.

"No. They left yesterday afternoon while Mademoiselle was . . . out," she said in a chastising tone.

"Did they talk with the inspector?"

"I do not know, Mademoiselle."

A real fountain of information, I thought sarcastically.

"Where would Mademoiselle like her breakfast tray?"

Frustration and irritation always brought out my belligerent nature. "Don't bother with a tray. I'm going to breakfast downstairs." If the master of the house thought I would wait to be invited into the main part of the house, he soon would discover that I could not be so easily avoided. I rather relished the idea of meeting him face to face, a kind of test for myself and perhaps a disconcerting one for him.

With Nela following at my heels, we traversed the labyrinth of corridors and

reached the main staircase without
incident. The closer we came to the breakfast room, the weaker my resolve became.
If Nela hadn't been there, I know I would
have turned heel and fled before I reached
the doorway. My mouth was suddenly dry
and a thumping under my ribcage belied
the arrogant jut of my chin. I feared I might
be betrayed by inner feelings which I could
not control. I had always prided myself on
being a "thinking" person but as my legs
suddenly became weak, I realized that
rational thought had nothing to do with the
way I felt about Raoul de Lamareau.

When I entered the breakfast room, I saw
that Inspector Davail was sitting at the
table with Raoul. The two men rose and I
felt that my entrance was akin to Daniel
entering the lion's den. Both men welcomed
me with cold eyes and stiff nods of greeting.

"I . . . I thought I would like to breakfast
downstairs this morning," I said with less
aplomb than I would have wished. In order
to give myself time to gain my composure, I
walked over to the sideboard and made my
selections. Nela hovered at my elbow and
quickly filled a warmed plate with my
choices. Nervousness made me select twice
the amount of food I usually ate, and I knew
I would never be able to consume all of it.

When I returned to the table, Raoul

viewed the plate of kidneys, sausage, eggs, truffles, biscuits, and sugared rolls and a mocking smile tugged at the corner of his mouth. "Are you eating for one day . . . or a week, Alysha?" he teased.

"I like a healthy breakfast," I retorted and forced myself to meet his eyes. The lively, soft twinkle there completely demoralized me. I had been ready to flay him with caustic remarks but the tender look he gave me obliterated such intention. The passionate moments in his arms swept over me. Even as I shoved the memory away, it crumbled my defenses as effectively as a gentle wind disperses the seeds of a feathery weed.

He dismissed Nela and as he held my chair, his hands touched my shoulders. A flare of warmth sped away from the point of contact. I knew then that my only hope was to get away from Raoul de Lamareau as soon as possible. "How soon will I be able to leave, Inspector?" I asked bluntly as Raoul sat down again and I met Davail's impassive stare across the table.

The policeman's agate eyes were just as I remembered, sharply honed and piercing, and I felt something inside me wither under their pointed gaze. "Some things cannot be hurried, Mademoiselle. One must be sure that all the circumstances are truly what

they seem." He lifted a delicate porcelain
cup to his thin lips and kept his stare
fastened upon me. Apparently he had
intruded upon Raoul's breakfast and joined
him in a cup of coffee. I had the feeling I
had been one of the topics of conversation.

Raoul confirmed it when he said, "I was
just telling the inspector that suspecting
you of participating in the burglary was
ridiculous. It is perfectly natural that you
would have slept heavily from the medicine
you were taking."

His tone was casual but I knew he was
warning me. He wanted me to stay with the
lie that I had not left my room the night of
the burglary. I kept my eyes on my plate to
keep from showing my anger to the
inspector. How dare Raoul use me for his
own despicable ends! My emotions were
riding a seesaw. In another minute, they
would be out of control . . . and I knew I
must not let that happen. "Yes," I said as
evenly as I could. There was no way to
retract the lie now. "I heard nothing, saw
nothing." That at least was the truth and
I managed to look directly into the policeman's face as I repeated, "I know nothing
about the burglary."

The inspector took another sip of coffee
without answering.

"I see that you have taken off the bandage

from your wrist," said Raoul. "Is it healed then?" His tone was warm and solicitous, not the kind of attention I needed to keep my hackles up against him.

"Yes. The swelling is gone and there is no pain."

"Good. Then I see no reason why you cannot go on to Paris as you had planned— with the inspector's permission, of course." Raoul gave the policeman a patronizing smile.

The bite of sausage in my mouth refused to go down. *He wanted to be rid of me as quickly as possible.* The bitter truth mocked my fantasy that he shared the deep feelings that raged within me. I was nothing to him. Not even a momentary fancy. He could kiss me and set me aside as easily as he did an inanimate object. His casualness fired my obstinate nature. "Of course, I would want to consult with Dr. Duboise," I said while some inner mocking voice reminded me that this was exactly what I had wanted—to be gone as soon as possible.

The inspector nodded. "I think it would be well for Mademoiselle to remain here a few more days."

I knew then that Inspector Davail was not satisfied that I was as innocent as I pretended to be.

"Yes, of course. The doctor should give

his permission," said Raoul quickly.
"Perhaps you would like to take a carriage
for a nice ride through the countryside,
Alysha. I'm sure you don't want to stay
cooped up in the chateau all day."

I stared at him. Why was he being so
solicitous? "May I take the children?" I
asked, testing the suspicion.

"Yes, of course. They'd love an outing. I'll
order a carriage to be brought around." He
smiled but a shadow flickered deep in his
eyes, belying his congeniality. His thoughts
were racing off in another direction, I could
tell. *He wants me out of the way.* The pre-
monition was as clear as water reflecting
bright sun.

My eyes jerked to the inspector. He
nodded his head in agreement. "Mademoiselle might enjoy seeing our small village."
His smile seemed calculating and somehow
threatening.

For a moment I wanted to retreat back to
my isolated room. Danger was like the faint
whiff of an indefinable scent. Before I could
identify it, the impression was gone and I
almost laughed at myself. For someone who
had prided herself on being completely
rational about her feelings and thoughts, I
was acting more and more against my true
nature. "Fine. Thank you, Monsieur de
Lamareau," I said formally as if his lips had

never burned my skin with their fiery warmth. "No carriage, if you don't mind. If there is a small trap and a reliable horse, I would rather drive myself."

"You don't trust the carriage? I assure you that nothing will happen like the last time."

"How can you be sure? Unless you know what made the other horse go *fou*?" I answered pointedly. The inspector's eyes traveled from my face to Raoul's. Those sharp black eyes took in everything. I hated myself for parading my suspicions in front of him. I had spoken before I thought. Now it was too late.

For a moment, Raoul didn't respond. His eyes narrowed. "Do I infer from that remark that you think I had something to do with the accident, Mademoiselle Grant?"

This time his tone was formal, angry, and perhaps laced with disappointment and regret. It destroyed all the intimacy that had been between us. We were like two opposing factions trying to bring the other down. I wanted to deny my suspicions but I couldn't. In spite of what my heart said, my rational mind would not let me discount the possibility. "I'm just wondering why you can give me such assurances? Unless the cause of the acccident is known. Has there been some evidence—?" I said hopefully.

"We think the horse was drugged, Mademoiselle," responded the inspector, carefully setting down his cup.

I dared not look at Raoul's face nor at the inspector's. I was afraid that the vision of Raoul standing by the horse when we pulled into the station was written on my forehead. The evidence seemed to bear out the sickening truth that Raoul de Lamareau was responsible. I must have paled for the policeman leaned forward. "Is there something that you wish to tell me, Mademoiselle?"

The moment had come. Now was the time to tell Davail about my impression that the horse had been nudging Raoul's hand just moments before it went wild in its traces. I moistened my lips. If I had not looked at Raoul before I spoke, my accusations would have come flowing out in relief but my eyes searched his face and my resolve dissipated. I had thought myself under his spell before. Now I knew it. Words choked in my throat without ever reaching my lips. He reached over and covered my hand with his and all was lost. I could not destroy the bewildering magnetic force rising between us by accusing him in front of the inspector.

"No . . . nothing," I murmured, my hand

trembling in Raoul's a moment before I withdrew it.

The inspector leaned back in his chair with a sigh.

Raoul smiled. "I'll have a small buggy brought around, Alysha. And old Belle. You can be sure she'll take you to the village and back without harm."

This time I did not question his assurance.

Annette and André came pouring out of the front door and joined me in the high-wheeled buggy like two renegade school-children escaping from a tedious class-room. My spirits rose instantly. Amid their excited chatter and laughter, I sent the dappled gray mare trotting away from the chateau and down a smooth, narrow road to the village. I was much better at driving horses than riding them. Sister Mary Josette at the school had sent me into the village with a small wagon almost every week to collect supplies from the local merchants. It was an outing that lent some stability to my life and I felt necessary and important as I discharged the routine errand.

The reins felt comfortable in my hands and solid Belle needed little guiding. I suspected she had made the trip thousands of times. Soft wind blowing against my face and playfully lifting hair under my bonnet was the catharsis I needed and I found myself laughing with Annette and André as rocks sprung out from under the wheels and soft puffs of dust accompanied our progress down the road.

Both children were in good spirits and from something Annette said, I determined that her Uncle Raoul had assured them that their mother was recovering from some illness and would be home soon. They seemed to accept her absence without undue concern and I wondered how many times Yvonne had left her children because of her heavy drinking. They must be used to her volatile moods but I knew that her paranoid tendencies had taken their toll on Annette. I smiled at her pretty face under a peacock blue bonnet that matched her dress. Her large eyes were bright and shiny. She seemed more relaxed than any time since we'd left the school. Sitting close to me with her little brother on the other side, she returned my smile as we bumped along in the well-sprung buggy.

André was a winsome, bright little boy and my heart tightened every time I looked at him because of his resemblance to Raoul. His brown eyes were feathered with black like his uncle's, soft and velvet, and capable

of the same kind of captivating gentleness.
As he laughed and bounced in the seat, I
wanted to hug him and ruffle his thick,
wavy hair.

A brief rain during the night had
freshened everything, lending a sweetness
to the air. Puddles of water remained in
rutted depressions along the side of the
road and we laughed at a flock of black
birds taking their baths with a flutter of
wings and dipping tails. The countryside
was the kind found in a French Impres-
sionist painting, soft colors blending one
with the other, greens and blues accented
by an occasional burst of red and orange.
The children waved a greeting to workers
in the fields as they stopped their work for
a moment and watched the buggy rumbling
by. Since the revolution, much of the land
had been turned back to the peasants and
had been broken up into small farms, each
carefully tended for the crops which
provided their livelihood. Farmhouses sat
back from the road, their chimneys and
steep slate roofs showing above clusters of
green trees.

As we passed an orchard of cherry trees, I
was startled to see a familiar figure
strolling beneath them—Dr. Duboise! Then
I remembered he had said he was
vacationing nearby. He turned at the sound

of our buggy approaching and I waved and
impulsively turned the horse into the small
road leading past the orchard.

"Bonjour." I waved and he smiled broad-
ly in return and started toward the buggy.
When he came to a small wooden fence, he
climbed over it with a clumsiness that was
comical. Annette smothered a giggle behind
her gloved hands and André laughed openly
as Dr. Duboise hoisted his ample derrière
and stocky legs over the top railing and
then dropped to the ground in more of an
awkward fall than a jump. His trousers
stretched at the seams and I would not have
been surprised to see a rent in them as he
clumsily navigated the rough boards.

"Good morning . . . good morning." He
beamed through his square glasses as he
came over to my side of the buggy. "What a
nice surprise to see you out and about,
Mademoiselle Grant. You are feeling better
then?" His practiced eye went to my
unbandaged wrist. He reached out and took
it. *"Bon!* It is well now? No pain?"

"It feels fine."

"And your head?"

I untied the streamers on my hat. His
gentle, pudgy hands lifted the hair from my
forehead. *"Tres bon!* Just a little dis-
coloration remains. In a few days all signs
of it will be gone. No marks left on your

lovely forehead. Your beauty will not be diminished in any way." His gentle blue eyes sparkled and brought a laugh to my own lips.

"You flatter me, Monsieur."

"And why not? You are a beautiful young woman. Any man would be amiss not to tell you so." Then he sighed. "I guess this means that you are discharged as my patient. You will be leaving us now. Such a pity. I wish you well in your new position."

His words brought back the upheaval which had engulfed me. Before I could say anything, Annette spoke up. "Mademoiselle Grant is not going for a long time. She is going to stay here." Her large eyes were pleading. "Aren't you?"

"For a little while." I did not say that I was virtually a prisoner in the chateau until Inspector Davail dismissed me.

"Well, then. Maybe we will see each other again? As friends . . . instead of doctor, patient?"

"I would like that," I said honestly.

"Remember what I told you. I'm here if you need me."

For some foolish reason, my eyes flooded with tears. His round, smiling face blurred for a moment before I blinked back the fullness. "*Merci*," I managed in a choked voice.

The doctor spoke to the children and gave me a chance to compose myself. Then he waved to us as I turned the buggy around and guided Belle back to the village road.

"He's nice," said Annette. "I like him better than Dr. Vanderley."

"Me, too," said André and then began to laugh. "But he's too fat to climb fences." The picture of him hoisting himself over the fence caused us all to laugh.

Meeting Dr. Duboise had added to the merriment of the day. André continued to bounce in the spring seat, eagerly pointing out ducks in the rushes of small stream as we went across a wooden bridge. "*Regardez!*" he shouted. "Bang bang," he shouted and aimed his pretend gun. Both Annette and I laughed at the great hunter. He was a delightful youngster and I prayed that he would not lose his *joie de vivre* as he grew older. Once Raoul had been as free and spontanteous as André, I thought, and I resented the responsibilities that had taken it from him.

The rippling stream was clear enough to tempt any fisherman and was very much like the one flowing through the woods where Raoul had taken me. I wondered idly if Raoul ever fished from the mossy bank where he had held me in his arms. The thought was a cue to bring back the

tingling, breathless sensation I had experienced when he kissed me. How artful he
had been—persuasive, seductive. How easy
it would be to give in to his practiced
charms. I could not believe how I had
allowed him to manipulate me. At the
breakfast table I had been completely
under his will and the knowledge made me
angry with myself. I should have spoken up
to the inspector. Why had I held back?
Perhaps I knew the answer to that question
but chose not to acknowledge it. Instead, I
resolved I would not allow Raoul de
Lamareau to dictate my actions or
emotions from now on. At that moment, I
felt quite capable of carrying out my
decision.

As we approached the small village of
Chambleau, small houses appeared closer
together, each shaded by tall trees with
sparse trunks and leafy clusters at the top.
Each house had only two or three rooms, no
flooring, with a single fireplace providing
the only heating. I knew that soot and
smoke filled the interiors. I saw an old
woman herding a cow into a room of the
house which must shelter livestock, a
common practice when there was no barn.
The French farmer treated his goats,
chickens and cows like members of the
family. Small gardens provided the

mainstay of beans, cabbage, and corn for
gruel. A few small grapevines bore the
fruit which was used for brewing tart
homemade wine. Low, multicolored stone
walls bordered each side of the road; white
wisteria vines frothed over walls and green
ivy softened the harsh exteriors of the
small, roughly hewn houses. The scene was
a pastoral one found all over France and I
loved it.

When we reached a small, central square
at the heart of the village I reined the horse
in the shade of tall maple and chestnut
trees. Green grass along the roadside would
keep Belle happy while we enjoyed
ourselves.

André ran over to watch a game of *boules*
laid out on the village square. Spectators of
all ages called out encouragement or
commented on the success or failure of a
team to send the cast-iron bowls sailing on
the ground toward the *cochannet*, a round
wooden ball. The team to get their bowls
closest to the *cochannet* earned the most
points. Some of the men were quite adept at
knocking the opponent's bowl out of the
way while securing their own position
closest to the wooden ball. Annette and
André cheered and I found myself laughing
with the rest of the spectators as two
wizened little men defeated two husky,

young men half their age.

We left the square as a new team was being organized to challenge the winners. Chambleau was laid out in the pattern of most French villages. On one side of the square stood the *mairie*, the town hall, and on the opposite side, the village church with its adjoining burial ground. A tavern and small inn stood on the corner and there was a bustle of people in and out of small, traditional shops where peasant women filled their mesh baskets with daily purchases. A *boulangerie* which scented the air with fresh bread drew us like bees after nectar to glass cabinets filled with the most tempting of pastries.

Without hesitation, Annette and André agreed with my suggestion that we should purchase pastries and glasses of cool, fresh milk. Then we could enjoy our refreshments in the shade of old, gnarled trees stretching over the small round tables and chairs crowded into an outdoor café.

We started to weave our way through the crowd toward a table set in a far corner and a gentleman rose from his chair to allow us passage by his table. My lips curved in an automatic "thank you" smile and then froze. For a moment I was completely disoriented.

The familiar face frowned at me for a

moment as if not believing his own eyes and then the gentleman swept off his hat, revealing thick brown hair now laced with gray. His shoulders were as broad as I remembered and when he spoke, the loud booming voice brought instant recognition.

"*Mon Dieu!* It's pretty Alysha all grown up. Looking like the image of her mother."

Maurice Travois, my mother's former lover, dealer in valuable objets d'art and antique furniture, embraced me.

Chapter Twelve

I couldn't believe it. The past rushed back
and I was that little girl again, basking in
his broad smile. My lips trembled and I was
grateful for the chair he slipped under my
rubbery legs. André and Annette were
waiting at a corner table and I gave them a
wave to say I would join them in a minute.

Fortunately Maurice Travois filled the
emotional moment of reunion with
expressions of his own surprise, giving me
a chance to get my own feelings under

control. As always his expensive, tailored suit had a rumpled look and a black cravat was askew at his thick neck.

"What a wonderful surprise, my petite Alysha." He laughed and his thick bushy eyebrows raised in questioning arches. "And what are you doing here? Where is your charming mother? *Mon Dieu!* It's been six years or more. When I left, you were a budding girl of twelve and now—" He clucked in appreciation. "As pretty as your mother ever was." He nodded. "The same fair looks to stir a man's blood, *n'est-ce pas?*"

He winked and his remark instantly dissolved my first flush of pleasure at seeing him. I did not like any references that I was like my mother. Her beauty was something I did not envy. What had happened between me and Raoul was a warning signal that I might be susceptible to the same passion-filled quagmires. I had tried my best not to look like her. It must be the soft fair hair framing my face, I thought. If I'd had it drawn back and hidden under my bonnet in its usual style, he might not have mentioned the resemblance. "When did you get back from Italy?" I asked, managing to find my voice at last.

"Oh, nearly two years ago. My wife died

while we were out of the country. As soon as my own health improved, I came back to take limited charge of my business again. And your dear mother? Where is she?"

"With a friend . . . in southern France."

He nodded with a knowing smile. "I thought as much. And you? Are you governess to those children?" he asked, indicating Annette and André.

"No. Just Annette's schoolmate. I accompanied her home from our school in Switzerland." I decided not to burden him with an account of the accident which had kept me here. I was never one to share the personal aspects of my life and Maurice Travois seemed too much of a stranger after all these years to unburden myself. "I'm visiting at her family's chateau for a few days . . . before I go on to Paris. I have a job waiting for me there, or I hope I have—" My voice faltered. "I'm going to work for Monsieur Roget, the *couturier*."

"A *grisette*? Oh, my dear child. You should be able to do better than that. A lovely intelligent girl, like yourself. Such menial work is not for you. *Mais, non.*" His craggy face furrowed with displeasure. "I always said you should have been a boy. Quick mind, eager to learn." He gave a booming laugh. "You used to pry all kinds of information out of me. Like a sponge, you were, wanting to know everything."

I smiled back, remembering how we had spent hours together while we traveled from one location to another to collect his merchandise.

"I enjoyed your company very much, Alysha, and your quick mind. You were like the child I never had."

"You were very kind to me," I said gratefully. I remembered how much I had missed him when he was jerked out of our lives so abruptly. For many nights, my pillow was wet with tears. "I missed you very much."

"And I missed you. If I had not been at death's door for so many months, I would have made certain that you were not left impoverished. My wife took control of everything. I was not well enough to oppose her." He shrugged. "Well, the past cannot be recovered. I often wondered what had happened to you, Alysha. I hoped for the best."

"I was sent to a boarding school in Switzerland when my mother—" I faltered.

"A new protector?" he finished tactfully.

"Younger . . . and he didn't want me around."

He clucked in disapproval. "His bad luck. You were a delight. Your vibrant company was always a joy. And more intelligent than many of the adults whose company I was forced to endure. No, you must not waste your life bending over some inane sewing."

"I'm afraid I have no choice. Even though I am well-educated, my background is such that no respectable family would accept me as a governess. Sister Josette always cautioned me that because of my background I must not expect too much out of life and that I should be grateful for what it offered."

"Rubbish! You were not made for such insipid resignation. My fiery little Alysha is not cut from such passive cloth. You have your mother's beauty but there is much more behind those velvet blue eyes than a superficial concern with feminine fripperies. You should not waste such talent."

I gave an impatient shrug. It was easy for him to say what I should do with my life but the truth was that a woman without the protection of an acceptable family could not make her own terms. "I fear that my choices are very limited."

"You always had a natural eye for line and form. Surprising for one so young. Better than the assistant I now have." He raised one unruly eyebrow and I could tell that he was quickly turning over something in his mind. Then he laughed again. "Why

not? It would be like old times. You come to
work for me, Alysha. I'll pay you ten times
more than any *grisette* earns in a year.
Yes," he beamed. "It will be like old times.
The two of us traveling here and abroad.
You will be a kind of companion—"

"What?" I stammered, trying to follow
his shifting conversation.

"I'm offering you a job, Alysha. You be
my assistant. Travel with me the way we
used to. I'll teach you what you need to
know. Strictly a platonic arrangement, of
course," he assured me as he sighed. "I'm
too old for a romantic liaison."

"No, I couldn't," I said automatically as if
such a protest was the only answer under
the circumstances. He had been my
mother's lover. I could not align myself
with him. People would think the worst.

"And why not? You work hard for me—I
pay you well. What could be better? You
like me, *n'est-ce pas?*"

"Yes, but—" My first, negative response
seemed foolish as the idea took root. Why
not? What could be better? I would be
doing something that I enjoyed, with
someone who cared for me. What did it
matter if people thought I was his mistress.
He would treat me well and give me a
chance to be independent. I shoved all
thoughts of Raoul to the back of my mind.

It would be better to work for Maurice
Travois than to live in constant regret over
something that could never be.

"That's better. A nice smile. It will be a
good arrangement for both of us."

I couldn't believe that my future was
about to take a wonderful new turn. I
wouldn't have to spend my days hunched
over some other woman's garment nor fight
off Monsieur Roget's advances. I must be
dreaming all of this, I thought even as
Maurice Travois's amused laughter reverberated in my ears. "Now, you looked
like the girl I used to know whose face
would light up like a thousand candles
when she opened her gifts at Christmas
time."

"You were very good to me," I murmured
with sudden tears welling up in my eyes.
"This all so sudden. I mean . . . I don't know
what to say."

"Say yes. You'd never make a seamstress,
Alysha. You were meant for better things. I
can teach you how to make money, lots of
it." He leaned forward and said in a
conspirator's tone, "The import-export
business is exciting and always a challenge.
Opportunities are everywhere. I have many
connections here and abroad to circumvent
the law. It's like taking money off a low
hanging tree."

With these words, the spell broke. My surge of happiness and relief instantly washed away like sand under a harsh wave. I felt cold as if a sudden chill had overtaken me. Maurice Travois's smile wavered.

"What is it, my dear?" He reached over and patted my hand. "You have lost the color in your cheeks."

"Why are you in Chambleau?" I asked in a choked voice but I knew the answer before he answered.

"The de Lamareau Collection. I understand some of it has been stolen. It's supposed to be one of the finest. Choice items were taken, I understand. They might still be here in the area. Sometimes thieves have no way to dispose of their stolen treasures. If I'm here in the vicinity, they might contact me. I have the means to take such bounty off their hands. There's more than one way to conduct a profitable business, *ma chérie.*" He winked at me and squeezed my hand. "I can make you a very rich lady, Alysha."

He was a dealer in stolen goods. I had suspected as much but this verification from his own lips was a shock. I didn't want it to be true. My childhood adoration had colored any moralistic judgments about him and I had accepted him as someone kind and warm and I had trusted him. Now

I had to accept the truth. He was no better than the thieves who carried out the robberies. And he offered me a chance to be a part of the business. I wanted to laugh but as hysterical laughter bubbled up, disappointment and anger kept me sitting in shocked silence.

"What is it? Are you ill?"

As I struggled for an appropriate answer, my gaze roved over Maurice Travois's broad shoulder. My heart lurched into the pit of my stomach. Inspector Davail stood watching us in the shadow of one of the huge trees.

I took my hand away from Monsieur Travois's but it was too late. The expression on the policeman's face was quite readable. *Accomplices.* He thought we were accomplices.

"What is the matter, *chérie?*" Maurice turned and followed my gaze. "Who is it? Is that man bothering you with his looks? I'll set his head lower on his shoulders," he growled. He pushed back his chair as if to get up and accost the inspector.

"No." I grabbed his sleeve. "That's Inspector Davail. I think he's been following me."

"The police . . . following you?" Monsieur Travois's forehead furrowed as he sat back down. "Why would he be following you?"

"Because . . . because, he thinks I had something to do with the theft."

I expected Maurice to throw back his head in his habitual way, and punctuate the gesture with that booming laughter of his. But he didn't. He kept his eyes steady on my face and asked quite solemnly, "Did you, Alysha?" There was a suppressed excitement in his voice that betrayed his eagerness.

"Of course not!"

He pursed his lips for a moment without speaking. Then he nodded as if my denial had meant nothing. "You're smart enough to have gotten yourself in a position of being on the inside and clever enough to have set up the burglary."

"I didn't do it!" I knew my voice was rising but I couldn't help it. I swallowed hard. "How dare you say such a thing!" My nails bit into my hands as I clenched them.

"If the police are following you . . . they must suspect something, my dear Alysha. But you've really gotten in over your head. The de Lamareau Collection," he laughed again. "You believe in starting big, *n'est-ce pas?*" There was a begrudging admiration in his tone.

"I had nothing to do with the robbery," I repeated very slowly. How many times had such a denial left my lips? It seemed that I was always denying guilt and it seemed that everyone was always brushing my denials aside.

He leaned forward. "Tell me everything and I'll take care of handling the merchandise. Who would have believed it? I knew you were as sharp as they came. I bet you engineered this whole thing. I'm proud of you. *Très superbe!*" He threw back his head and laughed like a proud parent.

My eyes fled to the spot where the inspector had been standing. The policeman was gone. I did not know whether to be relieved or frightened by his absence. He had seen all he needed to see. He must have known Maurice Travois was in the vicinity. At the breakfast table he had suggested that I take a ride to the village. He had wanted me to encounter Maurice Travois so he could verify what he had suspected.

My mind searched for something that would convince my mother's old lover that I was telling him the truth. Just like the inspector, he had made up his mind that I was involved in the burglary. All my denials counted for nothing. Suddenly I was angry at all of them. I was tired of trying to convince them of my innocence. Why waste my breath?

At that moment Annette and André came

over to the table. "You haven't eaten your
pastry," Annette chided me.

"No," I choked. "I'm not hungry."

"May I have it," asked André eagerly with
childish boldness.

I nodded and handed the sugared pastry
to him. Then I stood up. "It was nice to see
you again, Monsieur Travois," I said quite
formally, depending upon trite social
responses to get me through the moment.

His knowing glance went from me to the
children. "I understand. We will meet again
soon, Alysha, somewhere where we can
talk. *Bonjour*."

The inspector was waiting for me when
we got back to the chateau. As the children
bounded upstairs to their rooms, Frazer
halted me at the bottom of the stairs and
informed me in his officious tone that my
presence was requested in the library. I
was not surprised. All the way home, I had
dreaded the ordeal which I knew awaited
me. There was no escape from the
interrogation that the policeman would put
me through. Inspector Davail had seen me
with Monsieur Travois. Even though the
policeman could not have overheard our
conversation, he had seen the laughter on
Travois's lips and his hand engulfing mine.
There could be no doubt in anyone's mind

that we were close acquaintances. And the police would take it one step further—*we were also close associates.*

"Sit down, Mademoiselle."

I did as the small, rigid little man requested and folded my trembling hands in my lap. I had determined earlier that I would offer no explanations. I would only answer his questions as dispassionately as I could. Any emotional protests would be lost on this unemotional policeman who undoubtedly could pin squirming insects to a mounting board without any squeamishness. I felt like a helpless specimen as his black eyes bit into mine.

This vulnerable position was abhorrent to me and my natural belligerency instantly rose to counter it. I forgot about my determination to limit my remarks to brief answers to his questions. Once more my impulsive nature betrayed me. "You knew Monsieur Travois was in the village," I lashed out, as if Davail's actions were to be held accountable and not mine.

I thought I saw a glint of admiration in his eyes as if he much preferred a strong adversary to a simpering female dabbing her eyes with a sweet-scented hankie. I determined then that he would never reduce me to tears—never!

"*You* knew he was there, Mademoiselle.

Your need for an 'outing' was quite
convenient. And you most readily accepted
my suggestion of visiting the village. You
planned all along to meet him . . . only by
chance, of course." His tone was openly
sarcastic.

"That's not true. I had no idea Maurice
Travois was in the area."

He sighed and leaned forward in his
chair, clasping his bony, narrow hands on
the desk in front of him. "You have already
admitted your past association with
Monsieur Travois."

"Yes."

"A very smart move. Since I would have
discovered it for myself after a few
inquiries."

"I did not attempt to keep anything from
you. I was a child under his care from
the age of seven to twelve. That's all
the relationship there is between us. I
never saw Monsieur Travois after he
became ill and his wife took him to Italy to
recover. And you have no evidence to prove
that I have."

"Sometimes there is no need to look
beyond the present circumstances to find
the answers one seeks. I do not believe
in coincidence, Mademoiselle. Maurice
Travois is here for a definite purpose. He is
a very clever man. The Paris police have

suspected that he is a receiver of stolen goods for many years but have never been able to trace them directly to him."

"I know nothing about his business!"

The inspector gave me a weak imitation of a smile. "Then let me enlighten you. Maurice Travois is a master of funneling stolen furniture and antiques into the legitimate trade. He does it by selling such objects to 'closet collectors' who keep their acqusitions hidden from the general public. In that way, his customers become conspirators. They tell him what they want —and he finds it for them. I suspect that Jacques de Lamareau was one of his best customers. Maurice Travois is very clever. Some of the furniture he acquires is disguised by removing gilt, reshaping arms and legs, and covering chairs and settees with new fabric, but most of it is left intact and hidden away. Identification is very difficult."

"But if you know all this—?" I gasped.

"Why don't we arrest Monsieur Travois? Because he does not participate in the robberies himself. But I have hopes of finding someone who will lead me to his doorstep. Someone like you, Mademoiselle."

My laugh was weak but genuine. "There is little chance of that, Inspector. I have had no contact with Monsieur Travois until this morning. Unless you can find having milk and pastry in the company of an old friend an infraction of the law, you will never be able to connect me with any of his alleged nefarious activities."

"I am not so sure, Mademoiselle. Do you recognize this?" He held out a piece of paper.

"It's parchment, isn't it?" I took it, puzzled. It looked like the stationery which I had used to write my letters.

"Yes, parchment writing paper. We found it in the bedroom you now occupy. In the lap desk near your bed."

"Yes, I asked Nela to bring me paper and pen so I could write some letters. I fail to see why this should be of interest to you."

"Oh, it is of great interest to me, I assure you." He held up a sheet of paper with half of it torn away. Then he picked up a scrap of paper with scribbled black writing. "The same paper—" He put the two pieces together. "They match."

"I don't understand."

"The same paper. One piece found in your room . . . and the smaller one discarded on the floor of the gallery room. You've never seen this before?" He waved the small piece with writing on it.

"No." A feathery chill crept up my spine.

"What is it?"

The inspector's thin lips curved in satisfaction. "A shopping list. Very interesting, *n'est-ce pas*? The burglars passed up countless valuable items. They walked by silver tureens, priceless tapestries, matching chairs, and beautiful cabinets. They only took the items on this piece of paper. Someone had the opportunity to survey the contents of the house. Someone made a selection of items to be taken. Someone gave the list to the robbers. Someone made certain that easy entry into the house was provided for them. Someone did all of this, Mademoiselle."

It was obvious he thought he knew who that "someone" was. Even as a wave of weakness swept through my body, I jutted out my chin. "You can't think that I—"

"This torn sheet of paper was found in the hall outside your room. It matches the piece on which the note was written."

"I never saw it before!"

"You have the same kind of paper at your bedside."

"Other people in the house have access to the same kind of stationery," I lashed out as panic rose in waves under my rib cage. "I'll bet you'll find some like it in every *secrétaire* in the house."

The inspector was not impressed with my

challenge. "I told you, Mademoiselle, I don't believe in coincidences. You had access to pen and paper. You had the opportunity to view the hidden collection. Your presence in the house is contrived."

I laughed a high, bitter laugh. "You cannot possibly believe that I had anything to do with arranging a carriage accident that might have killed me?"

"The possibility of great rewards will often stimulate great risks."

"I will not sit here and be accused in this fashion. What you are suggesting is preposterous! Anyone in the house could have made that list. I wasn't the only one in the chateau that night who could have let the burglars in—"

'You are the only one with a past association with Maurice Travois. You are partners in this crime."

I lurched to my feet. "It's not true! You have no proof."

"Not yet . . . but I warn you, the scent of the fox is not far from the hunting hounds, Mademoiselle."

As if I could feel his hot, threatening breath upon my neck, I turned and fled the room.

He let me go but as I bounded out the door, I heard a satisfied intake of air that might have been a pleased chuckle. His net could reach out and snare me any time he was ready. I could almost see the small, satisfied smile on his lips as I fled upstairs to the sanctuary of a murdered man's room.

Chapter Thirteen

I did not leave my room until evening. All afternoon I waited for the inspector to send his men after me. I thought about trying to get away but such wild imaginings were the result of mounting panic. I had nowhere to run.

About dusk, I was sitting in the window seat, staring out upon the chateau grounds when I saw two riders emerging from the woods. I recognized Raoul's lithe, graceful figure immediately as he rode his chestnut stallion. A small dark-haired woman rode at his side and my breath caught. *Yvonne—* she was coming back home. Had they been together all day? The memory of her sobbing "I love you . . . I love you" made me apprehensive. What was the relationship between them? Raoul seemed protective of her even after she had tried to shoot him. Had he lied about their relationship? Were they really lovers?

When Nela returned with an invitation to join Madame de Lamareau and Monsieur de Lamareau for dinner, I could not still my desire to see them together. Some masochistic need to torture myself made me send Nela back with my acceptance.

I had nothing in my wardrobe that would allow me to dress formally for dinner. My school wardrobe was lacking in such finery. I chose a simple forest green Sunday gown which set off my fairness and accented the smallness of my waist. Small green beads decorated a modest neckline and the pointed cuffs lying over my wrists. I didn't need the confining lacing suffered by most women and I was pleased that the lines of my dress were enhanced by the fullness of my breasts and rounded hips. The material was worn in spots but I reassured myself that I would be sitting most of the time and the soft gaslight would be kind to my appearance.

I let Nela have her way with my hair. She brushed the pale silken strands into a topknot of curls upon my head, leaving soft waves upon my forehead to cover the fading cut. The style made my face seem softer, like my mother's. But my expression was not hers, I thought with some reassurance. My eyes were too direct, my mouth too firm, and the jut of my chin too pugnacious. No, I had none of my mother's coquetry. I could not flutter my eyelids or keep my mouth curved in a seductive smile. I did not know how to keep a man fawning and attentive. I lacked any of the feminine finesse to keep a man like Raoul de Lamareau interested in me. Well, so much the better, I lectured myself. He was the most lying, deceitful, maddening person I had ever met. And it was time I stopped letting him manipulate me.

Armed with this determination, I followed Nela downstairs to a small parlor adjoining the dining room. My heart was like a wild hummingbird in my throat as I entered.

Raoul was already there, standing before a small cabinet which held a tray of glasses and liquors. My eyes slid over his smooth, broad back molded by the dark cloth of his dress coat with tails sharply cut away from

the front of the jacket. The lines of his
matching trousers were smooth and wide
enough to allow grace of movement and
still hint at the firm, muscular legs beneath.
At my entrance, he turned around and I saw
he wore a ruffled shirt and a black cravat.
His dark hair shone blue-black in the
gaslight and for a moment his brown eyes
seemed almost velvet in texture. There was
a lack of tension in his facial muscles and I
wondered if Yvonne could be the reason for
his good humor.

"*Bonsoir, Alysha*," he greeted me. I'm
glad you're down early. We can have a
drink before Yvonne arrives. I do not want
to tempt her now that she has regained her
balance. Wine? Sherry? We have some
special white wine from Bordeaux."

"Fine." I sat down on a Louis XVI sofa set
in front of a marble fireplace and looked at
the portrait of a man above the mantel. For
a moment my heart caught. The handsome,
dark-haired Frenchman looked so much
like Raoul that for a moment I didn't realize
that the bone structure of the man was
much larger.

"My brother," volunteered Raoul, following my gaze. He handed me a fluted
goblet and sat down beside me. "The family
resemblance is quite evident."

I nodded in agreement. "I noticed that

André has the same bone structure. The same dark eyes, the same intensity of expression."

"And the same abominable temperament?"

"I thought he was teasing but I couldn't be sure. "No, I find him quite pleasant."

"And you find me—?"

"Impossible," I said before I thought.

He laughed. "You can never be accused of polite, social hypocrisy, Alysha. Do you always say what you think? Doesn't it get you into trouble?"

"Always." And then I began to relax in spite of myself. His confident, easy manner could gentle the most skittish colt and charm the most reluctant woman.

"I bet you were an impossible child."

His gaze centered on me and the teasing smile inspired me to tell him about my favorite childish pastime of listening to people gossip and repeating it at the most inopportune moment. "I got my backside paddled more than once for repeating the truth instead of ducking the question."

"I find it refreshing." As he chuckled, he reached up and, with his fingertips, lightly traced the curve of my chin. "Everything about you is unexpected, my dear Alysha. I never know if the next time I see you, you're going to be a starchy prude, an

exasperating fool, or a very sensuous
femme fatale."

My lips trembled as I turned away frm
his touch. I took a deep sip of my wine. I
must not allow him to do this to me. My
vow that he would not manipulate me had
already begun to shrivel up like dry leaves
and would soon be only powdered dust.
Every tingling sense in my body was totally
aware of him: his touch, the faint spicy
smell of his toiletries; dark, velvet eyes that
shone with the faint smile on his lips; that
deep resonant voice that caressed my name
when it came softly from his throat.

"Alysha—" He turned my face towards
his.

Even though I willed myself to look away
from his face poised so close to mine, I
could not take my eyes from his. I parted
my lips but words would not come. In the
next instant his mouth had claimed mine.
His tongue wandered over my lips as if
caught by the sweetness of wine drops
lingering there. A teasing fierceness
pervaded the long kiss.

I could not draw away. For a long
moment his mouth worked mine with a
compelling possessiveness that made me
lean into him. My breathing was shallow
and my heart quickened. Even though only
a few seconds had passed since his lips met

mine, when he drew away, I felt as if the
world had been revolving at a mad rate for
an eternity.

"Alysha, love," he whispered in a thick
voice. "You must go away."

The unexpected entreaty was like a wash
of ice water. I wanted him to beg me to stay
with him no matter what hurricane forces
raged around us. I wanted to hear vows of
his love and protection—not abrupt
entreaties that I should go away.

I did not have time to formulate a tart
reply because there was a rustle in the hall
and Yvonne appeared in the doorway. I
wondered if she had been there earlier or if
she had just reached the drawing room the
moment after Raoul drew away. I could not
tell from her face which showed signs of
her dissipation. Bloated cheeks, puffy
eyelids and an unhealthy color ruined a
natural beauty that must have been hers.
Her gown was fashionably cut to reveal her
full breasts and there was something
sensuous about her rounded curves and
feminine vulnerability as she walked into
the room.

Raoul was instantly on his feet and moved
toward her in a solicitous manner that
seemed to shut out everything that had
happened between us a moment before. It
was as if the passionate kiss had never

happened. His expression was controlled, with no lingering passion in his eyes or the curve of his lips. *You must go away.* Why? Did I present a threat to someone like Yvonne? Or Raoul himself? What was he afraid I might find out?

He raised Yvonne's hand and kissed it. "You look lovely tonight, *ma chère, Yvonne.* Come you must greet our house guest." He talked as one would to a child, tender, placating, and almost pleading. He guided her over to where I sat.

Raoul de Lamareau could change his outward demeanor with alarming speed, I thought, stunned. He was a chameleon. My emotions were still tumbling in chaos, like a foaming cataract over steep rapids while he calmly smiled down at Yvonne, composed and solicitous as if she had never been far from his thoughts. His eyes searched her face and seemed reassured with what he found there. As she greeted me, her eyes were clear and I could see no outward sign that she had been drinking.

"I must apologize, Mademoiselle Grant," Yvonne said quickly as if to set aside our last meeting as quickly as possible. "I regret my behavior yesterday and offer no excuses. Please forgive me." Even though her words were politely apologetic, a fierce hardness in her eyes raked my face and made me ill at ease. I was almost certain she must have witnessed Raoul kissing me.

"No apologies necessary," I said quickly, cursing the embarrassed warmth creeping up into my face. "I'm glad that . . . that you're feeling better," I finished lamely.

"*Merci.*" Her frigid, controlled behavior was a contrast to the woman I had first seen sobbing on Maurey's arm and the fanatical drunkard of the hunting lodge who had tried to kill Raoul and then sobbed, "I love you . . . I love you."

Although her petite figure was no longer slender, she wore her gown well, a fashionable dress of yellow satin, trimmed with velvet rouleaux around the flounces that fell from her bare shoulders and in layered ruffles on her sleeves. An embroidered panel decorated her skirt and was drawn to the back in a gathered bustle. She had obviously taken care with her toiletries. Her raven hair was clean and shiny and drawn into a high pompadour which gave height to her small figure. In spite of these outward changes, a hint of a tormented woman remained. She made me uneasy.

"I'm sure that dinner is about to be served," Raoul said quickly as if he did not want to linger over our unfinished drinks. "Alysha," he held out one arm to me and

with Yvonne on the other side, he
conducted us through an archway into a
formal dining room. He placed Yvonne at
the head of the table, with me on her right,
and then he took a place on her left. Everything he did seemed to be bent on
reassuring her that she was indeed the
mistress of the house and he was only there
to serve her.

I had never seen this side of him. Almost
subservient. He placated Yvonne when she
voiced any complaint and smoothed over an
embarrassment when her trembling hand
upset a water goblet as she reached for it.
His manner was not relaxed or casual and I
knew that he was not even tasting the food
or drink served to us by fawning servants.
His nervousness transmitted itself to me.

I let the superficial dinner conversation
wash over me and jumped when Yvonne
suddenly addressed me in a strident,
accusing voice. "Tell me, Mam'selle Grant,
why you are trying to turn my children
against me?"

The acid accusation was so sudden, it
caused my jaw to drop in bewilderment. "I
. . . I don't know what you mean, Madame.
I'm fond of Annette and André but I—"

"But she could never take a mother's
place," finished Raoul smoothly. I felt the
tension that visibly stiffened his shoulders.

"Why did you come here?" Yvonne's eyes revealed raw, smoldering hatred as she glared at me. All pretense of polite congeniality was gone. Her hand was like a claw on her water glass.

"To see Annette home from school. Sister Mary Josette asked me. I wrote you a letter explaining when we would be here."

"I never got it." Accusing eyes raked Raoul's face. "I suppose you kept it from me like you do everything else. Anyway, I don't believe it. You brought her here, my dear, whoring brother-in-law. You're not satisfied just to bed Louise, now you have to have some cheap—"

"That's enough!" His voice was like the pound of a gavel coming down upon her last word. "Mademoiselle Grant is a guest in this house . . . and you'll treat her like one."

She smiled maliciously. "I do think you protest too much, my dear Raoul. The two of you are in this together, aren't you? She plays up to my children, you try to keep me quiet and docile—while you steal the de Lamareau collection for yourself!"

"You forget yourself, Madame. Only respect for my brother's wife keeps me from ramming such lies down your throat."

Yvonne laughed, a tight, hysterical laugh. "If you respected him so much, why did you kill him?"

I thought Raoul was going to grab her by the shoulders and shake her senseless. Instead, he took a deep breath as if fighting for control. "That will be enough."

Her mouth twisted in an ugly grimace. "You thought I would fall into your arms and marry you after Jacques' death, didn't you? You had it all planned. And when I refused to marry you, you decided to kill me. All your kind concern about my health is only a pretense to get your own way. You hate me . . . you want me dead—"

"That's not true. Your imagination has run away with you, Yvonne."

She gave a bitter laugh. "My dear brother-in-law, you'll use me and my children any way you can to satisfy your greedy needs. And I'll never marry you . . . never! I spit on you and your whore!" She lurched to her feet and fled the room.

I stared across the table at Raoul. He sat frozen for a moment, his eyes glazed, and then he put his head in his hands and I could not see his face. I was at a loss as to what to do or say. His vulnerability wrenched at me and I wanted to go around to his chair and stroke his bowed head, comfort him, try to lessen the hurt of the vile things that had been said. I feared such impulsive action would only turn his angry eyes upon me. He was not a man to show his weaknesses and he would not forgive me for responding to them. Bewildering feelings for him poured over me with such intensity that I was shaken. I bit my lower lip to keep tears from spilling down my cheeks.

When he raised his head a moment later, a mask was on his face. He gave me a wry smile and shook his head. "Well, I guess that's enough dramatics for the evening, Alysha. I suggest we enjoy the rest of our dinner if we can."

"I'm sorry," I said feebly.

"For what? For whom? Me? Yvonne? My dead brother? Don't disturb yourself. The situation is not of your making."

"I think Yvonne might have seen . . . you kiss me."

"Yes, I'm sorry for that." Then his eyes softened. "Not for the kiss. That was a moment of happiness which I must cherish as something warm and beautiful."

"Then why did you say that I must go away?"

"I have no choice, my love. What I want most in my heart must give way to what I think is best for you. You must not stay here. I should have put you back on the train that first day."

"Did you send me to the village this morning to meet Maurice Travois?"

"Who?"

"Maurice Travois. I told you about him. My mother's lover."

"Oh, the one that stimulated your interest in—" He stooped. "*Mon Dieu!* He's here? In Chambleau? Why?"

"That's what Inspector Davail would like to know." I could not be sure whether or not Raoul was pretending innocence or whether he truly did not know about Maurice Travois's presence in the village. My feelings were in such a turmoil, I could not be sure of anything.

"I don't understand."

"The inspector is certain that I am in league with him, that I helped set up the burglary. He has it all worked out. Apparently, he knows that Travois handles stolen goods, primarily for other 'closet collectors' like your brother, Jacques. It all fits into a neat, incriminating pattern. He may arrest me at any moment."

"Alysha! *Ma chérie.*" He was around the table in an instant and pulled me up into his arms. His lips touched my forehead lovingly as he murmured reassuringly, "I won't let him touch you. You must not worry any more. Whatever has happened is no concern of yours."

I wanted to laugh and cry at the same time. No concern of mine! How could he say such a thing?

"Come." He drew us past two waiting servants whose eyes had grown wide as they stood motionless and observed all the dramatics that had taken place. Gossip and speculation about what had happened in the dining room would run rampant in the servants' hall tonight, I thought. I didn't care. It was enough that Raoul had brushed aside any suggestion that I was Travois's accomplice. He had reacted to the suggestion in a loving, protective way and I knew I was like parched earth soaking up the affection and assurance which he gave me.

He kept his arm around me as we mounted the stairs and wound our way through the unused west wing. When we reached my door, he drew me into his arms and kissed me with the same intensity that I had felt in the drawing room. "May I come in?" he asked quietly when he lifted his lips from mine.

I knew what he was asking. The moment had come when I must deny my feelings for him or give them rein. Out of the upheaval of my emotions only one thing was clear. Even though I was half-frightened of him, I could not still the devastating whirlwind of emotions that engulfed me when I was near him. I wanted to touch him . . . feel his tender arms pulling me close . . . reel under

the pressure of his kisses and give myself to
him.

"Yes," I croaked in a near-whisper.

He shut the door behind us, locked it,
then leaned up against it and drew me into
his arms once again. He kissed me gently
but deeply, pulling my lips into his warm,
receptive mouth as if devouring the
sweetness there. His hand cupped the back
of my head, his fingers threading the soft
curls that tumbled from a silken crown. As
his questing tongue touched mine, a
surging, primitive hunger responded
within me. A moan escaped my lips when he
lifted his mouth for a brief second. I feared
that he might set me away from him as he
had done before and my arms slid up
around his neck in a captive embrace.

He kissed me again and then, with his
mouth pressed against mine, he lifted me
up in his arms. When he gently laid me on
the bed, I tightened my arms around his
neck and pulled him down beside me. My
eyes were closed as his hands slipped from
my shoulders to cup the fullness of my
breasts. I felt the front fastenings give way
and then his head was buried in the soft
crevice. For a moment I stiffened. I had
never felt a man's intimate caress before,
not this sure, tantalizing command of my
breasts as his fingers gently kneaded them.

"It's all right," he whispered. "Your body was made for love, *ma chérie.*" His lips touched the rosy bud of a nipple and his tongue lightly flicked it into a hardening apex of sensation.

There was no light in the room except that shining through the tall, narrow windows from a golden benign moon. As if spreading a benediction upon us, its dappled light spilled upon the floor and a few moments later touched our naked bodies with a golden glow. My eyes searched his face and I lost myself in his passion-laden gaze. His eyes and hands traveled from my rounded breasts, down over the firm smoothness of my waist and buttocks and his loving gaze followed the touch of his hands upon my thighs.

"I please you?" I asked, for I feared that he might find me wanting.

His desirous eyes came back to my questioning face. "You please me." He drew a tremulous breath. "You please me."

"And you please me," I offered with a foolish smile. As I looked upon his nakedness, I reveled in the clean sweep of his torso, his muscular thighs and the soft dark hair upon his loins and chest. No statue by Michelangelo had ever done more justice to the perfection of the human male, I thought. Raoul de Lamareau was hand-

somely beautiful. I shivered with pure joy
and wondrous expectation. I did not know
the ritual of making love. My naiveté might
have made me awkward and fearful if I had
not been filled with such passion for this
man. He had captured all my senses and
filled me with wonderment. My body
responded with a knowledge all its own. My
lover would lead and I would follow. Any
apprehension was lost in a mounting desire
that he was deftly arousing within me.
When his lips descended repeatedly upon
mine, I parted my mouth and welcomed the
rising thrusts of his tongue.

As his hands and lips caressed my body,
an indefinable hunger made me arch my
body against his. When I thought I could
not stand the devouring need his passion
had aroused, he swept my legs apart with
one of his. Even in the throes of desire, I felt
a stab of alarm. "No," I gasped. I did not
know how it was with a man and woman. I
knew nothing about the union of their
bodies in this mysterious rapture. I wanted
to turn back. "No, please—"

He kissed me again, lying quietly upon
me. "I will be gentle," he promised.

Sweat gathered on his forehead as he
held back his own passion. I knew then that
he would never take me selfishly and dis-

regard my pleasure for his. "Do you want me?"

I had never felt such wanting before. "Yes, I love you," I whispered. A quick thrust brought a cry of pain to my lips. Then the momentary discomfort was lost in a building fulfillment as I strained to press my hips hard against his demanding thighs. His rhythmic thrusts carried me upward on a spiral of indescribable pleasure and when the burst of exploding sensation came, my body shuddered from the impact.

Raoul met my release with a shuddering that left him spent upon me. Then he pressed his cheek against mine, murmuring endearments that matched the intensity of joy that burst through me.

After a while, he slipped away from me but continued to cradle me against his shoulder, stroking my hair, and murmuring endearments. *"Bien?"*

I smiled. *"C'est bien."* Nothing could have been better.

No matter what happened to me the rest of my life, for this one moment, I had experienced a miracle of completeness, wholeness, contentment. All the empty years had been swept away.

Chapter Fourteen

I do not know when Raoul slipped away from my room. The bed was still warm when I awoke and dawn was glazing the mullioned windows with a rosy pink. For a moment I stretched my legs like a contented cat, delighting in the wondrous aftermath of a night of love. As I remembered how we had explored each other's bodies, a rosy flush that matched the glow of sunrise stole into my cheeks. Had it really happened? Had I been as uninhibited in my ardor as I now remembered? How would I ever face my lover in the bold light of day? A more sophisticated woman would be able to handle these things, but I could not. My euphoria began to dissipate. Maybe the night had been no more to him than a momentary pleasure. He had made no promises for the future. Even though I had lost my heart to him, Raoul de Lamareau still remained a bewildering and rather frightening enigma.

Sighing, I reached down to the foot of the bed where Nela had laid out my night dress. I slipped it on. After I had tied the ribbon into a bow at its high neck, I lay there looking up on the graying ceiling. In the growing light of morning, all the uncertainty of my present situation poured over me. What was I going to do? After what had happened between Raoul and me, could I ever tell the inspector the truth? How could I admit that Raoul had told me to lie? Or confess that I suspected he might have been responsible for the carriage accident? Even as I examined the questions in my confused mind, I knew the one answer to all of them. No, I could not. My earlier determination not to be manipulated or exploited by Raoul mocked me. What had happened between us had new, poignant consequences. He had secured my silence as surely as if he had placed a gag over my mouth.

When Nela brought in my breakfast tray, she pursed her lips in a knowing manner. The rumpled bed and my loose, tousled hair upon the pillow were evidence enough of the romantic tryst of the night before. The whole chateau probably knew where the master had spent the night, I reasoned with a flicker of uneasiness. The dining room servants had witnessed the scene with Yvonne and had seen our departure together. I wondered if Raoul waited in the breakfast room for me to join him.

As if Nela read my thoughts, she said, "The master rode out early this morning. He was in the stables before dawn." An edge of accusation was there in her tone. Did Nela feel I had betrayed the mistress of the house? Did they know of her feelings for Raoul? Was Nela as well as her sister, Alveretta, devoted to Yvonne and did they look upon me as a threat? The thought that all the servants might be in league against me suddenly chilled me. Would they fill the inspector's ears and protect the de Lamareau family at all costs? I suddenly felt surrounded by enemies.

"*Merci*," I murmured in an uncertain voice as Nela poured my coffee from a tiny steaming pot and took the lid from a serving dish. Then she filled my plate with generous serving of eggs Benedict, a buttered croissant and fresh berries in clabbered cream. I did not look at her as I ate.

When she asked me about what I wished to wear, I answered her inquiries in an even tone as if I were accustomed to waking up in a bed still warm from a lover's passion. I chose a light blue dimity gown that had been my favorite for several summers. It was another hand-me-down from my mother and quite out of style now with its full sleeves and gathered skirt which was made to be worn with layers of crinoline instead of several soft batiste petticoats. I always liked the freedom that the full skirt gave me and this spring I had freshened the gown with a new ribbon trimming which matched tiny rose flowers in the print.

I instructed Nela to lace one of the extra ribbons in my hair and she pursed her lips in a knowing fashion. As I watched her in the mirror, my eyes were unusually bright and my cheeks flushed. I felt a deep tremulous quivering inside me as if some metamorphosis had taken place which frightened me.

After my toiletries were complete, I decided to go downstairs and wait for Raoul to return. I had to find out what last night meant to him. Would he declare his affections—or be ready to use my love against me?

I reached the lower hall just as Frazer opened the front door and admitted Maurey Montaigne. "Morning, Frazer," he said breezily. "Nothing like an early morning ride to make one feel fit. Is Mademoiselle—" Then he stopped, a smile spreading across his boyish face as he saw me poised near the foot of the stairs. "Alysha! I was just going to ask if you were receiving visitors this morning? You look lovely. That is the perfect shade of blue for your eyes. They are as deep and luminous as I remembered. I am here to claim my walk in the garden." He bowed deeply and kissed my hand.

I had to laugh at his effusive compliments about my summer dress of three seasons. In spite of myself, I appreciated Maurey's practiced compliments. "You are *très galant*," I responded with a mock formality that made us both grin.

"And you have your bonnet and gloves in hand as if intending to view the gardens without me," he chided. "Shame . . . shame."

I didn't want to admit that I was on my way to the stables to await Raoul's return. "Not at all," I lied. "My sixth sense told me

you would be arriving this morning." For
some reason, I was relieved to put off the
moment when I would meet Raoul's eyes
again and learn whether or not last night
had any serious effect on him. I feared I
might find him as handsomely aloof as
always—and for that I could wait.

I tied the blue streamers of my simple
straw bonnet and took Maurey's arm. We
left by the front door and walked under the
front arched portico until we reached the
side of the chateau and went down a wide
flight of stairs leading into the gardens. The
intricate pattern of clipped hedges was
heightened by masses of riotous flowers
planted in specific color patterns. Some of
the evergreen hedges were only knee-high
while others came as high as a man's head.
Intricate mazes made of hedges were
popular in French landscapes because they
were pleasing when viewed from above and
baffled the senses when walking among
them.

Maurey kept up a gay monologue about
beautiful gardens he had seen at chateaus
along the Seine and explained why he preferred the classical beauty of fountains to
slow-moving streams and man-made lakes.
I had very little to contribute to the topic
but I soon gathered that Maurey was one
who enjoyed an attentive audience more

than a lively exchange of ideas.

As we walked, I was enjoying the warm
sun and easy conversation, when the
pleasure was destroyed by angry voices
floating down from a terrace above us. I
jerked my eyes upward. A small wall and
masses of greenery blocked the view. I
could not see who was there but Yvonne's
hysterical screaming chilled my veins like
ice water.

"You slept with her! Don't lie to me! You
weren't in your room all night! How dare
you bring your cheap little whores under
my roof!"

There was nothing I could do to avoid
eavesdropping. When I recognized Raoul's
resonant angry tones, my breath caught in
my throat. "You had best watch yourself,
Yvonne. My patience is at an end. I am prepared to put a stop to these hysterical
ravings, I warn you."

"Don't think you can threaten me! I'll
have the *gendarmerie* down on you in a
minute." She gave a high-pitched laugh.
There was no sign of drunken speech. If she
had been drinking, it did not lace her
vitriolic words. "I'll show you and that
conniving trollop what the law can do to
you. How long has she been your mistress?
Stop it! Get your hands off of me—"

"I'll shake your head off your shoulders

if I have to," he growled. "I'm warning you, Yvonne. I've taken all I can from you. Either you straighten up or I'll—"

She sobbed. "Kill me . . . like you killed Jacques?"

Raoul swore. "You stupid woman! I'm surprised you haven't ruined everything with your drunken blabbering. Now listen to me . . . listen well! You straighten up or I'll call Dr. Vanderley—"

"No," she cried. "No, you wouldn't."

"Yes, I would. I'll do what I have to do, Yvonne. Shut you away if necessary. I'm warning you for the last time. You behave yourself. Keep your goddamn mouth shut. I'll not tolerate your drunken interference in my affairs."

"You lying, no good bastard, I'll kill her—"

The sound of his hand upon her cheek was like a sharp report. Yvonne cried out and then she must have crumpled in his arms, sobbing. Their voices lowered and then footsteps faded away into the house.

I couldn't look at Maurey. My heartbeat was racing in my throat. Perspiration broke out on the palms of my hands. I was embarrassed, shattered by the threats I had heard, fearful of a violence that was strong enough to sweep us all into a holocaust.

Maurey gave an embarrassed laugh.

"Yvonne seems to be at it again. When she's drinking, she lets her imagination have full rein." I knew that he was gallantly protecting my reputation. Even if he believed that I had spent the night with Raoul, he was too much the French gentleman to indicate that he believed Yvonne's raving.

He took my arm and led me farther into the garden. I walked beside him, numb and unseeing. I felt sick to my stomach and I knew I was as pale as the white roses blooming around a raised sundial which caught the morning shadows.

"Yvonne has always been a fool when it comes to Raoul," said Maurey, giving me time to compose myself. "Everyone was surprised when she married Jacques, but, of course, he was the older brother with the inheritance and Raoul was nearly ten years younger. It wasn't a happy marriage. Jacques loved only one thing—his avaricious collecting. He ignored her and the children. Shut himself off from his family for weeks at a time, hoarding and gloating over his secret acquisitions. In a way I'm glad someone stole some of them. Serves him right. Anyway, don't mind Yvonne's hysterical jealousy. She's maliciously attacked my sister, Louise, the same way. No one believes anything she says." He paused in front of a wrought-iron bench set near a fountain aged with green moss. "Would you care to sit here for a moment?"

I nodded and gratefully let myself lean back against it as Maurey sat down beside me. He began talking about water lilies and the paintings of Renoir. "He's my favorite, although Monet's figures have an individual charm that add to his work. Have you ever seen one of his originals? I wouldn't be surprised if there isn't one hidden away in Jacques's collection. You didn't notice any, did you, when you evaluated the collection?"

The question broke through my upheaval of emotions. I had been listening to his conversation with only part of my mind. Now, I focused my attention on his eager face. "Evaluated the collection? I don't know what you're talking about!"

"Sorry. Guess I spoke out of turn. Louise said that the inspector was pretty sure that you had looked over everything in the west wing." His light brown eyes were no longer merry, but somber and questioning. "You could tell me, Alysha. I would be willing to buy a Renoir at a good price. I would never tell anyone that you were responsible for getting it to me. I'm not interested in any of the other things that were taken. Porcelain vases are not my style."

I swallowed back a growing lump in my throat. *Maurey believed I had a part in the robbery.* I managed an amused laugh. "Sorry to disappoint you. I have no intention of turning thief now or ever." He was no longer the amusing, entertaining young admirer. I saw his friendship as calculated, contrived, and motivated by his own selfish needs. It was really humorous, I thought. It was too bad that I couldn't lightly toss off his offer to buy stolen goods from me but laughter died in my chest and tears welled up in my eyes.

"Chérie, je regrette—" He took my hand and looked anxiously into my burning face. "Forgive me. It was Louise, my sister. She's the one who put me up to making the offer. I see now that it was an unforgivable insinuation. Of course, you are innocent. My sister is always one to spread rumors. She told Inspector Davail about your soiled gown that day we had tea . . . and your bandage, as if you had been touching dusty things. She made a big thing out of discovering you in the drawing room, near the vases that were stolen. I'm afraid she persuaded me that you might—"

"Don't!" I couldn't take any more. At least I thought I couldn't, but at that moment Maurey leaned over and brushed a kiss on the side of my forehead—just as

Raoul came into sight on the other side of
the small pond.

As his eyes met mine, there was nothing
of the passionate lover who had bathed my
body with kisses and flamed it with his own
desire. He looked at me as if there were
nothing but wintry disdain flowing through
his veins. His voice was crisp and accusing.
"I thought I glimpsed you from the terrace
room but I couldn't be sure." He waited as
if he wanted me to deny that I was truly
sitting there with Maurey at my side and
heat rising up in my cheeks, knowing he
had misinterpreted the kiss Maurey had
unexpectedly given me.

Maurey was instantly on his feet. "Alysha
had promised me a walk in the garden," he
said quickly. "I rode over early this
morning to claim a few minutes of her
company." His brown eyes flickered to me,
beseeching that I say nothing about his
offer to buy a stolen painting.

Raoul intercepted the glance and I knew
with a sinking heart that he mistook it for
some romantic entreaty. My eyes begged
him. *There's nothing to be angry about.
Please, please tell me that you love me.
Don't reject me with those cold eyes.* But my
silent pleas went unheard.

"I see. Well, please forgive my intrusion,"
he said stiffly. "I'll leave you two to your

private enjoyment." He started to turn away.

I rose with a rush. "No, wait a moment. Please, we need to talk."

Raoul gave me a curt nod of his head. "Perhaps later. Right now I must ride into the village. I want to have a talk with Dr. Vanderley."

My heart curled into an aching ball as he walked away towards the stables. If Maurey hadn't been there I would have run after him and begged him to explain the horrid words I had overheard between him and Yvonne but Maurey had his hand on my arm.

"He's going to go through with it," said Maurey in a whispered tone. "He's going to have Yvonne committed—and take everything for himself. I wonder if my sister's had anything to do with his decision. She's determined to have him. They're lovers, you know."

Maurey's words reverberated in my head the rest of the day. They were a mockery to the night of love which I had treasured as something pure and wonderful. Yvonne's remarks, and the knowledge that Louise had probably lain in Raoul's arms under this very roof, made me view what had happened as a cheap and tawdry liaison. All my life,

I had struggled to deny the romantic, passionate nature of my mother. I had prided myself that my English, rational mind dominated my actions. I had always considered myself a "thinking" person who was not governed by capricious feelings. All of that had been swept away. I was as foolish as my mother. With the slightest encouragement I would become Raoul de Lamareau's mistress. Such was the state of my infatuation that I knew I would be tempted to take him under any circumstances. He had reduced me to an emotional beggar, willing to accept him as he was and discount all the unanswered questions. My foolish heart believed that circumstances vindicated his harshness toward Yvonne. After all, she had tried to kill him. My irrational feelings would not let me look too closely into the possible reasons for this rancor. I could not believe that he had shot her husband and yet the warning I had overheard that morning indicated that he was afraid that Yvonne's hysteria might bring trouble.

As I closeted myself in the horrid room which spoke of a dead man's presence, it seemed to me that his selfish eccentricity permeated the very air I breathed. His murdered spirit would not let anyone in the house rest in peace. Even in death, he made his presence known. It was as if his tortured spirit were forever destined to guard the possessions that he had greedily amassed. It seemed to reach out and touch everyone.

I tried to read but the book I had brought from school did not hold my interest. It seemed a lifetime ago that I had packed it in my luggage, thinking I would have it to read when I found some lodgings in Paris. Now, the words blurred and I could not think of any reality beyond the present moment. I heard the children in the garden but my spirits were too leaden to join them.

An uneasy anxiety grew as I speculated on what Inspector Davail would have to say to me the next time we met. Would Maurice Travois try to see me again? He had promised as much when I left the café. How could he believe I was in league with those who had burglarized the chateau? There had been an admiring glint in his eyes when he had suggested it. I prayed that he would not compromise me any more in this situation than his presence in the area had already.

As the day went by, my nerves were stretched like a flaxen thread ready to snap. When evening came and Raoul still had not come to see me, I refused to cower any

longer in my room, waiting. The thought of
eating a solitary meal was too abhorrent,
especially in my desolate mood. I freshened
my hair and told Nela I would dine with
Monsieur de Lamareau.

Her face was expressionless although I
knew that, if she were willing, she could tell
me a great deal about what went on in the
house. It would be useless to question her.
Nela's silence was like a wall and I knew I
could not breach it. I wondered if she were
as distant to Louise Montaigne when she
stayed at the chateau or, some taunting
voice added, *any other women whom Raoul
brought here for his pleasure.*

As Nela and I emerged through the door
on the main landing, Annette rushed into
my arms, burying her head against my
shoulder, weeping as if her heart would
break. "Mama has run off. Her maid,
Alveretta, can't find her in the house anywhere."

I stroked the girl's dark hair trying to
soothe her. I didn't know what to say as my
mind grappled with the situation. Yvonne
had probably gone back to the hunting
lodge, I reasoned. She probably had more
liquor hidden there. After this morning's
fight with Raoul, she would undoubtedly
turn to drink for consolation. "Your
mother's all right. I'm sure she is. Come,

let's go downstairs. We'll have a cup of tea while we wait for the servants to find her."

I was certain they would find her at the lodge. Then I remembered the guns that were kept there and the near tragedy when Raoul had tried to reason with her. Fear that she might be waiting for him to come after her made my hand tremble as I poured our tea from a tray brought in by Nela.

We had finished our second cup when Alveretta and another male servant returned to the house. They came to the sitting room looking for Raoul. "Madame de Lamareau is not at the hunting lodge," Alveretta said, looking at me for some direction. "Do you think we should start scouring the woods for her, Mademoiselle?"

I didn't know what to say. A thought like a piercing arrow struck me. *Could it be that Raoul had returned with Dr. Vanderley and they had taken her away as he had threatened?*

All three servants, Nela, Alveretta, and a middle-aged man in stable clothes, waited for my answer. They watched the questions flickering on my face and waited for some direction. Without Yvonne and Raoul in the house, there was an absence of authority and whether I liked it or not, it seemed that the servants had chosen me to fill it.

Annette began sobbing again and I struggled to make some kind of decision. If Raoul had taken Yvonne away, he would be furious if I launched a full-scale search in the woods for her and alerted everyone in the area to her absence. On the other and, if she were wandering in a drunken state through the copse, she ought to be found before the chill of a dark night overtook her. It was already past the eight o'clock dinner hour. Annette added her pleading, waiting eyes to the others leveled upon me.

"You are certain she is nowhere in the house?" I addressed my questions to Alveretta.

"Yes, Mademoiselle. We have been searching the house and gardens all afternoon. Madame slipped away right after lunch when I thought she was napping. I wouldn't have left her alone but I—"

I waved away the rest of her contrite explanation. At the moment, placing the blame was not of the utmost importance. "Could someone like Monsieur de Lamareau have taken her . . . for an outing?" I asked, carefully choosing my words. "Did you leave her alone that long?"

The guilty look Alveretta sent the fair-haired, burly man from the stables told me that the servant had been gone quite a bit

longer than she was ready to admit.
Undoubtedly, there had been some dallying
in the stable between the two of them. I
wasn't going to belabor the point. "I just
need to know if someone could have
approached Madame in her room and
accompanied her from the house," I
assured her. "It would not be wise to raise
an alarm for Madame if she is in the
company of friends at the moment.
Monsieur Montaigne, for instance."

"No, mam'selle. He left alone," said the
stableman. "I watched him take the bridle
path through the woods. It's a shortcut to
his home, you know."

"And Monsieur de Lamareau? Has
anyone seen him come back from the
village?"

All three shook their heads. Their
ignorance didn't mean that he hadn't come
back with the doctor and quiety and
furtively taken Yvonne away. Right now
she could be shut away in some secluded
institution. I was caught in a bewildering
maelstrom of speculation. *Had Yvonne run
away on her own—or had she been taken*? I
was like someone blindfolded trying to
determine a proper aim on a target. Finally,
I stiffened my shoulders and made my
decision. "I think we ought to send out a
search party. We must find Madame before

she is completely lost in the darkness of the
night. Would you see to it?" I addressed the
stableman. "Do what is necessary to find
her," I ordered as one in authority. The
responsibility rested uneasily on my
shoulders but Annette's tearful whimpering strengthened my resolve.

"Oui, mademoiselle. I'll alert the
groundworkers and the stableboys. We'll
have a dozen men searching for her *tout de
suite.*

The children and I waited in the sitting
room, Annette on one side of me and André
on the other. The French mantel clock
ticked away the minutes. I tried to keep the
children's attention on something else but I
knew that only one thought was uppermost
in all our minds. Where was Yvonne de
Lamareau?

It seemed like an eternity but it had been
less than two hours when they brought
Yvonne home, her body limp and her chest
barely moving with shallow breathing as
the stableman carried her in.

They had found her half-submerged in a
small stream, almost lifeless. She had
either fallen or been struck in the head with
a sharp rock and was unconscious. If they

had not found her as quickly as they had, the feeble breath of life that remained would have been quietly silenced.

Chapter Fifteen

They took Yvonne upstairs to her room and I sent for Dr. Duboise. The mantle of responsibility had been thrust upon me and I had to assume it in the way I thought best. I knew nothing of Dr. Vanderley, the family doctor, and the fact that Raoul had gone to him to talk about Yvonne made me reach out for Dr. Duboise. I put aside any apprehension over Raoul's probable displeasure. An ugly suspicion that somehow he had been responsible for

Yvonne's condition made me grateful to
have someone like Dr. Duboise in charge. I
could not believe that what had happened
to her had been an accident. I did not share
my suspicions with Dr. Duboise but he was
quite solemn after he had examined her.

"Very serious. The head wound . . .
exposure—" He shook his head. *Très grave.*

"Had she been drinking?" I asked boldly.

His eyebrows raised in surprise. "*Oui.*
The smell of spirits was on her breath.
Madame de Lamareau is a . . . drinker?"

I nodded.

He let out his breath in relief. "Well, then,
that could explain what happened. She was
not herself . . . wandered into the woods,
fell and struck her head. A tragic accident."

I did not respond to his reassuring words.
Even though I wanted to believe that
Yvonne had brought this dire condition
upon herself, I could not. Dr. Duboise had
not heard the angry threats Raoul had
made against her that morning. Her
husband had met a tragic death and now
she lay between life and death herself. She
had thought Raoul capable of murder—and
I found myself almost convinced that her
accusations could be true.

"What is it, Mademoiselle? Your heart
looks heavy. You do not believe she harmed
herself in this way?"

"I don't know what to believe." I blinked rapidly to keep back a fullness in my eyes. He patted my shoulder and his kindly blue eyes anxiously searched my face. It was all I could do not to lean against him for fatherly comfort.

"Where is Monsieur de Lamareau?" he asked as if going right to the heart of my turmoil.

"I don't know. He left early this morning." I wasn't going to speculate on whether or not he had returned without anyone seeing him, coaxed Yvonne from the house, and left her on the banks of the stream to die. The scenario was so troubling that I had to close my eyes against it.

"You have done all you can, Mademoiselle. Go to your room. I will see to the patient. Take the sleeping powder I left for you—"

"No. I must see to the children. And I want to be here when m'sieur returns." As anger fueled my body, strength returned to my voice.

The doctor did not insist. He seemed to know that there were dragons of my own that must be slain before I could follow his advice.

I was in André's room when I heard Raoul's voice in the hall. I was reading a

fairy tale to the boy with only half of my
mind and I stumbled over the next sentence
as my body went rigid. André watched me
with wide eyes and I tried to smile
reassuringly as I went on and finished the
story.

Then I bent over and kissed him. "Now,
you go to sleep."

"Stay here. Like you did before."

I had to smile at his innocence. He had no
idea what it had cost me to stay by his bedside the night of the burglary. "I'll come
back and make sure you're asleep before I
go to my room. Your sister's already asleep
so close your eyes and think about the
brave knight in the story."

"Is Mama going to be all right?"

"It is in God's hands." The phrase was a
favorite of Sister Josette and it came easily
to my lips. I tucked the covers around him.
For a moment I was furious with Yvonne
for the way she had ignored her children.
Both Annette and André had been cheated
of her loving care. She used them to absorb
her own emotional tirades, filling them
with anxiety and bewilderment. They
deserved better.

There was no one in the hall as I came
out. I wavered indecisively. Should I seek
out Raoul? Just then Alveretta came along
the hall from Yvonne's room. I asked her if

the doctor and Monsieur de Lamareau were there.

"No, mam'selle. A nurse has arrived to see to Madame." Her small eyes, so much like Nela's, suddenly filled with tears. "It is my fault. All my fault. If only—"

"You must not blame yourself, Alveretta. No one can foresee these things. You are not responsible."

But who is? That was the dagger-like question that accompanied me downstairs to the main hall. *"Où est Monseuir de Lamareau?"* I asked Frazer as he appeared with a tray of drinks from the back of the house.

"In the library, mam'selle. With the doctor."

I wanted to hear what they had to say to each other so I brazenly followed Frazer into the room. My steps faltered almost immediately. If I could have turned and fled unnoticed I would have but I had committed myself to the impulsive intrusion. There was nothing I could do but stand my ground.

Louise Montaigne was sitting on the leather couch beside Raoul. The closeness of their bodies reeked of intimacy. They were both dressed in riding attire, dusty and showing signs of an extended time on horseback. *He had spent the day with her.*

Last night he had held me in his arms, made love until dawn, and then deliberately sought her.

"Alysha?" His expression was guarded, defensive, and I had the impression that for once his aristocratic composure had deserted him. He looked thoroughly shaken and as he came to his feet, I had the impression that he was braced for whatever tirade I was about to unleash upon him. My own emotional turmoil was such that I could not say a word.

Dr. Duboise took in my ashen face and guided me to a chair beside his own. "Sit down, Mademoiselle. You are in time to join us in a drink. Such a trying time, for everyone. I have just been telling M'sieur that Madame's condition is very grave. She lingers with a thread of life that could be snapped with one quiet breath."

"She brought it upon herself," said Louise with a narrowing of her russet brown eyes. "We have been worried about her for a long time, haven't we, darling? We did our best but you cannot help someone who is weak and hysterical—"

"That's enough, Louise," Raoul said sharply. He took his drink from Frazer and stood by the fireplace. I saw then that his boots were dirty and a tiny green leaf was stuck to a reddish clump of mud.

*He had been in the woods. My God, were
he and Louise in this together?* I felt faint
and took a deep sip of the brandy Dr.
Duboise had placed in my hands. I sent him
a grateful look and his composed, unruffled
expression gave me strength.

"I can't understand how she was able to
leave the house unsupervised," said Raoul.
"And where did she get the liquor? She was
sober when I left this morning. Alveretta
has always been dependable." His jaw
clenched and for a moment I believed that
he was as bewildered by what had
happened as I was. Then I remembered how
well he lied. Last night, I had believed that
nothing could make me doubt him again. I
took another deep, grateful sip of the fiery
liquid that was returning some warmth to
my limbs.

"I realize," said Dr. Duboise, "that you
will undoubtedly want to call in your
family physician. I was happy to respond to
Mademoiselle Grant's distress but as you
know I am vacationing here with my
brother and—" He gave a slight, apologetic
shrug of his shoulders.

"Of course, Dr. Duboise. We are indebted
to you for your generous response. If you
would be willing to render your services
until Dr. Vanderley returns to the area, I
would be most appreciative. Dr. Vanderley

is out of town for a few days and—"

Not hearing the rest of his sentence, I finished it in my own mind. *He had gone to make arrangements for Yvonne's commitment but the doctor was out of town.* This knowledge was like a weight balanced against the suspicion that he and Louise had struck Yvonne and left her for dead. Had they tried to murder Yvonne because Raoul had been unable to make arrangements for her commitment? And why? For the first time I wondered if Louise had been involved in Jacques's death. Maybe it was she whom Raoul was trying to protect—if he hadn't done the deed himself.

"Of course, I will be happy to administer to Madame as best I can," responded the doctor graciously as he pushed his square spectacles back up on his nose. "For another day or two, only. Now, if you will excuse me, I will check on my patient and then return again tomorrow morning to see if there is any change." Dr. Duboise smiled at me. "There is color in your cheeks now, Mademoiselle. Get a good night's rest. Do not worry about matters which are not your responsibility." I thought there was a warning in this last admonition as if he knew that I was unable to put aside my suspicions about what had happened. Did he fear for my own safety?

After he was gone, I quickly excused myself.

"No, please stay. I want to talk with you, Alysha. Louise, if you will excuse us. Your usual guest room has been prepared." He held out his hand to the auburn-haired beauty and eased her to her feet. Then he bent and kissed her cheek. "Sleep well, I'll see you in the morning."

Her eyes were liked chipped bits of ice as they raked my face. Then her lips curved in a malicious smile. "Men. They will amuse themselves, won't they?" Then she swept out as if remaining would be beneath her dignity.

I had flushed under her knowing gaze. I felt cheap and tawdry and angry. "We have nothing to say to each other, m'sieur," I flared, clenching my fists.

"We have to talk."

I jerked away from his touch. "We have nothing to say to each other. I'm going to my room." I turned to flounce away but he stopped me with firm hands on my shoulders and swung me back to face him.

"Please." The word was said softly in a pleading tone I had never heard him use before. "Please. I'm trying to understand what has happened. I woke up this morning thinking that Browning was right, 'God's in his heaven, all's right with the world,' and then I see you in the garden with Maurey kissing your forehead . . . *Mon Dieu*, I wanted to kill him." Raoul's hand bit into my shoulders.

"Maurey . . . you thought—?" *He had been jealous of Maurey*. I didn't know whether to laugh or beat my fists against his chest for his stupidity.

"Alysha, *ma chérie*, how could you dally with him the morning after we—"

"I wasn't 'dallying' or doing anything else with him," I flared. "He asked me to take a walk in the garden. Then we heard you and Yvonne quarreling—" I saw the muscles in his cheeks tighten and I knew then that he had been unaware of our presence below the terrace. "We heard everything. Yvonne's malicious remarks about me and . . . your threats." My voice quivered. I searched his eyes as if I could read what lay behind their guarded darkness. I didn't want to accuse him but I couldn't help it. The thing that lay between us was ugly and malignant. I had to verify it. "Did you carry out the threat to silence Yvonne? Did you leave her in the copse for dead?"

I could have struck him and the sudden stiffening of his body would not have been any greater. He dropped his hands from my shoulders as if the touch was suddenly abhorrent. I wished I could have called the words back but some stubborn fiber in my being made me level firm eyes upon his face as I waited for his answer.

Through taut, cold lips, he said, "If you can accuse me of such a thing, Mademoiselle, there is nothing to be said between us."

Before I could justify the question, he brushed by me and left me biting into my lower lip and staring at the rug through swelling tears. I would have gladly suffered his verbal abuse if only he had denied the accusation, but he hadn't. His riding clothes and soiled boots were evidence that he had picked up dirt and leaves while walking on dank ground. Both he and Louise looked slightly disheveled. Even as I silently begged him to deny it, he had avoided a direct answer and had not given me any explanation of his activities that day. As always, he had left me with a frightening sense that he was capable of doing whatever was necessary to carry out his own nefarious plans.

I slept little that night. As if death were in the house, I huddled in bed and trembled with a chill. I could not get any warmth into my body even though I wore my robe to bed and pulled the covers up around me. I wondered if Yvonne had died and her spirit was blowing a cold breath upon me. Lying there in her murdered husband's room, I could imagine his troubled spirit uniting with hers to wreak havoc upon those who had harmed them. I knew such images were "night thoughts" and I struggled to put them from me and close my mind to images of vengeful ghosts. There was enough terror in reality. I did not need to look to the world of spirits for fear strong enough to thicken my blood like clabbered cream.

If Yvonne died, Inspector Davail would be turning us even more tightly on his rack of inquisition. I dreaded the morning and feared the night. When I heard a mewing outside my door, I got up and let Beau into the room. Gratefully, I clutched him to me, and buried my cheek against his soft fur. Some warmth eased back into my body and finally I slept.

Yvonne had made it through the night. Glad to have something to do, I took the children out in the garden to get them away from the hushed, sick-room atmosphere that permeated the chateau. The elderly *bonne de'enfant*, Mavis, readily gave them up, grateful that I had assumed temporary charge of them. She had come to the household with Yvonne and I could tell that the white-haired woman was almost beside herself with worry over her mistress.

We played with André's ball upon the smooth green lawn and sat at the corner of a large pond and watched goldfish as they slipped golden bodies through the foaming water. I arranged for a picnic lunch to be prepared and we sat out in the warm sunshine eating pâté sandwiches and fresh green grapes that were as sweet as the wine they made.

"I think Mama is going to die," said André with the blunt honesty of children. "She looks dead already."

"She's very ill," I said quietly. Dr. Duboise had told me that morning that there had been no change during the night. He feared that if she didn't rally soon, pneumonia was likely to set in. In her weakened condition, she could never fight off such a serious complication.

Annette put her fist to her mouth as if to choke back a sob. I put my arms around her shoulders and bent my head to hers. I wondered if Annette was questioning whether or not her mother had really wandered away by herself. Others in the house could have overheard the same argu-

ment on the terrace between her mother
and uncle. Once the inspector started
asking questions all of it would come out.
"We'll have to wait and see," I said, as
much to myself as to the children.

The day went slowly. I did not see Raoul.
I felt poised on the edge of a chasm that
would engulf me at any moment. The
inspector had not interrogated me any
more but I felt uneasy. Was he collecting
evidence against me and would he, at any
moment, level his charges against me?

Late in the afternoon, Nela came to tell
me there was a gentleman visitor waiting
for me in the small parlor, and I knew the
moment had come. I braced myself for the
policeman's snares of lies and circum-
stantial evidence.

I sailed into the room with my head high
and my chin jutted out as if prepared for
any battle. My warlike demeanor dissolved
in a rush of surprise. It was not Inspector
Davail but Maurice Travois who waited for
me. His presence was a cue for old affection
to sweep over me. I went into his arms for a
hug before I remembered that his illicit
activities had tarnished my respect for him.

"What . . . what are you doing here?" I
gasped, surprised, happy, and nervous
about his presence. Did he truly believe I

was a conspirator in the burglary?

He gave his burly laugh. "I came to see you, of course. Does that surprise you? No, don't think of it as business, Alysha. Pure pleasure. Finding you again after all these years. I know I rushed things when we first met. Foolish of me. I've come to mend my fences. Jumped to conclusions, I did. Well, now, sit down and let me look at you. A fine young woman. Your mother should be very proud of you. How is Nicole?" His thick eyebrows matted together. "Sorry about the way things happened. I wanted to put things right by you and your mother but—" he shrugged. "My wife saw the chance to dominate me while I was helpless to do anything about it. I thought about both of you and wished you well. I was very fond of you and your mother."

His expression of affection took me by surprise but love survives on the smallest nourishment. Suddenly, I was a child again and old feelings rushed back. I felt the heavy emotional burden I had been carrying lighten. I could not change him nor what he was but neither could I reject him. Old ties were too strong. He began to entertain me with stories about a recent trip to the Orient and I found myself laughing at the picture of him standing in a sinking Chinese sampan with his trousers hiked up to his fat knees to keep them from getting wet.

My laughter must have floated out into the hall, an abrasive sound in the silent, waiting house. Frazer passed by the open doorway with a stern reprimand on his face and a moment later Raoul appeared. I knew the sound of my laughter must have brought him there. My face was suddenly warm with embarrassment. "Please forgive me. I forgot myself." Then I said to Maurice quickly, "Madame de Lamareau lies seriously ill."

"Oh, *je regrette*." Then he stood up and addressed Raoul. "It is my fault, Monsieur, I fear that I am responsible for Alysha's merriment. No insult was intended. I am Maurice Travois, an old friend. I met her in the village yesterday."

"Yes, she told me." Raoul's eyes narrowed a fraction as he looked from me to Travois. Then he held out his hand. "Glad to meet you, m'sieur. Please, be seated. I did not mean to intrude."

"Not at all. Please join us," I said quickly.

At first, I thought he was going to refuse but he returned Maurice's broad smile and I could see that he was going to play the congenial host. Very smoothly, Raoul led the conversation into a discussion of the import business.

Raoul seemed quite knowledgeable about foreign markets, especially where the exportation of French wines was concerned. I found their discussion lively and informative. I began to relax. Monsieur Travois continued to entertain us with his stories and I was not surprised when Raoul invited him to stay and dine with us. I was pleased and yet uneasy when Monsieur Travois accepted.

I should not have worried. Louise did not join us and the meal went very well. For the first time, I felt I could say what I wanted and both men would accept my contribution. I always enjoyed matching my intellectual wits with others. The table conversation skirted any references to the burglary or Yvonne's accident and I lost myself in the enjoyment of good food and conversation. I was sorry when it was over and Maurice bade me goodbye with an affectionate hug.

"We must not lose contact with each other this time, my dear Alysha. And thank you, M'sieur, for your hospitality."

"Won't you join me in the library for a brandy while your rented carriage is brought around?" invited Raoul.

I was not included in the invitation. There was nothing I could do but excuse myself. I made my way upstairs to visit Annette and

André and read them a bedtime story. They were glad to see me and we all sat cross-legged on Annette's bed while I read to them. My thoughts kept coming back to the two men in the library and I wondered what they were talking about. My ears seemed to burn but that certainly could have been my imagination.

After I finished the story and patiently endured their delaying tactics, I kissed the children good night and made my way back downstairs.

I had decided that if the two men were still talking, I would join them, invitation or not. When I reached the library, the door was open. I peeked in and was disappointed to find it empty.

I started to turn around and then a slightly open door to the terrace caught my eye. With a quickening pulse, I wondered if Raoul could be outside on the terrace, breathing in the night air. Without questioning the impulse, I searched the moonlit terrace for his slender figure. I was disapointed. There was no sign of him.

I walked to the stone parapet and stared down into the garden. Suddenly I saw Raoul, taking a path toward the main fountain. Without analyzing my behavior, I hurried along the terrace until I came to a wide expanse of stairs leading down into the formal garden.

He was out of sight now, but I headed in the direction I thought he had taken. I was about to despair that I wouldn't find him in the circuitous paths and the maze of evergreen hedges when I heard voices. I slowed my steps. It was Monsieur Travois's voice, hushed but still booming. Why had they thought it best to continue their conversation out here in the garden? I eased forward, suddenly furtive about my movements. If they did not want to be overheard, I had no intention of alerting them to my presence.

"I've given you my final offer," Maurice Travois's voice was firm. "There is a great deal of risk in disposing of such celebrated items. You are really in no position to bargain with me. If you—"

I had moved closer and the end of his sentence was cut off as I stepped upon a loose rock and it skidded out from under my foot.

"What was that?" he asked.

There was an exchange of muffled voices and then a double pair of footsteps moved in my direction. *They were coming after me!* I spun around and sped down the bordered path between high hedges but in my haste and fright, my sense of direction was faulty. Instead of finding my way out of the maze

of evergreen hedges, I had trapped myself
in a dead end. There was no way to
run—except right back into their arms. Fear
raced through me. I had heard too much.
My suspicions had been confirmed. Raoul
had arranged the burglary and was now
meeting with Monsieur Travois to dispose
of the loot. I wondered where he had hidden
it all. *The hunting lodge?* The answer came
from out of nowhere.

I cursed myself for the fool I was. I fell to
the ground and rolled as far back under the
bushes as I could manage. Luckily I had
worn my dark brown jacket and skirt. The
color would not betray me. I held my breath
and scrunched my eyes tightly as I had done
as a child to keep myself hidden from
searching eyes.

Footsteps crunched on the path, they
came closer and paused for a moment. Had
they seen me? I waited for rough hands to
reach down and drag me out. Nothing. A
moment of agonizing silence. Then the footsteps retreated. I heard a muffled conversation just on the other side of hedge where I
lay frozen. Then they moved away as if
searching other nearby paths. Finally all
the noise faded away.

Had they gone? Or were they waiting for
me to emerge? What would they do to me?
In any other situation, I would have

depended upon Travois's past affection for me to keep me from harm but I knew that such a hope was childish. As for Raoul, I didn't know his true feelings for me—I never had. To think that I would be able to deflect him from any course he had taken was even more foolish than to show myself.

I lay there trying to sort out what I must do. I couldn't be certain that the two men had not glimpsed my flying skirts as I evaded them in the maze. My head and shoulders could have been seen above the hedge. They might be waiting for me to come back in the house. No, I could not return to the chateau. I reasoned that Yvonne must have found out what was going on. Perhaps she had discovered the stolen cache in the hunting lodge or barn and now she lay dying from the same hands that would deal with me if they found me.

Where could I go? The village was within walking distance. Tears crept out from under my closed lids and I felt such desolation that I couldn't force myself to move from my hiding place. Heartache was like a paralyzing disease. I don't know how long I cowered there. My emotional upheaval blotted out any sense of time. Finally, my stiff body demanded release from its hunched position.

As quietly as I could, I eased to my feet. I

was afraid to stand upright for fear that
one of the men might be watching for such
a clue as to my whereabouts. With furtive,
cautious steps, I moved forward out of the
boxed square made by the hedges. I was
completely disoriented and chanced a quick
look over the hedge to see with alarm that I
was heading back toward the chateau
which looked like a gray, waiting beast in
the moonlight.

I reversed my direction. The outbuildings
were nearby and I heard the sound of a
horse's hooves. Was it Raoul? The
horseman was heading away from the
chateau. Maybe he was going to the hunting
lodge to remove the evidence. That meant
that Maurice Travois was the one still
there, probably waiting for me to reappear.

I knew I could outrun him if he saw me
and my spirits rose. Like a brown shadow
playing upon the ground, I ran through the
gardens and skirted along the edge of trees
planted along the sides of the chateau.

I could see Maurice Travois's rented
carriage waiting at the front door. Every
moment I expected to hear my name
shouted and my flight brought to a sudden
halt but the fear only lent swiftness to my
flying feet.

The front gate was open as if waiting for
Monsieur Travois's departure. My breath

came in burning stabs as I lifted my skirts and ran away from the chateau in the direction of Chambleau.

My spirits rose as I left the chateau behind and I saw a narrow country road twisting ahead of me. I had escaped safely! I would find the inspector and tell him to search the hunting lodge for the stolen objects. I suddenly had a wonderful sense of victory—but it was short-lived. In my haste, my foot struck a rock, slipped out from under me, and down I went on my twisted ankle.

For a moment I sat in the middle of the road, writhing with the sharp pain. Then the sound of carriage wheels approaching from the direction of the chateau brought me limping to my feet.

Chapter Sixteen

In desperation, I hobbled to the edge of the
road and threw myself down in the uneven
long grass that bordered it. I lay as quietly
as I could only a few feet from where the
wheels of the carriage would rumble by. I
closed my eyes and waited, praying that my
prone body blended in with the grass and
uneven ground. I knew that in a few more
minutes, the bobbing lanterns on the
carriage would catch me in the radius of
their light and I did not know if I would

remain concealed as the carriage whipped
by or if a glance to the side of the road
would reveal me lying there as clearly as an
ornament on a Christmas tree.

I held my breath and it seemed an
eternity before the carriage reached me. I
cringed as flying horse's hooves seemed
close enough to kick me in the head. The
wheels spun pebbles and dust over me. I
glimpsed the black vehicle as it went by. It
was Maurice Travois's rented carriage, all
right. Apparently, he had given up the
search and was heading back to his
accommodations in town. Raoul had ridden
off in the direction of the hunting lodge and
Monsieur Travois had gone back to the
village. Perhaps they would double back on
their tracks when they found no sign of the
eavesdropper they had heard in the garden.
Did they know it was me?

I was furious with myself for my
clumsiness. Tears of pain and heartache
swelled up and I was filled with the urgency
that I must not let my pursuers find me
alone on the dark road. But where should I
go? To the village where I might run
directly into Travois or back to the chateau
where Raoul might have returned to wait
for me? Either direction presented danger.
Then I remembered that it was only a short
distance to the farmhouse that Dr. Duboise

had rented.

I found a crooked stick nearby to help ease the pressure on my swelling ankle as I hobbled and winced and moved down the shadowy road at a snail's pace. I knew that the doctor had been at the chateau earlier examining Yvonne but he was surely home by now. I prayed that all this painful, laborious walking would not be for naught.

My nerves were so raw-edged that when a night owl came screeching out of one of the trees, I nearly sank to my knees in paralyzing fright. Overhead a grid of branches allowed only slivers of moonlight to fall upon the ground and its ever-changing, flickering pattern seemed alive and threatening. In my emotional state, I sensed danger on every side. Even the night silence broken only by my shuffling steps was ominous and like a loud scraper upon my nerves. My breath was coming in short gasps and my heart was racing madly as I reached the lane leading to the farmhouse where Dr. Duboise was staying.

The house was further from the road than I remembered the day I glimpsed it from the orchard when the doctor had chatted with me and the children. As I stumbled toward it, I could only see the silhouette of the cottage's tiled roof against the black-purple sky. Then, finally, while I was still some distance from the house, a reassuring light in the lower window gave me new energy. The pain in my ankle seemed less as I hobbled up a flagged path and gave a frantic pound on the door knocker.

"Dr. Duboise?" My voice rose in near panic as I called his name. "Dr. Duboise?" I knocked again.

I heard steps and the thick door swung open. I thought his full face and blue eyes the most beautiful sight I had ever seen. For a moment, I couldn't speak and tears escaped down the curve of my cheek.

"*Mon Dieu!* What is it, Mademoiselle? What has happened? Has Madame de Lamareau—?"

I shook my head and limped through the open door.

"You have hurt your ankle."

I nodded again. All the things I needed to tell him were lodged in my throat. Instead of talking, I started to cry.

He quickly took charge, helping me across the hall into a warm, homey room where a discarded book and pipe told me he had been sitting in a large chair by the fire. He led me to it and I fell back gratefully into the soft seat still warm from his body. For a moment I closed my eyes against the fullness there and took several deep breaths into my lungs. I must not give way now. I blinked back my tears, firmed my chin, and bit my lip as I endeavored to get control of myself.

Dr. Duboise knelt down, slipped my shoe off and his gentle hands probed my injured foot. I winced at his touch and he murmured reassurances.

"Nothing broken. Just a twist. Really, Mademoiselle, you must not collect more injuries to keep me here," he teased. "I am flattered but even a beautiful lady like yourself cannot tempt me to stay here forever."

His merry blue eyes and jiggling double chins settled my rising hysteria. I managed a weak grin. The comfortable room and his protective, bedside manner were the things I needed to get my emotions under control.

"That's better. Now just sit there while I get a wrapping for your ankle. And some tea. The best medicine in the world."

"Dr. Duboise . . . something has happened," I said, leaning forward and looking up at him with the anxiety I felt churning inside. "I must tell you—"

"In a moment. First the bandage and cup of tea. I insist. Doctor's orders." He bustled out and I heard distinct sounds as if he were putting a kettle on to boil. I leaned back in the chair, closed my eyes and tried

to organize the things that must be said.
There were homey smells in the house that
soothed me as I sat there; the smell of sweet
pipe tobacco, homemade bread and scents
from garden flowers in wide-necked vases.
Some sanity seemed to return to my chaotic
world and my breathing and heartbeat
began to return to normal.

In a few moments he was back with a
bandage which he deftly wound around my
ankle. "That will hold it firm. And now the
tea."

Like a little, stout woman entertaining
company, he came back with a tray and set
it on a small table near me. The teapot was
of solid earthenware and so were the heavy
mugs. Nothing fancy, but the spicy tea had
a hint of oranges in it and I gratefully let
the hot liquid bring some warmth back into
my body. I realized then that I was stone-
cold, like a statue, and the hot cup in my
hand almost seared my skin. I kept my eyes
on the cup as I sipped it, only paying
marginal attention to the doctor's chatter
about the merits of herbal teas. I refused
thick slices of bread and butter which he
tried to force on me.

"My stomach is . . . queasy," I said. Had it
been only a few hours ago that I had sat at a
dinner table enjoying a lovely meal with
Raoul and Maurice Travois? It seemed

another lifetime that I had laughed and
chatted with them. How cleverly they had
fooled me! Travois had come to see Raoul—
not me. Between the time I had seen
Travois yesterday and this evening, he had
found out that Monsieur de Lamareau was
the one he should be dealing with. I
remembered that I had been the one to tell
Raoul that the dealer was in the village. He
must have contacted him at once and
invited him to the chateau to talk over
business. The remarks I had overheard
were evidence that some bargaining was
taking place over the stolen items.

I set down my cup. I had to tell Dr.
Duboise what had happened before Raoul
could figure out that I would turn to the
doctor for help. He knew how much I liked
Dr. Duboise. Once my absence was noted,
Raoul would deduce that I had been the one
in the garden and it wouldn't be long before
it occurred to him that I might have run
here.

The doctor sighed as he sat in a
companion chair facing me. The furniture
in the room was of the comfortable, unpre-
tentious variety, nothing too fancy and it
showed signs of wear. Dr. Duboise's ample
figure seemed in harmony with the setting
as he put his feet up on a lumpy footstool
and settled his hands comfortably on his fat

stomach. "All right, my dear. I think it's best you tell me what is causing the anxiety mirrored on your face. Perhaps I can help but I warn you I am no doctor for affairs of the heart."

I blinked. Had my infatuation with Raoul been as obvious as that? I felt myself flushing with embarrassment. Then I took a deep breath. I knew that pride had no place in the charges that I must level against Raoul de Lamareau. "Something has happened . . . I overheard a conversation . . . in the garden . . . which confirms my suspicion that Monsieur de Lamareau is responsible for the chateau theft . . . and that my former protector, Maurice Travois, is about to receive them."

Dr. Duboise listened to my disjointed speech with his usual placid expression. I thought he was smothering a smile at my dramatics. "My goodness, this is a serious matter, after all."

"It is!" I flared. "You must believe me, Dr. Duboise. Raoul de Lamareau is likely to come here after me any moment. I think he rode off toward the hunting lodge . . . probably to move the stolen objects . . . I think Yvonne discovered them . . . and that's why she met with an 'accident.'"

"Come, my dear. I fear you have let your imagination have a long rein. Let's stick to

facts and not suppositions, Mademoiselle.
I'm afraid you have let your suspicions
tumble wildly in every direction." He
seemed to be humoring me as he coaxed.
"Now tell me exactly what happened in the
garden."

I described how I had seen Raoul leave
the house and my efforts to overtake him. I
repeated Monsieur Travois's words and
told him how I had accidentally made a
noise which sent the two men hunting for
me. "I hid under the hedge until they were
gone. I heard a horse leaving the stables . . .
then I ran away from the chateau. I was
going to go to the village to find the
inspector but I turned my ankle . . . and
came here."

"And a good thing you did. This is not
something a young girl should handle
alone." He seemed to be weighing my
words. Was he trying to decide if I was just
a foolish young girl in love with a well-
respected gentleman like Raoul de
Lamareau? He could relegate my
allegations to the status of a lovesick fool
who was seeking revenge for some slight or
rejection.

"It's true . . . every bit of it. You must
believe me!"

"Now, now. No need to get upset,
Mademoiselle. We should talk this thing

through and see what must be done." His
forehead wrinkled thoughtfully. "I heard
about the robbery, of course. And you think
Monsieur Travois is here to receive the
stolen items . . . from Raoul de Lamareau."

I nodded. "I met Maurice Travois in the
village. My mother and I lived with him
when I was a child." I told Duboise about
accompanying Travois on trips and the
interest in art and antiques which he had
stimulated in me. "Inspector Davail was
ready to use that knowledge against me."

"You?" The doctor looked as if he were
going to burst into full laughter. "My dear,
you really must be joking. You, a thief?"

I nodded, irritated by his amused
dismissal of my statement. My tone was
rather strident as I said, "The inspector
accused me of having accomplices who
arranged for my presence in the chateau so
I could view Jacques de Lamareau's private
collection." It was a relief to spill it all out.
"He found a list left by the robbers. A kind
of shopping list, written on the same paper
which I had used for some letters. The
pieces matched. I know now that Raoul
must have taken it from my room." My lips
trembled. "And he made me lie about being
in my room the night of the burglary."

"And you weren't there?" asked Dr.
Duboise in surprise. I could tell he was

wondering whose bed I had shared. It seemed to me those benign eyes were sharp enough to detect the night of passion I had shared with the master of the house.

"I stayed with André, the six-year-old. He was upset because he didn't know where his mother had gone. Raoul had taken her to the hunting lodge because she was drunk and verbally abusive." I didn't tell him that Yvonne had tried to kill Raoul. Even now, I couldn't think rationally about the lies he had told me, the way he had elicited my sympathy—and then betrayed me.

"I don't understand why you think Monsieur de Lamareau would harm his sister-in-law."

"I think she found out he was responsible for the theft. Maybe she came across the stolen things at the hunting lodge. He had been keeping her there—because she drinks so heavily."

He nodded. "Yes, a victim of drink. I suspected as much. A strong odor of whiskey was on her breath and I fear that her intake of alcohol is partially responsible for the deep coma. When I examined her a few hours ago, I found her pulse much weaker. If she doesn't rally soon—" He shook his head. "Such a pity. I cannot believe that Monsieur de Lamareau is responsible."

"Did you know that her husband,
Jacques, was murdered?"

"Are you serious? I haven't been here
long enough to pick up on all the
happenings in the area. Murdered? How
was he killed?" He peered at me through
his square spectacles.

"Shot. The police decided it must have
been a poacher but Yvonne is still accusing
Raoul of killing her husband. She has even
convinced her daughter of it. Annette is
terrified that the whole family is in
danger."

"Can Madame be telling the truth?" The
doctor seemed horrified by such a
supposition.

"I don't know what to think. After what
has happened—" My voice trailed off. How
could I put aside the tenderness I had felt
in Raoul's arms and judge him dispassionately? My own feelings were at war,
lashing me like a fagot of nettles.

"And the police? They are satisfied that
Monsieur de Lamareau is not guilty of
killing his brother?"

"I don't know. Inspector Davail may be
waiting for more evidence to show up.
Maybe there was an earlier burglary
attempt by Raoul and Jacques discovered
it. He might have been killed to hush it up."
I put my hands up to my head. "I don't

know, I can't think any more." Then I brought them down quickly. "What are we going to do? Maurice Travois will remove the evidence from here and there will be no proof. And if they are hunting for me—?"

As if my words were a signal, the sound of a horse galloping toward the house made me gasp.

"Steady . . . steady," the doctor said, attempting to soothe me as he stood up.

"Raoul! Maybe he's come! What shall I do?"

"I will take care of Monsieur de Lamareau," he said calmly. "We must have more time to decide what would be best under the circumstances. For the moment, I will hide you, Mademoiselle."

"Thank you . . . thank you."

The doctor went quickly to a door leading into the kitchen. "Philippe! Come! You must carry Mademoiselle upstairs." Then he turned to me. "My brother. He will take care of you while I turn away my visitor. You're not to worry . . . not to worry." His smile was reassuring. "Leave everything in my hands." Then he told a round-shouldered, lean, sinewy man who entered from the kitchen to carry me upstairs to the back bedroom.

His brother was the antithesis of Dr. Duboise. Looking like a laborer who had never read a book, he swept me up in his thick arms with the indifference of a paid servant. He didn't look at my face as he carried me upstairs and into a back bedroom where he set me down on a soft, feather bed. He must have been in his forties, like Dr. Duboise, I thought, but his eyes were not soft and merry. They were hard like faded blue marbles. I could not help but draw back from his touch. Wordlessly, he turned and , with steps as soft as a cat's, disappeared down some back stairs that must have led directly to the kitchen below.

I strained to hear sounds from the front hall. I heard the door open and Raoul's muffled voice. I had been right. He had come after me. My whole body seemed to suddenly tremble. I couldn't hear what they were saying. The distance was too great. Pressing my fist against my mouth, I sobbed, "Raoul . . . Raoul." Such was my weakness that even now I longed to rush into his arms and recapture the wondrous magic that shut out the world and all its ugliness.

Whatever the doctor had said must have satisfied him for I heard the door shut and the sound of horse's hooves fading away from the house. He had gone. I was safe. He would not know that I had found sanctuary here and that Dr. Duboise would be the one to bring the law down upon him. I needed to do nothing more. This knowledge was of little comfort. My victory over him was a hollow thing—empty, devoid of everything except a searing heartache.

I sat there on the bed, my eyes dry and all emotion drained away as if my body were blessedly detached from the stark reality that surrounded me. My mind refused to acknowledge the guilt I felt for destroying the man I loved. I couldn't feel anything at the moment. Tears had dried on my cheeks. I felt an insidious chill to the marrow of my bones.

When the doctor bustled into the room, he took one look at my ashen face and said quickly, "It is all right, my dear. He has gone. You can relax now. There is no reason for him to believe I lied. No one will know you are here until we are ready."

"You must send your brother for Inspector Davail."

"There is no need to be hasty, Mademoiselle. You have put yourself in my hands. You will do what I say." His voice was suddenly without his usual warmth. An indefinable emotion had crept into it. A kind of hardness that brought my head up.

I stared at his face and for a moment in my confused state, I thought his eyes were his brother's. Then I blinked and saw that I was mistaken. They still had their soft, reassuring glint. Once again I was letting my imagination run away with me. My nerves had been stretched tightly for too long. I let my shoulders slump and gave in to bone-deep fatigue.

"You must rest now," he said. "A good night's sleep and you will be able to look at things a lot more clearly."

"Yes," I agreed wearily. I needed time to think. I couldn't understand why I suddenly felt uneasy. Nothing had changed and yet intuitively, I sensed that something important had escaped my notice and was tugging at me for recognition.

The doctor slipped off my other shoe and then reached for the fastening on my long jacket.

"No." I stopped his hand.

He gave an amused chuckle. "Please, Mademoiselle, do not concern yourself. I am a doctor. I want to help you get comfortable. You do not want to sleep in your dress, *n'est-ce pas*?"

"I can't sleep here," I heard myself say as if some inner voice was suddenly in command.

"But, of course, you can. What better place? You do not want to go back to the chateau, *n'est-ce pas*?" He raised a questioning eyebrow.

He was right. I could not go back there. Not until everything was settled. Once the truth had been given to Inspector Davail, I would be free to go but until then . . .

Dr. Duboise nodded as if reading my thoughts. "It is too late to do anything tonight. In the morning, we will talk again, Now, you must sleep."

"I'll never be able to sleep."

He smiled indulgently. "But, of course, you will. Please undress and get into bed. I will return when you are discreetly covered with blankets up to your neck," he teased as if amused by my modesty.

I nodded and he bounced out of the room. I stared after him, wondering why I could not rid myself of growing uneasiness. I undressed and slipped under the covers, wearing only my chemise and drawers. I was confused. Something was not right. I had thought that once I told Dr. Duboise what had happened, he would want to notify the police at once. Instead, he seemed to be in no hurry to pass on the information that I had given him. *He didn't believe me.* That was it! The truth was like a blow to the stomach. He was humoring me. Like the inspector, he thought that I was lying, making up stories for some nefarious reason of my own. *Maybe he thought I was*

guilty. He had laughed when I told him that
the inspector was about to arrest me for
the theft but maybe my distraught
condition had made him consider the
charges valid. He was not going to put
himself in an embarrassing position by
relating anything to the police until he had
made up his mind about me. To accuse
Raoul de Lamareau of burglarizing his own
home was a grave act and he wasn't going
to make such a serious charge based solely
on the evidence of a rather hysterical young
woman.

"It's true," I lashed out as he came back
into the room with his medical bag. "I am
not making all of this up."

He patted my hand. "I'm sure you're not,
Mademoiselle, but we must move slowly.
These are dangerous waters. A great deal is
at risk here. It is good you came to me. I
will handle everything. Now you must
sleep—" He took a bottle of brown
medicine. I recognized the smell as he
opened the lid.

"No, I don't want laudanum," I protested.

"You must take it. Open your mouth. I do
not want to call my brother to force you but
I will if I must." There was nothing of his
usual gentleness in the warning. I knew he
meant what he said. Even though crinkles
remained around his eyes, they were not

smiling. I swallowed the liquid before I could summon the strength to question him.

"I . . . I don't understand—" I said aloud, with a new surge of apprehension.

"Understand what, Mademoiselle? You came here for help and I am happy to be of service. You have done the right thing under the circumstances. Now I must make certain that *I* do the right thing." He was smiling again but for some reason it seemed false, like a mask he put on and took off at will.

"You have to believe me." I knew my voice was rising hysterically.

"Oh, I believe you."

"Then—why? Why won't you go to the police? Now? Tonight?"

"Because, my dear Alysha, I am not ready to have the police snooping about. It is most fortunate that you came here with your suspicions, *n'est-ce pas?*" He gave a cheery laugh but it chilled my blood. "Most fortunate."

My God! It couldn't be.

Could it?

Chapter Seventeen

I had little time to handle the sudden roaring of new dangers but I knew with sweeping awareness that Dr. Duboise was not what he seemed. It was too late to rectify my horrible mistake. I had run right into his clutches as surely as a frantic insect flies into a spider's net. I cursed myself for the fool I had been. I had been so desperate for friendship that I had never looked behind his opportune presence at the time of the accident. I had never asked

Leona Karr

myself about his personal life. I had taken
everything he had told me at face value. He
had said he was vacationing in the area
with his brother and I had accepted the
statement without question. I had limited
my suspicions to those who lived at the
chateau and the Montaignes. *But it was Dr.
Duboise who had come and gone freely the
days preceding the burglary.*

As the laudanum took effect, I struggled
against an overwhelming weakness that
swept through my limbs, making them feel
detached, light, seeming to float away from
the rest of my body. My fuzzy thoughts
reeled inside my head like a swarm of
locusts. For the first time, as my vision
blurred, I looked up and saw beyond Dr.
Duboise's outwardly smiling, good-natured
exterior. I knew with sickening certainty
that behind those benign blue eyes was a
calculating man who was unscrupulous
and cunning. In appearance his hard,
dispassionate brother was the epitome of
what lay beneath Dr. Duboise's jovial,
chubby figure. I knew I must get away but
the strong dose of medicine which the
doctor had given me sapped my will. His
pudgy face swirled in my blurred vision. I
tried to move my thick lips to scream at
him, but nothing came out. I thought I
heard him laugh as he tucked the covers

around me in a paternal fashion. Then the weight of my eyelids closed my eyes and I was sucked away into a whirling gray nothingness.

When my eyes fluttered open again, I could not at first remember where I was. As I lay there, the sloped ceiling with its dark rafters was foreign to me. The homey odor of baked bread seemed unfamiliar for I had become used to the smell of dust and leather of the chateau bedroom. I turned with a jerk and the feather mattress on which I lay sank in an unfamiliar way under my body. Bright light flowed through a small window under the eaves and the sharp stabs of sunlight hurt my eyes. I groaned as I closed them against an ache that revolved like a grinder's wheel in my heavy head. My tongue was thick and dry and a bitter taste came up from my throat with a wave of nausea. I had trouble raising my hand to press against my forehead. What had happened? I couldn't think clearly. Where was I? Why was a sense of panic lodged like a heavy stone in my weighted chest?

"Ah, our pretty Mademoiselle is waking up. And how are we feeling today?"

The familiar voice was a reassuring sound. My eyes fluttered open again and I saw my doctor's smiling face bending near me. I was relaxed as I felt his touch upon me. His merry blue eyes peered at me through his square glasses and then I saw he was about to spoon more liquid out of a brown bottle.

"No," I protested in a guttural whisper. A twist of panic turned to raw terror. Although my memory was still lost in gray foggy mists, I reacted instinctively. I tried to push him away but the muscles in my arms were flaccid and without strength. I managed to turn my head away but that was all. "No—" I protested again but he turned my head back with a firm hand.

"*Oui.* It is not time yet for you to be up and about, Mademoiselle. You need more rest." His kind, patronizing tone was accompanied by a full smile that was no longer reassuring—but terrifying.

My befuddled brain would not function properly but I knew that I must not allow myself to be drugged again. "No . . . No!" This time the guttural whisper rose into an hysterical protest.

"Mademoiselle. Calm yourself."

"It was you . . . you arranged the robbery," I gasped.

He only smiled.

"And the accident . . . you . . . you—" My thick tongue rolled in my mouth.

He nodded. "I had to have access to the house to decide what items would be taken and to arrange for a door to be left unlatched. I am sorry, Mademoiselle, that you turned out to be my patient. We did not know you would be on the train with the young girl. We learned through a servant at the chateau that she was expected home that afternoon. Since she escaped the over-turned carriage unscathed it was fortunate for us that your injuries required medical attention."

"You used me." There was so much I didn't understand but the pieces were beginning to shape inside my befuddled head.

"There are some things that can't be helped. You must take your medicine like a good girl—" He leaned over me.

Once more I raised my arms in a feeble effort at defense and tried to clamp my mouth shut as tightly as I could. He deftly pushed my weak arms out of his way and grabbed my nose in a firm pinch, shutting off my air. When I opened my mouth to gasp a breath, he poured in the liquid. I sputtered and gasped but my attempts to spit it out were to no avail. The treacherous laudanum slipped down my throat. I felt hot tears streaming down my cheeks.

With a terrifying sense of helplessness, I

tried to raise my head from the pillow,
willing my limbs to move, but my strongest
effort was useless. In less than a minute the
bed beneath me tipped in a dizzy fashion. My
eyes widened and dark rafters in the ceiling
began to gyrate, crossing and making weird
patterns as they moved in my drugged
vision. Suddenly the ceiling came down
upon me, the walls came in, my breath was
shut off and screams caught in my throat.
There was no escape as a maddening
vertigo finally drew me away from tortured
hallucinations—and I slipped away once
more into a drugged state.

When I fought my way back to
consciousness the second time, it was dark
again. Some intuitive acuity kept me lying
still, without any movement to alert anyone
to the fact that I was coming out of the thick
clouds of sedation. I allowed my brain to
start functioning as something apart from
the drugged, disjointed body that en-
compassed it. At first, random images
floated about like dry leaves tossed in the
air, whirling in wild disarray and then
coming to rest in bewildering patterns that
demanded new interpretations. Somewhere
I had gone wrong. My mind wrestled with
the events that had brought me to this
drugged state in Dr. Duboise's farmhouse.

I struggled with the memory of why I was here, a drugged prisoner, helpless and completely at his mercy. I had seen Raoul leave the chateau, I was certain of that. My attempts to catch up with him in the garden had failed. Why? It seemed obvious now that he had taken a different direction than the one I had taken when he disappeared from my view. When I heard voices, I had assumed that he was the one meeting with Maurice Travois but it must have been Dr. Duboise, my befuddled brain reasoned. Yes, it must have happened that way. As I crouched in the shadows and recognized Travois's voice talking to someone, I had not heard the responding voice. When I had betrayed my presence, only hushed whispering followed. When I lay hiding under the hedge, I had not seen the two men who searched the maze for me. *I had just assumed it was Raoul and Maurice Travois.*

I blinked back warm tears as I realized my fatal mistake. Raoul must have gone straight to the barn to saddle his horse, falsely assuming that Maurice had left in his rented carriage, when, in fact, Maurice had lingered to meet someone in the garden. It must have been Raoul I heard ride off on his horse when I huddled under the hedge.

It had been Dr. Duboise in the garden

with Maurice Travois. I knew the doctor had been at the chateau earlier, visiting Yvonne. Travois could have arranged to meet him there and the visit to the chateau had been contrived; his real purpose had not been to see me but to confer with Dr. Duboise in a setting which would not link the two of them. As I accepted this scenario as a strong possibility, hope began to flicker in my breast. *Raoul was innocent of my vile accusations*. He could have taken a ride, come back to the chateau and found me gone. Since he knew my affection for Dr. Duboise, he had promptly come looking for me here—and been deftly turned away. "Oh, Raoul, darling." My stupidity overcame me. My willfulness and distrust had plunged me into a quicksand of treachery and danger.

I could not lie there like a senseless beast waiting for the slaughter. Slowly I raised my eyelids a narrow slant. I couldn't see anything for a moment. Darkness filled the room. It was night. How long had I slept? Dr. Duboise could have given me dose upon dose of laudanum to keep me drugged while he arranged affairs to his advantage. I still could not believe he had fooled me so completely. The carriage accident had been arranged. He had admitted it. He had been at the station and must have given something to the horse while the carriage driver was collecting our luggage and Raoul was helping us down from the train. The doctor had provided his own accident so he would be on hand to offer his help. It was Annette he had expected to treat in order to gain admittance into the house. The fact that it was I who was injured turned out to be an added bonus when Raoul placed me in the deserted wing. On his daily visits he had access to the stationery in my room, the crowded gallery across the hall and he was also able to leave a window or door unlatched for easy entry. He had given me medicine to make me sleep heavily so there would be no danger of my overhearing the burglary taking place across the hall. No wonder he had been startled when I told him I had not been in my room that night.

I had been such a fool. My desperate need for someone to care about me had led me to accept Duboise's outward congeniality at face value. I had misplaced my trust completely. Like a frightened animal, I had run straight into the hunter's snare. But it was not too late. Strength flowed back into my resilient body as I lay there in the darkness and realized that my life was in deep peril. At the right time, the doctor would make certain that I did not live to tell about my drugged imprisonment. I was sure that he was keeping me alive for some nefarious reason which would work to his advantage, otherwise he would have already disposed of me. I must not lie here and placidly accept his diabolical scheming.

All my senses strained to ascertain if anyone were sitting in the darkened room waiting for me to stir. My slanted eyes opened wider as no hint of breathing or movement touched my ears and nostrils. Then I heard voices and loud noises floating up through my window from the yard below.

At first I thought I would faint dead away when I tried to get to a sitting position. The bed rocked under me and my head floated away from my body. Only an act of will kept me sitting there until the dizziness began to lessen. Very slowly I eased to my feet and, like someone reeling from drink, I stood up unsteadily. My rubbery limbs threatened to bend and drop me to the floor. Terror fueled my body with abnormal strength and I staggered over to the window. Either because my ankle had healed itself or enough laudanum remained in my body to blot out the pain, I could limp on it without sharp pain.

Weak and dizzy, I leaned up against the

window frame and I peered out the small dormer window. I was looking down on the back of the house and a small clearing between it and the barn. Just below, in a lantern's yellow glow, someone on horseback came into the radius of light. Dr. Duboise's brother! I recognized his rangy build as he began to unsaddle the horse. He was talking to someone just out of my vision. Then the figure moved forward and I saw Dr. Duboise. The doctor gestured with his hands as if giving his brother some kind of direction. I wondered where the brother had been. To the village? To dig a grave? I knew with frightening certainty that whatever the errand had been, it had to do with me.

As the brother led the horse into the barn, the doctor took the lantern and I heard a door close below my room, perhaps the kitchen. Almost immediately footsteps sounded on the back stairs.

In a drunken stagger, I lurched back to the bed and had just managed to get under the covers as he came into the room. I tried to feign sleep but unfortunately my breathing was coming in gasps as my chest rose and fell rapidly.

"Ah, our patient is awake," he said with infuriating insight.

I knew that it would do no good to feign

sleep. He was too perceptive to be fooled. I opened my eyes as he set a lantern near the bed. My mind whirled frantically. I must not allow myself to be drugged again.

As if he read the determination in my clenched jaw and rounded eyes, he smiled benevolently at me. "Relax, Mademoiselle." And then he drew a small pistol from his jacket pocket. "I would prefer not to shoot you while you are fully conscious but—" He shrugged. "I suppose in the long run it won't make any difference . . . to me."

"You . . . you wouldn't shoot me."

"Ah, Mademoiselle is so young . . . and foolish." He shook his head sadly. "Of course, I would shoot you. I have not pursued a passion for beautiful things without making some sacrifices along the way. You see, I also have a dedication for collecting rare and expensive possessions. Just like Jacques de Lamareau. I watched him for a good many years buy objects that I wanted. He kept them all for himself. I, however, am willing to share some of my treasures with others. For a price, of course," he said as if wanting me to know that he was a good businessman as well as a connoisseur of beautiful things.

"Let me go, and I won't say anything. You can have the things you stole. Please . . . please . . . just let me go."

His double chin bounced as he shook his head regretfully. "I couldn't chance it, Mademoiselle." His smile was sad. "I would have preferred to have the young girl injured in the accident. But since it was you, it is a pity that you were unable to go to Paris after the burglary as you had planned. I had no idea that the foolish inspector would center his suspicions upon you. Now, there is no help for it. I must make certain you do not give my little operation away. My brother and I have been very successful for several years. He would not like it if I gave in to any soft feelings. Now, you must take some more of your medicine. It will be easier for you that way."

"How can you do this? You are a doctor!"

"Ah, yes, a doctor. My profession is a blind spot in everyone's eyes. That's what makes everything so easy." He grinned in satisfaction. "People like me."

He was congenial, pleasant, and even smiled as he leveled his pistol at me. My stomach turned over in revulsion. His good-natured madness was terrifying and paralyzing. His pleasant manner was so effective that it was difficult to recognize the treachery that lay within.

"Now, my dear, will it be the gun or a nice dose of peaceful sleep?" He waited for my answer politely as if he were waiting for my choice of tea or cake.

"Sleep," I said hoarsely. It was my only chance. A bullet would determine my fate in a split second.

"Bon!" he said as if proud of my choice. With the gun within his reach on the table, he spooned an even larger dose of laudanum into my mouth. I tried to hold it there without swallowing, but he quickly gave my throat a quick jab and as I gasped, the drug passed down my throat.

Once again he tucked the covers around me and stood up. "Sleep well. It will not be much longer, Mademoiselle. Then it will be all over for you." As if this were a reassuring benediction, he left the room, closing the door behind him and I heard his footsteps fading away. He must have gone to his bedroom at the front of the house.

Instantly, I was out of bed, throwing myself down on the floor and reaching under the bed. "Thank God," I breathed as I brought out a chamber pot which habitually lurked under most beds. Outdoor facilities were not the rule for common folk who lived in farmhouses.

I leaned over the pot. Then I rammed a finger down my throat and forced myself to gag. In the next instant my queasy stomach responded and I began to retch. In deep heaves, I brought up the medicine and bitter stomach bile. The meal I had eaten with Raoul and Maurice Travois was long gone. Dizzy, I clutched the rounded edges of the pot and prayed that the closed door would shut out the sounds of my gagging.

At last I was spent. I feared that some of the medication might have been absorbed or remained in my stomach but as the moments passed, my head became clearer. I took deep breaths to settle my racing heartbeat.

My body stiffened. I froze and held my breath. The back door banged shut and I heard heavy steps on the stairs. The brother.

I heard an interchange of muffled voices in the hall. I caught bits and pieces. "Get some sleep . . . wake you about two o'clock . . . safe to move her then."

The footsteps receded to the front of the house. I sat quietly, without moving. *Safe to move her then.* Like a death knell, the words reverberated in my head. I knew I had to get away before they came after me. But could I escape from the house without bringing my captors down upon me?

I had to wait until I was certain they slept. Even though rising panic screamed at me to rush out of the room and down the stairs, I knew such haste would be folly. My only hope lay in a quiet, stealthy exit from my room while they slept.

I eased to my feet and reached for my clothes which Dr. Duboise had tossed over a nearby chair. My fingers trembled at the fastenings. I ignored the one shoe that lay beside the bed. The other was downstairs where the doctor had removed it upon my arrival. It didn't matter. I would go barefooted. The bandage that the doctor had wrapped around my ankle would not take either my white loomed hose or a shoe, anyway.

Now that I had moved about on my ankle, it began to throb in persistent warning that I should not be putting my weight on it. How could I possibly walk for any distance on it? The answer was obvious. I couldn't. If I were to make good my escape, it would not be on my own two legs. I had watched the brother unsaddle a horse and lead it into the barn. If I could make it that far undetected, I was confident that I could put a halter on it and ride bareback away from the farmhouse. But first, I would have to get to the barn.

I cursed the creaking boards in my room as I finished dressing and sat on the edge of the bed. I knew that settling boards would sound much louder on the stairs. Since I had been able to hear footsteps coming and going so clearly, I feared that even my light steps might alert my captors to my intended escape. There was nothing I could do but pray that both of them would be sleeping too deeply to hear my furtive movements.

I watched shadows outside my window as large trees moved like dark dancers in rhythm with the night winds. Now that I knew that I had misjudged Raoul, I could think about him with a sense of joy and relief. I still did not understand much of his behavior but for the first time I knew that I trusted him, totally and completely. I wondered what he was thinking about my disappearance. Maybe Dr. Duboise had put out the word that I had left for Paris. If so, Raoul would be hurt and angry and he might not be looking for me at all. I knew that Dr. Duboise would arrange to use my disappearance to his advantage. I did not know how he planned to dispose of my body. If I were not successful in escaping, Raoul might never know the truth. This realization brought more strength to my determination to get safely away from Dr. Duboise's murderous intent.

At last, I felt enough time had gone by for both partners to be asleep. If I were going to escape, it would have to be now. I stood up, wiping my perspiring hands on my skirt and wincing as I limped to the closed door. I eased it open a crack and listened.

Only the night sounds of wind against the house, settling beams and branches scraping against the stone exterior broke the hushed silence. No human sound of movement intruded upon the slumbering old house. It was now or never. The longer I waited, the less chance I would have to make it out of my room, down the back stairs, and out to the barn. I had no idea how soon Dr. Duboise would be up again nor what time of night it was.

As I eased out into the hall, my eyes tried to adjust to the shadowy darkness. My brief glimpses of the interior when I was carried up the stairs had been vague and I couldn't remember how much furniture there had been in the hall. I knew that I must not bump against anything as I moved cautiously forward. A window on a stair landing gave filtered light at the far end of the corridor but I wanted to use the back, kitchen stairs which I now knew led directly downstairs to the back door. There was no light at all as I poised at the top of the back stairs. Only a dark abyss beckoned me toward the narrow, twisting staircase. One false move and I would tumble headfirst to the bottom.

I held my breath and started down. Each

step was an eternity of torture for despite
the careful easing from one to the next, the
uncarpeted steps creaked. The dark tunnel
seemed to go on forever. I could see no light
at the bottom. A door must close off the
staircase from the kitchen, I reasoned. At
the bottom step, I reached out and touched
wood. I had been right. If I'd had a lantern, I
would have readily seen where the
doorknob might be, but in total darkness, I
could only feel and when my hand hit the
knob, it made a noise that seemed like an
explosion in the slumbering house.

Anxiety made me open the door with less
caution than I should have exercised and I
was thankful that it swung easily on its
hinges. I limped into a large kitchen which I
determined took up almost all of the back
of the house. I stood immobile for several
seconds until I got my bearings and could
distinguish chairs, table, workbench,
cupboards, and cooking stove. Then I made
for the back door. Very carefully I turned
the worn doorknob but the door did not
open. It was locked! My eyes fell to the
keyhole. Thank God, a skeleton key
protruded from the lock. Afraid to breathe,
I turned it carefully. With a soft click the
bolt pulled back.

In the next instant I was outside in a
small clearing between the house and the

barn, standing almost in the same spot where I had looked down upon the two brothers earlier. I hobbled toward the barn in a frantic gait as if the devil himself were after me. The main door of the barn was closed and even though I heaved against it with all my feeble weight, it would not budge. I was not going to be able to get in the barn that way. Exasperated, I stepped back and spied a small door which I assumed led to the tack room. It opened easily. Once inside, I blinked to see where I was and how I could get into the barn where I heard horses moving about in stalls.

My eyes began to adjust and the interior came into shadowy focus. Moonlight through a dirty window fell upon a long, narrow room. It was crowded, but not with saddles, halters nor grain. A pair of Louise XIV chairs were half-covered with sheets and several packing barrels and containers stood open. Light through a dirty window was strong enough to touch one of the open boxes. My trembling legs almost gave out on me. Nestled in a bed of cloth, the top of an amethyst vase caught the light and gleamed back at me.

In the next instant all thoughts of the discovery were swept from my mind. I swung around as a soft movement behind

me alerted me to someone else's presence. I
had only a glimpse of an impassive face as
Dr. Duboise's brother shot a fist out and the
blow nearly lifted my head from my
shoulders before I crumpled in a heap at
his feet.

Chapter Eighteen

I didn't lose consciousness from the harsh blow to my chin. My ears rang and my eyes seemed to float back in my head but I was aware of his rough hands upon me from the moment I hit the floor. I was like a rag doll when he jerked me to my feet and I wobbled without any strength in my legs. He swore an ugly oath and flung me back to the floor in obvious disgust. Rough hands bound my arms and legs and then tossed me in a corner amid the stolen furniture and packing containers like a chicken trussed up and ready for slaughter. Then he left me.

I could not believe I had failed so miserably. Creaking boards had given me away or my clumsy opening and closing of doors had alerted him to my escape. As I lay there, anger more than fear dominated my emotions, anger at myself for having failed and fury at the two men who were treating me so callously. I had never thought myself a violent person, but as my head throbbed from the vicious blow Dr. Duboise's brother had given me, I thought I could kill them both . . . and gladly.

"Shame, shame, Mademoiselle," chided Dr. Duboise a while later when he shone a lantern down upon me. He was fully dressed and I knew whatever plan he had designed for my demise was still going to be carried out. "It's unfortunate that you did not take the easy way out . . . sleep your way into sweet oblivion. You surprise me, Mademoiselle. That was very clever of you to vomit the medicine. I did not expect such resourcefulness or I would have locked the bedroom door. Now, you have brought an unpleasant experience upon yourself. It is unfortunate but I quickly lose patience with people who try to best me. Now you will have to face the gun while you are fully conscious."

I waited for his pudgy hand to draw a gun from his jacket pocket and level it at me and I could not contain my look of surprise when he didn't.

"Not here, Mademoiselle," he said, following the movement of my eyes. He gave a merry chuckle. "Your obsession with the hunting lodge gave me an idea, you see. If the police found your body and some object taken from the burglary in the barn at the lodge, they would come to the same conclusion that you did—Raoul de Lamareau arranged for the theft and stored the booty there. When they find you shot, they will assume that either there was a falling out among thieves and Raoul killed you—or that you discovered his hidden cache and he killed you. Either way, a nice tidy solution, *n'est-ce pas*?"

"I think it is as abominable as you are!"

He shook his head. "Such a fiery temperament. And very shrewd. Imagine you trying to trick me like that. Luckily my brother is a light sleeper. He knows every creak in this old house. It was folly of you to try and escape, Mademoiselle." He chuckled dangerously.

"What did you expect me to do? Meekly accept the evils of your twisted mind? You are mad . . . mad . . . mad! You pretend to be a doctor—"

"I am a doctor, Mademoiselle!" He drew himself up. "A very good doctor. For years I treated the most wealthy patients in Paris. I saw the way they lived—opulence, abundance, riches, and never turning their hand to one bit of work. I saved their lives— and for what? More gambling, whoring, and treating everyone else in the world as dirt under their feet. So, I decided I would relieve them of a few of their possessions. Not indiscriminately, of course, just select pieces which I fancied or thought someone else might desire. I disposed of them myself very carefully but this time I am going to let Monsieur Travois handle the things I don't want. He has foreign contacts which I don't have and it will be safer to have some of these things out of the country. His presence in the area was a fortunate happenstance. When I sent a message for him to meet with me at the chateau, he came most willingly. He's a shrewd businessman but so am I. We will come to terms agreeable to both of us. I have told him to return to Paris and I will turn the merchandise over to him when we reach Paris."

"But how will you get the things out of here? The police have been alerted to look for stolen items."

"I always plan ahead, Mademoiselle. That is one of the reasons for my unbelievable success. When I arrived here to rent this farmhouse, I brought padded furniture and many packing barrels and cartons. I will be taking them back with me—only not with the same contents. Instead of cheap earthenware dishes, delicate porcelain figures will be packed in the barrels and an antique chair will be padded to look like my old easy chair." He beamed. "Everything will look the same on the outside. The same men will handle them for me without question. You see I instructed my brother not to steal more than the items I had on the list. Greediness is folly. I'll keep what I want for my personal collection and give Monsieur Travois the rest to sell."

"And Monsieur Travois has agreed to all of this?"

"But, of course. I sent word to him last night by my brother informing him that our timetable has been moved up. He was saddened to learn that you were ready to run to the *genmarderie* with the information. He was hoping that it wasn't you who had overheard our conversation. Yes, he was disappointed, Mademoiselle. You should not have been intent on betraying him to the police—"

"But I was afraid. I thought it was Raoul

who was with him and I believed he had tried to kill Yvonne so—"

Dr. Duboise waved his hand as if the explanation bored him. "No matter. Now, I must decide which objet d'art to sacrifice. Such a shame. If only you hadn't come here to seek sanctuary, both of us could have been spared this unfortunate turn of events."

"It's your fault! Why did you offer to be my friend?" I lashed out at him.

He looked surprised. "Because I liked you."

"But only enough to kill me," I said sarcastically as sobs caught in my throat.

"I did not plan to kill you, Mademoiselle. You brought that on yourself," he said in a scolding tone. "You should not have been eavesdropping upon my conversation with Maurice Travois. All of this could have been avoided. It was very unwise of you to upset my plans this way."

I don't think I had ever hated him as much as I did then. With all the righteous judgment of a god, he had decided the blame was mine. He would kill me without any pangs of remorse or guilt. I knew it would be folly to appeal to him on any emotional level and my ability to talk my way out of most situations would not help me in this moment of life and death. I could not discern any weakness in his self-righteous attitude. Frantically I worked my hands which were bound behind me but the knot held firm. The harsh rope sawed into my flesh and I felt the warm trickling of blood easing down my fingers. My legs were tied tightly together at the ankles and even though I could squirm on the ground, such efforts only depleted my energy and failed to extricate me from my bonds.

In the soft light of a lantern, I watched him search among some packing cartons. He lifted out several stolen objects and then shook his head and put them back again. It was obvious that he could not bear to part with any of them. I watched him uncover an ebony statue of a Madonna and Child, about two feet high. I recognized it as the work of a seventh century sculptor and one of the missing Italian treasures. With a loving touch, he stroked the smooth lines of the statue as one would caress a child. Then he shook his head. "No, I cannot part with this one."

Sighing heavily, he put it back and then reached into the box containing the amethyst vases and drew out one of them. Once more his hands stroked its glazed smoothness, following the balanced curve of a thin neck down its rounded sides to the fullness of its decorated center. "Yes, I will have to part with one of these vases. The other I will keep and this one will undoubtedly be returned to its place on the fireplace mantel.''

I thought I saw a glint of moisture in his benign blue eyes. His expression turned my blood cold. No grieving parent ever lost a loved one with more raw desolation than showed on his face at that moment. I wanted to scream at him that the thing he held in his hands was only baked clay without flesh and nerves and the spark of life which he had dedicated himself to preserve. How could he agonize over the loss of an object when he was prepared to snuff out my life without an ounce of remorse? I did not know how to appeal to him because his behavior was beyond my understanding. I wanted to accuse him of being more concerned about the safety of a vase than the preservation of a human life. Such accusations withered on my lips for I knew they would be useless. For the first time, I felt utter and complete despair. My stubborn, belligerent nature seemed to fail me at that moment.

"And now, Mademoiselle, it is time to take a little ride. I will carefully wrap this beautiful vase in a saddlebag so it will not suffer from the ensuing events. We must keep it safe at all costs."

He would blow my head off but he would not allow a scratch to mar the porcelain vase. I wanted to laugh hysterically at the incongruity of his actions.

He disappeared through the small door and immediately I heard voices from the adjoining barn. The sounds of a horse being saddled warned me that I was about to be taken from the farmhouse to the hunting lodge. I struggled with my bonds again in frantic helplessness. If only I could get away. Fiery rings of pain circled my wrists as I jerked, pulled, and twisted. The ropes held firm.

I let my head fall forward in defeat. It was no use. There was no escape. I had lost my chance when Dr. Duboise's brother followed me out of the house.

Why had I allowed Dr. Duboise to send Raoul away when he came for me? What a fool I'd been and now that stubborn willfulness was going to cost me my life. There was no ray of hope that we might be seen on the way to the lodge. I knew no one was there now that Yvonne lay dying at the chateau. My logical mind told me it would be too much of a coincidence to expect Raoul to be roving about in exactly the right place to save me from the doctor's diabolical intent. *Raoul . . . Raoul.* He would never know for certain that I wasn't a part

of the conspiracy. He would think the worst
of me. Somehow this thought was as awful
as the fate that awaited me. If only we could
have set things right between us . . .

"Now, then, Mademoiselle. A gag over
your mouth, your body in a large mill sack,
and we will be on our way. We will circle
the chateau and approach the lodge from
the Montaigne side of the property.
Although I don't expect anyone to be about
at this late hour, I am not taking any
chances."

As he spoke his brother jerked me up into
a sitting position, fastened a wide strip of
cloth across my mouth and tied it firmly at
the back of my head. Now that I couldn't
talk, screams collected in my throat. I
thought I would choke from my own saliva
and my thickening tongue as the cloth filled
my mouth. Muscles in my throat contracted
and I feared I might vomit into my closed
mouth. But the worst was yet to come.

"Now the sack," said Dr. Duboise.

He watched as his brother hoisted me up
into a sitting position and pulled a large
woven sack over my head. It still smelled of
grain. My nostrils filled with the dust and
wheat particles left in the sack. Air evaded
me as I drew it in in dusty snorts. I writhed
as the sack was drawn tight at my ankles
and tied there. Then he threw me over his

shoulder like the weighted sack I was.

I wanted to scream, cry and kick—but I could do nothing. My head wobbled upside-down as he carried me out of the barn. The next instant I was slung over the haunches of a horse. It moved nervously with the unexpected weight and my head bobbed on one side of the animal while my feet dangled off the other side.

"I should be back in a couple of hours," said Dr. Duboise to his brother. "Finish packing these things. I want to be ready when the morning train pulls in. I've arranged for a dray wagon to load everything at seven o'clock. See that it's ready."

His brother grunted something in reply.

"Don't worry. I'll take care of her. It will go smoothly. No one will connect us with her or the stolen vase."

I felt him settle his fat buttocks in the saddle. With me firmly tied in place behind him, he kicked the horse into a trot. With each rise and fall of the animal's haunches, every bone in my body seemed destined to splinter and fall apart. Silent groans echoed in my ears. Every second was pure agony. My head bounced as blood rushed into it and each jolt pressed all the air out of my aching lungs. I wished then that I had taken the laudanum as Dr. Duboise had suggested for it would have been much easier if I had been unconscious and oblivious to what was happening.

I tried to fill my mind with forced activity to keep it off the agonizing discomfort of riding upside-down while the horse jolted me to pieces. Dr. Duboise had said we were going the long way around to the hunting lodge. I tried to anticipate what would happen once we got there. Would I have a chance for any kind of escape or would he shoot me while I lay bound hand and foot? My head thumped and the lack of breath brought increasing pain into my chest. My distress grew to a point that I was praying we would soon reach the lodge so I would not have to endure any more torture.

I knew when we had reached the deep copse of trees for sharp branches jabbed into the woven sack and brought new pain to my body. I could hear nothing but horse's hooves upon the deadfall that littered the bridle path. It was a soft rhythmic sound and I knew we must be approaching the lodge. The horse slowed to a walk and it was a blessed relief not to be bounced around as before. My body seemed more tolerant of the discomfort and I was grateful that I was still able to think and feel. It was an assurance that death had not yet overtaken me.

When the horse suddenly stopped, I knew we had reached the lodge. My wild hope that someone might intercept us before we reached it was shattered as Dr. Duboise's quiet voice assured me, "We are here, Mademoiselle. The lodge is dark and deserted. I will lead the horse into the barn. Then all will be well."

All will be well. His soothing, friendly tone had not changed from that first moment when I opened my eyes after the carriage accident and heard him say, "Just lie still, Mademoiselle. Everything's going to be all right." I had believed him then and put my complete trust in his friendship. Now, he was still reassuring me that everything was going to be all right. I wanted to laugh hysterically. Unspoken cries and sobs rose in my chest like unleashed wings of frantic birds cutting and bruising my insides.

I heard his footsteps as he led the horse inside. I waited expectantly. Dear God, what was he doing? Was he going to shoot me while I hung like dead meat over the horse's back? No, he would not endanger the horse. I had a few more minutes of life.

It seemed an eternity before he finally cut me free and let me drop to the ground. When he took off the sack, I saw that he had lit a dusty lantern which hung from one of

the rafters. It gave muted light through its
dirty chimney, sending elongated shadows
into the dark corners of the barn. At one
time the long, narrow building must have
been filled with sleek horses used for
hunting but now the gates on the stalls
hung crookedly, the littered floors had not
been mucked out, and old dry straw mingled
with dirt and refuse among discarded bales
of hay. I suspected that bats and pigeons
inhabited the abandoned loft and rats and
mice roamed freely in and out of the
abandoned structure.

I begged with my eyes for Dr. Duboise to
take the gag from my mouth but my silent
pleas were either ignored or misunderstood for he paid me little attention as
I lay in a crumpled heap where he had
dragged me.

His attention was centered on something
else more important. I watched him
carefully take the soft bag from where it
had been tied on his saddle horn and draw
out the delicate vase. He breathed a sigh of
relief as he dusted it with the sleeve of his
jacket. He must have been worried that the
bounce of the horse would harm it. His full
lips parted in a smile as lantern light
burnished the delicate glaze and
highlighted its loveliness. Once more his
sensuous loving touch brought cold shivers

up my spine.

He stood for several minutes, holding the vase and looking about. Then he spied a pile of three bales of hay near where I lay and he walked over and very gently nestled the vase on the top one. Its beauty demanded velvet, not straw, as a setting but even these mundane surroundings could not diminish its vibrant amethyst color. As if lost for a moment in its beauty, Dr. Duboise gazed at it, completely ignoring my crumpled figure on the floor beside his booted feet.

I tensed for I knew the moment was approaching when he would turn his attention back to me. As if my thoughts penetrated his fascination with the vase, he sighed and then looked down at me.

I thought his sudden stiffening was caused by something he saw in me but I suddenly realized when his head jerked up that he must have heard someone coming. He grabbed the pistol from his jacket pocket and spun around, facing the half-opened stable door.

My heart began to beat thunderously. Steps! Someone was coming. Raoul? Had he found me? I fixed my eyes on the opening barn door, wanting to shout a warning that Dr. Duboise had a gun leveled at him but my cries were muffled and gargled behind the tight gag. As I stared

mesmerized with fear, a familiar, craggy
face poked his head around the corner and
then lumbered into view.

Maurice Travois. Dr. Duboise's accomplice.

Dr. Duboise lowered the gun and
demanded angrily, "What are you doing
here? I thought we had arranged to meet in
Paris. I told you I had matters to take care
of first."

Monsieur Travois nodded his thick
graying head. My spurt of hope died.
Another meeting of the conspirators. I had
last heard them in the garden and now I
saw them both clearly as they stood talking
to one another. If I had had any lingering
doubts about them being in league with
each other, they vanished at that moment.
Monsieur Travois had wanted the stolen
items enough to come to Chambleau to get
them. He must be here to make certain that
everything went as planned.

"I don't need any help," snapped the
doctor. "It isn't wise for us to be together. I
can take care of this little matter. I must
sacrifice one of the vases. We need to leave
some evidence here with the body."

Travois nodded. Then his eyes moved to
where I lay in a crumpled heap on the dirty
floor. "Your brother told me that you were
going to bring her here," he said in a con-

versational tone. "Is it necessary to truss her up like some fowl ready for Sunday dinner?"

"She tried to escape. She's a wily one, threw up the medicine I gave her, and slipped out of the house. Fortunately, my brother is a light sleeper. He caught her in the barn."

As Dr. Duboise talked, Monsieur Travois walked over to where I lay. He bent down and removed the biting gag from my mouth.

I searched his expression for some hint of compassion. "Please—" I croaked.

"Why did you come here?" The doctor frowned.

"I couldn't sleep so I hired a driver to take me out to the farmhouse and discovered you had already gone. Your brother told me your plan so I came here. You see, when your brother came to see me earlier tonight, he told me that there would be a slight delay because you had an important loose end to take care of. He gave me the message that I was to go back to Paris and you would contact me later. I accepted your instructions at first and then I slowly realized that it was possible you meant to harm Alysha. I came to stop you." Then he smiled at me. "*Ma chérie*, you didn't think I would trade you for a pair of Venetian vases, did you?"

Dr. Boise raised his gun. "Step back, Monsieur Travois, I can't allow any sloppy sentimentality to complicate our business arrangement. I am going to kill Mademoiselle Grant and leave her here with the stolen vase. Inspector Davail already suspects her of being in league with the burglars. This will confirm it and I wouldn't be surprised if Raoul de Lamareau isn't arrested as her accomplice and murderer. It seems that he is already under a shadow for the death of his brother and the near-death of Madame de Lamareau. It is all working out perfectly and I will not suffer your interference."

"And if I refuse to cooperate?" Monsieur Travois threw back his broad head in an open challenge. I was reminded of a bull ready to charge.

Dr. Duboise looked ready for the challenge. "Then I will have to leave you here for the police to find. Two conspirators instead of one."

"How about three?" smiled Monsieur Travois. "You see, my dear doctor, I sent word to the chateau that I was coming here. I'm certain that Monsieur de Lamareau will be joining us shortly."

Dr. Duboise stiffened. "You're bluffing and I—"

"No, he isn't." A deep voice from the

depths of the stable halted the doctor's next
word. Raoul stepped into view holding a
hunting rifle in his hands. "Drop your gun,
m'sieur, or I'll blow your head off."

He had come! For a moment nothing else
registered. I dared not even breathe for fear
of turning the balance against us. Monsieur
Travois remained motionless, watching the
doctor's finger tightening on the trigger.

"Don't do it," Travois said quickly. "He
won't miss you with that shotgun. Your
pistol will not be accurate at that distance."

For a long, long moment, Dr. Duboise did
not move and then very slowly he lowered
his pistol—*and aimed it directly at my head*.
He smiled and said very gently, "If you do
not drop *your* rifle, Monsieur, it will not be
my head but Mademoiselle Grant's which
will splatter brains upon the wall." His soft
lips curved in a triumphant smile. "Drop it!
Now. My finger gets heavy and might slip
at any moment."

Raoul did not move.

The weighted moment was an eternity. I
knew, as Raoul knew, that once he dropped
the rifle it would be all over for all of us. In
that frozen moment, an idea was conceived
in terror.

I screamed, "The vase!" With all the
strength I could muster I bent my knees
and thrust my bound legs forward,

ramming my feet into the pile of baled hay.

The vase on top of the pile tottered and started to fall.

With a cry, Dr. Duboise leaped forward to grab the wobbling vase—but he never made it.

Raoul fired.

They fell together, the vase and the slain doctor. Ironically Dr. Duboise's pudgy body cushioned the amethyst vase's fall as it landed on his fat body and then rolled to the floor and lay beside him.

Raoul was beside me in an instant, freeing my bonds, pulling me close in protective arms that promised never to let me go again.

Chapter Nineteen

My exhausted and battered body kept me from fully recovering for several days after my ordeal. The physical and emotional drain of the traumatic events had taken their toll.

Dr. Vanderley was called in to see me and I found him to be an older gentleman, very professional, and I cursed myself for not having allowed him to treat me at the time of the accident. I had unwittingly played right into Duboise's hands by insisting that he be my doctor.

During the time that I recovered from the
ordeal that Dr. Duboise had put me
through, a hushed mourning fell upon the
chateau for Yvonne de Lamareau had
quietly passed away without ever regaining
consciousness. I knew now that she had
brought on the tragedy by her own drunken
actions. My beloved Raoul sat by my bed
and answered all my questions. The love in
his eyes put all my fears to rest. My
suspicions were a thing of the past.

I was no longer in the deserted west wing
but Raoul had placed me in a lovely
bedroom overlooking the main section of
the garden. "I put you in Jacques's old room
to try and protect you from Yvonne's
insane jealousy. I didn't trust her drunken
hysteria not to engulf you in our problems.
Even a new maid was a cue for her to
accuse me of bringing the girl into the
house for my own pleasure. Once I saw you,
I knew that she would vent her jealousy on
you and I wanted to avoid such unpleasant-
ness if I could. It seemed the best arrangement after the accident. That's why I didn't
want you interacting with the family. Since
I knew how violent Yvonne could be when
she got on one of her drunken tirades, I
decided that it was better for you to be
isolated. I could have gladly spanked you

when I found you had gone to the lodge after I had taken precautions to keep her there—and away from you."

"I'm sorry. I guess I was pretty stubborn—"

"And uncooperative, willful, opinionated, dogmatic—" he grinned "—and divinely enchanting. You'll never know what hell I went through when you disappeared without a trace. I took a ride after dinner to sort out my thoughts. I knew that you believed I was responsible for Yvonne's condition. And I felt responsible myself— not because I had harmed her but because I should have taken better care of her. I promised my brother and then—"

I covered his hand with mine. "It wasn't your fault."

"I should have had her committed to a private home much earlier but because of the children, I hoped that—"

"I know. You were more than fair with her, taking all her abuse, wild accusations, and her attempts to turn Annette and André against you. I've talked to them and explained that their mother was ill. She lied to them when she said you wished them harm. Children are very wise and will make the right decisions if given a chance. It may take time but they will come around . . . and love you as much as I do."

I leaned back, warmly content in the circle of his arms as he sat on the bed beside me. "I'm sorry. I guess I made it difficult for everyone."

"Yes, my beloved, you drove me out of my mind . . . in more ways than one."

"But how was I to know? Annette told me even before I met you that you had killed her father—"

"Yvonne shot Jacques in one of her drunken rages and left him for dead. I heard the shot and reached him as he lay dying. He told me that he and Yvonne had been quarreling and she followed him into the woods and shot him. He made me promise to protect her from the law and take care of her. She had always been infatuated with me and married Jacques when I told her that she could never be the one I loved. Her jealous hatred made her lie to her children and accuse me of having murdered their father . . . and of trying to force her to marry me. All lies . . . I tried to keep the police away from her, and not let anyone know the truth. That's why I wanted you to lie about her being gone from the chateau the night of the burglary. I knew she could never stand up to intense questioning and I had promised Jacques not to let anyone know she was responsible for his death. When she pulled a gun on you that day in the lodge, I knew that I must do something before she brought harm to someone else or to herself.''

"And you went to talk to Dr. Vanderley?"

"Yes, I thought we could put her in a private home until she could regain control of herself. But he was out of town. I was so upset I rode over to talk to Louise. She has been willing to try and help Yvonne all along—''

"Because she's in love with you," I added bluntly.

He nodded, his expression thoughtful. "At one time, we were close but I knew that I would never marry her so I withdrew from the relationship. I think Yvonne realized that I didn't love Louise and so she never tried to harm her—not the way she might have harmed you. I had to watch everything I did and said so she wouldn't go off on some dangerous bent. I cannot say that I'm sorry it's over. I'm telling you all of this but the truth must never come out—''

"But it is not fair that you should live under such a cloud.''

"It does not matter . . . if it protects the children. They must not be burdened by their mother's actions. She is gone now and all of us can begin living new lives." He lightly kissed my cheek and then the corners of my mouth in a tantalizing way.

"When you're feeling better, I'll share some of those new plans with you," he murmured.

"I'm not going on to Paris to work for Monsieur Roget?" I said with feigned surprise, giggling foolishly like someone in love.

"No. I took care of everything. I sent word that you had been unavoidably, permanently detained. I have a proposal speech all rehearsed when you're ready to hear it."

"I'm ready," I coaxed with feminine coquetry as a delicious warmth sped through me.

He cleared his throat in mock solemnity. "My dear Mademoiselle Grant, I would be honored if you would be my wife as soon as you are able to stand on those two lovely legs."

"Does that mean that I'd have to love, honor, and obey you?"

"Yes."

"Would you settle for two out of three?"

He laughed deeply. "That's my enchanting, exasperating Alysha. Life with you will never be dull." His eyes shone with promises that flamed my desire.

"If you'll take me as I am—"

"Gladly. I've already told Maurice Travois that there's going to be a wedding.

He made me promise that he'd be invited. You don't mind, do you?"

I shook my head. "I know that he's engaged in illicit dealings—but he came through for me. He was willing to gamble his own life to save mine."

"The inspector is not able to charge him with anything because he never touched the stolen goods . . . besides, he's decided to retire. The strain of almost being involved with a murderer was a warning that he had best quit his illegal activities before the law caught up with him."

"If he hadn't sent word by his hired driver that he was going to the lodge, I would have never reached you in time." He buried his face in my hair and I knew that he was fighting to keep his composure. His voice choked with emotion. "I love you so very much—"

"And I love you." My own voice was hoarse.

"And you're never going away. I've promised Annette and André that I would keep you here always."

"Always."

Beau, who had been stretched out lazily on my bed, stirred and then raised his head. He gazed at us for one long minute, then he lay back down with a purr of satisfaction.

THE BEST IN HISTORICAL ROMANCE

from LEISURE BOOKS

LOVE'S LEGACY by Rosemary Jordan. Irish lovers flee England's tyranny for a chance at happiness in America.
_____2422-5 $3.95US/$4.95CAN

UNTAMED DESIRE by Kim Hansen. An Eastern woman and a man as rugged as the West find passion and pleasure on the prairie.
_____2442-X $3.95US/$4.95CAN

EMBERS OF DESIRE by Patricia Pellicane. An innocent young lady and her Indian captor discover love in the turbulent times of the Revolutionary War.
_____2446-2 $3.95US/$4.95CAN

LOVE'S SAVAGE EMBRACE by Melissa Bowersock. A beautiful halfbreed's heart is torn between two worlds—and two lovers.
_____2151-X $3.75US/$4.50CAN

SWORD OF THE HEART by Maureen Kurr. Lovely Alix Beaucamp risks her sacred honor to win the heart of a mysterious dark knight.
_____2467-5 $3.95US/$4.95CAN

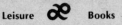